Carl Weber's Kingpins:

The Ultimate Hustle

Carl Weber's Kingpins:

The Ultimate Hustle

T. Friday

www.urbanbooks.net

Urban Books, LLC
300 Farmingdale Road, NY-Route 109
Farmingdale, NY 11735

Carl Weber's Kingpins: The Ultimate Hustle

ISBN 13: 978-1-64556-492-8

First Mass Market Printing November 2023
First Trade Paperback Printing November 2022
Printed in the United States of America

10 9 8 7 6 5 4 3 2 1

Distributed by Kensington Publishing Corp.
Submit Orders to:
Customer Service
400 Hahn Road
Westminster, MD 21157-4627
Phone: 1-800-733-3000
Fax: 1-800-659-2436

Carl Weber's Kingpins:

The Ultimate Hustle

T. Friday

Dedications

and

Acknowledgments

This book is dedicated to the five most important people in my life, my brat pack: Jordin, Jacob, Jacory, Jakayla, and Jalisa. Please understand that everything I do and every struggle I overcome is so that you guys don't have to worry about a thing. I love you guys, and don't ever forget it.

To my Blunt, you have been in my corner and stood by me for the last fifteen years, and although I be getting on your nerves, you never switched up on me. Our bond is unbreakable.

To Racquel Williams, you rock!!!! People always say make your first choice your best one, and I can say making you my first publisher was the best decision that I could have ever made. Over the few years of working with you I have learned so much in this industry. No matter what the situation is, you have had my back each and every way.

You have shown me nothing but love, and for that I truly appreciate you.

Jasmine Moore and Jennifer Dinwiddie, I appreciate you two for always being my listening ear when I talk about my characters as if they are real people. Y'all time is just around the corner.

To my Pen Sister Christine Davis, it's because of you that I'm doing something that I love. I really appreciate you and your grind.

To my wonderful readers and my supporters, I'm nothing without you guys. For the last four years and twenty-five books later, you guys have read and reviewed all of my books, and I appreciate each and every one of you guys. I really just want to say thank you from the bottom of my heart. It really touches my heart when I hear some of you say that I have become one of your favorite authors. You all make me keep going stronger.

To my dearest baby sister Amanda Jordin Hollis, my white chick, I love and miss you so much. I swear, fifteen years wasn't long enough to have you here with us. I'd give anything to hear your voice again.

To my mom Lisa and dad David, I wish you guys were here to see that I'm finally doing something that I love and know for a fact that you two would be proud. I love and miss you guys so much. Please continue to watch over the family.

Chapter 1

"Shot, shot, shot!" Chanel and Nicole playfully yelled over the loud music as they watched and cheered their friend Erica on. Erica was the life of the party as she tossed back three shots of Patrón down her throat, acting like she had something to prove.

No one looking at their table would have guessed that the three young ladies who sat around the booth were all faithful members of Missionary Baptist Church and the main one drinking and partying was the one and only 21-year-old Erica Collins—Pastor Eric Collins's one and only beloved daughter.

"Whew, that was straight fire. Let's get another round," Erica said, fanning her mouth before jumping up out of her seat and walking toward the bar.

Chanel stayed behind, babysitting her cup. Unlike Erica, she knew not to party too hard on Saturdays, especially when they had to be at Sunday school at 8:00 a.m. Nicole, on the other hand, was too busy texting her boo, Mekco. She was secretly ready to go and lie up under him.

Rolling her eyes, Chanel sipped her drink. "I hope we don't end up having to carry her home. Then we'll all end up in trouble with the pastor."

"Come on now, Chanel. Loosen up a li'l bit. She only gets a chance to be free and hang out every blue moon," Nicole explained, hoping their so-called friend would understand and cut Erica some slack. Knowing she had it the worst of the three of them put together being the preacher's kid (PK) and all, she deserved a good night out.

Seeing that Chanel's face was still twisted up in disappointment, Nicole walked off toward the dance floor. Mekco had just texted her, letting it be known that he had just made it. She wasn't in the mood to deal with Chanel's negative attitude. She really felt like if Chanel was going to be so uptight that night, then she should have stayed home reading her Bible or something.

Nicole had been Erica's best friend since the first grade and knew how her life could be with her strict dad. There wasn't anything wrong with loving the Lord, but Mr. Collins could be a little too godly at times with all the praying and prais-ing. Even with Erica being grown, Pastor Collins was not having his daughter out in the streets em-barrassing him or their church family with her foolishness. It was a miracle that he finally allowed

Erica to have the little freedom that she had now. Maybe it was because she had turned 21 and he overheard her talking to Nicole about moving in with her. He was scared that he was going to lose his baby girl for good. She still was on lockdown, but not the whole twenty-four hours a day and seven days a week. Pastor Collins had made sure to keep his daughter busy in the church as much as possible.

The days that Erica was allowed to spend the night at Nicole's house were the most important days of her life. That night was the first night that she had been out in over a month, and she was trying to enjoy herself to the fullest. The only rule that her father had was that she had to have herself in church every Sunday no matter what house she woke up in.

Chanel was new to the clique and had been at their church for two years. They had really just started letting her hang with them and into their secret lifestyle outside of the church. Sometimes she acted like she was cool with them, but tonight she seemed to only be around just to be nosy and to judge them. That was one reason why Nicole really didn't care too much to have her around. She would have stopped her coming around altogether, but Erica was blinded by her church-girl ways.

As Nicole walked off, she pulled out her phone and texted Mekco. She was ready for him to show his face and handle his business so they could spend the rest of the night together. After she pressed send, she felt someone grab her from behind, their strong arms wrapped around her waist. She was ready to go off until she looked down and saw "Detroit Brick Boyz" tattooed on the guy's hand. She took that moment to twerk on him so he could feel just what he had been missing since the last time they had hooked up.

"Hey, baby!" Nicole said while turning around and planting a kiss on her lover.

He could tell by the smile she wore on her face that he was missed. "Damn, baby, I missed your li'l sexy ass," Mekco said, giving her a hug and squeezing her ass. He had played his part in helping it grow, so he had no problem touching what was his, no matter who was around and watching.

"I missed you, baby. Are you ready to go now?" Nicole questioned.

"Not yet, bae. When my bro get here and the crew welcome him home, we getting the fuck out of here. I hope your girl not busted. My man needs her to be a bad bitch like you," Mekco jokingly teased.

"First off, I don't see anything funny, boy. You know I don't hang around no ugly girls, and you already know Erica is not ugly at all. And we ain't no bitches, so watch your mouth. Anyway, let me get back to my girls. Just text me when y'all about to come over."

Nicole gave Mekco a peck on his big, juicy lips before leaving him stuck in his nasty thoughts. He couldn't wait to get her home and make love to his girl. He had been so busy over the last two weeks getting things ready for his homeboy Pierre's homecoming and taking care of business that he barely had any time to just chill with Nicole.

It was crazy how the two were so different but had fallen in love with each other. Nicole felt comfortable around him even when he was showing his rough side and running in the streets. Something about him being a boss turned her on.

Erica and Nicole came back to the table at the same time. "Okay, ladies, I bought a few more shots for us, but looking around, I see I just wasted my dang money," Erica said, noticing that Chanel still had her first drink.

Nicole quickly butted in. "No, you didn't, boo," she said, killing two shots back-to-back. Seeing Mekco's sexy ass and knowing what was in store for her when she got home made her want to be drunk. There was something about drinking and fucking Mekco that she loved.

She turned to Chanel. "Come on, girl. You come to have fun or not?"

Chanel knew all the attention was on her now thanks to Nicole. She really wasn't feeling the night anymore. She looked down at her watch. "Look, it's almost eleven p.m. We should be leaving now. Y'all ready?"

Nicole gave Chanel a dirty look, then turned her attention to Erica. "Do you hear her? She always flaking on us. I still don't understand why you hang out with this wack-ass girl."

Erica tried not to laugh at Nicole's goofy ass, knowing that would have only egged her on, but at the same time she was right about Chanel. "Nicole, boo, chill out. Please."

"Come on, Chanel, this is the most fun that I've had in months. You don't have to drink, just chill with us a little longer," Erica begged.

"Look, I'm not really feeling this tonight. Maybe some other time."

That very moment Erica started to see what Nicole had been warning her about. "Well, Chanel, I guess it's a good thing you drove your own car, 'cause we are not ready to leave yet. Bye."

Nicole giggled to herself as Chanel grabbed her purse and stomped off. Erica didn't say another word as she picked up Chanel's drink to finish it off. "Shoot, I'm not about to waste my money." Both girls burst into laughter.

"I'm glad she's gone. Things were going to get a little awkward in a minute anyway," Nicole said, totally trying to ignore the face that Erica was giving her.

"What are you talking about, girl?" Erica asked, confused by her best friend's statement.

"Nothing, boo. Let's just chill out."

"No, Nicole, what you got up your sleeves? Please don't make me hurt your crazy self."

"Okay, boo. You know I've been dating my baby Mekco for a minute now, right? Well, he's here tonight with his homeboy, and I was thinking that maybe—"

Before she had a chance to finish her sentence, Erica cut her off. "No, no, no. The last time you tried to hook me up, the dumb boy worked my darn nerves within the first twenty minutes. I'm not dealing with that crap."

"Please, Erica, you'll be my best friend for life. Just talk to him, and if you don't feel anything, I promise I won't play Cupid anymore."

Listening to Nicole plead her case, she agreed to at least be nice and have a conversation with the guy. "Okay, Nicole, but this is the last time."

With a wide smile spread across her face, Nicole looked away from her phone and said, "Good, boo, 'cause they will be on their way over here in ten minutes."

"Welcome home!" the whole Detroit Brick Boyz squad yelled as they lifted their bottles and cups in the air. Their old leader had just come home from doing a six-year bid for a drug charge, and they were all there to celebrate with him. Well, all the ones who stayed loyal to him.

After six long years locked up, Mr. Pierre Miller, aka P in the streets, was finally a free man. His boy Mekco had been the one who kept things in order while he was behind bars. Mekco did exactly what he was supposed to do and made sure everything ran smoothly. Most importantly he made sure everyone in the crew ate. Along the way he had to body a couple of snakes, but as far as he knew they deserved whatever came their way.

When P walked out of the prison gates, Mekco had already had a place waiting for him and a ride in his driveway. Their dads had been business partners back in the day, so the two grew up more as family than just friends. They learned as small boys that being loyal should always be first if you were gonna make it in this life.

When Pierre got knocked, Mekco did the only thing that he thought was right. He stepped up and became the leader. He knew his job was to make his boss proud of him.

Mekco hit the streets and collected all the money that was due to P. Instead of putting that shit in his own pockets, he got his boy a lawyer, made sure his books stayed straight, and with the rest, he put the shit up in a safe place. He knew whenever his boy came home, he shouldn't have to ask anybody for shit. He tried his best to keep everyone in their crew on a straight path. They didn't need anyone else getting knocked.

On top of Mekco being loyal, P was also loyal. He never snitched on nobody he worked with. He did them six years without making anyone else pay for something they all were on the streets doing. P lived by the Meek Mill lyrics:

Before I snitch they gotta burn a hole in my tongue
Give me a hundred years in a hole on the sun

"Welcome home, my nigga. It took you long enough to get here. We turning up thinking your ass wasn't gonna show up to your own party," Brandon said with his words slurring.

P gazed his way and gave him a funny look. Back in the day, P didn't care too much for Brandon or his stepbrother Brian, and now they were celebrating his homecoming. P couldn't believe that Mekco had recruited these fools to roll with his crew. P decided not to be petty and just enjoy his night. He gave him a nod and then turned toward everyone else.

Brandon wasn't a fool, so instead of playing the tough guy, he sat there holding his drink like a bitch. His brother peeped everything and gave his brother a look that let Brandon know he should have said something. Brian hated how his brother was letting muthafuckas ho him.

Looking around at his old crew, Pierre couldn't help but smile. "I miss y'all niggas. I couldn't wait to get home and see y'all niggas for real doe. Sad to see a few didn't make it, but only the strong will survive this game."

"Damn, nigga, don't tell me you done got soft on us over the years," Mekco jokingly said.

"Right, this nigga giving out mushy-ass speeches and shit," Face added.

Pierre couldn't help but laugh at his best friend. "Man, fuck y'all niggas. Let's get some more bottles around this bitch. A real nigga home."

Everyone raised their drinks again and drank to a real nigga being home.

While everyone sat around enjoying themselves, Mekco pulled P to the side. "Ay, bro, I've been talking to this bad-ass shawty who's over there, and she got her homegirl with her. After six years I know some pussy is what you need. These niggas good over here. Let's bounce."

Thinking about what Mekco just said, he drowned his throat with the alcohol, not letting the burning sensation faze him. Standing up to leave, he admitted, "I been around all niggas for six punk-ass years. I see the crew doing good, so yeah, let's go see these bitches."

Mekco shot Nicole a quick text letting her know that he was on his way over to her booth. "Follow me, my nigga. They over there."

***

Nicole smiled as she placed her cell phone back into her handbag.

"Girl, I take it your boo on his way. That smile is not fooling nobody," Erica said.

"I swear, when you're in love and know that he loves you back just as much or even more, you can't help but smile," Nicole bragged.

Erica was happy for her friend and the love that she had found in Mekco. Nicole deserved to be happy especially after her last boyfriend, Denzel, dogged her out. After she dated him for five months, he had her believing that he was the one. But he couldn't hide his true intentions with her after she gave up her virginity.

"Damn, nigga, is that your girl or is she the one for me?" Pierre asked when he noticed that there was only one girl at the table. He had to admit that baby girl was a li'l cutie.

Mekco smirked. "Calm down, nigga. That's my fucking wife you over here lusting after. You wouldn't even know what to do with that. I don't know where her friend at, but she look just as good with her pretty brown skin."

P shook his head. He was ready to see what the hype was all about.

"Hey, baby, what's up?" Nicole asked as she stood up to give Mekco a hug and a passionate kiss. It was like no one was watching the way they showed their affection for one another. You would have never guessed that they were just together fifteen minutes ago.

Pulling away from her, Mekco turned toward P. "Hey, baby, this my bro P, and, P, this my baby Nicole."

"What's good, sis? You all right?"

"Hey, P, I'm happy to finally get a chance to meet you. Mekco talked so highly about you, I couldn't wait until I could put a face with the name."

"Now that we are all together, where is your homegirl?" Mekco questioned. He hoped Nicole's best friend didn't chicken out and go home. He knew she could be a good girl at times.

Nicole could tell that Mekco and P were worried about Erica's disappearance. "She just went to the restroom. She should be back in a minute."

After waiting for a good ten minutes and making small talk, Pierre excused himself and went over toward the bar. He was feeling like ol' girl was on some bullshit, and sitting around watching his homeboy and his bitch caked up wasn't in his plans as a good time. He took a seat and ordered a beer.

As he finally looked to his left, he saw a beautiful brown-skinned female. Matter of fact, she was drop-dead beautiful and had caught his eye. He tried not to keep staring, but it was hard for him not to do. The fitted blue dress that she wore hugged her body just right, and the splits on her side made him wonder if she wore any panties under the dress.

He finally picked up the nerve to walk over and shoot his shot.

"Excuse me, how you doing tonight?" he said nervously. Having been locked away for six years, he wasn't sure if things still worked the same as they did before.

Erica lifted her head up from the bar counter and saw who was trying to get her attention. At first glance, all she saw was a thuggish-looking guy with tattoos covering up most parts of his body that showed and who probably just wanted sex, but she wasn't giving shit up. After seeing his beautiful smile and pretty, platinum slugs, she couldn't help but smile and reach her hand out.

"Hey, I'm Erica."

"What's up, Erica? I'm P."

Erica stared at him strangely. "P, really? Do you have a real name?"

"Yeah, shawty, but we just met, and I can't trust you with my government yet," P said, laughing.

Erica couldn't help but join him in a laugh. "I see you have jokes, Mr. P."

After a good twenty minutes of conversation, they were joking and laughing together as if they were old friends. She laughed at so many jokes that she had forgotten all about her headache and feeling sick. The headache was what had her sitting at the bar in the first place. She couldn't make it back to the booth where her friend was waiting for her.

Feeling her phone vibrate, Erica dug in her purse to get it. She looked down and saw that it was Nicole calling. "Hey, boo, what's up?" she asked.

"Girl, where are you? Mekco's friend was waiting for you to come back to the table. I asked you to do me one favor and you start acting like Chanel's bogus self."

"Nicole, don't be mad. I got a li'l sick from those freaking drinks, so I took a seat at the bar. I swear, I couldn't even make it back there toward the table. I'm at the bar getting myself together. I'll be there in a minute."

"Okay, boo, don't be long. Love you."

"Love you too, Nicole."

Nicole grinned, then hung the phone up. "She said she'd be back in a minute, but anyway, where P go?"

Mekco was leaning back with his eyes closed. He was faded and didn't give a fuck where anyone was at. All he wanted to do was to get the fuck to the crib and lie up with Nicole.

Erica put her phone away. "I'm sorry. That was my homegirl. I was supposed to be meeting one of her boyfriend's friends. I wish I could stay and talk a little longer, but I already promised not to flake on her."

P laughed to himself. He knew exactly what she was talking about, and she was sitting there clueless. One thing that he could admit was that Erica was just as beautiful as her friend.

"Okay, shawty, that's cool. So you think I could put my number in your phone? That way if shit don't go right with ol' boy, you could hit me up."

P could tell that she was feeling him. She kept a smile on her face that was bright enough to put the sun out of business. She slowly pulled her phone back out and handed it to him. He quickly put his number in her phone. "Don't forget to call me, okay, shawty?"

"I won't," she mumbled as she watched him walk off toward the restrooms.

Erica hated that she had to leave the bar and return to the booth where Nicole was waiting for her. It was a surprise, but she was actually feeling P. There was something about his thuggish ways that intrigued her. From his tattoos to his teeth, she was wishing it was the next day so she could call him. One thing that made her really like him was the fact that he kept her laughing.

Making her way back toward the table, Erica sat down and said hi to Mekco. He said hi back. He was sort of happy to see her because that meant they could finally go.

"So where's your boy?" Erica dryly said.

"Man, your ass disappeared and hurt his feelings. There ain't no telling where that nigga went," Mekco said, causing the whole table to laugh.

Just then P walked up to the table. "What up doe?"

Erica looked at him strangely. "Oh my, did you follow me over here?" she frantically asked. She was hoping that he wasn't crazy like the last guy Nicole tried to hook her up with.

P took a seat right next to her. He knew what she was thinking, but he thought it was funny to make her sweat. P would have kept fucking with her, but Mekco and Nicole couldn't keep their laughter in.

"Don't start tripping, Erica. This is my bro P."

Erica gave the whole table a funny look before laughing herself.

"So I take it y'all two know each other?" Nicole asked with a smile. She could clearly tell that her friend was interested in P.

Erica had to admit, "Yeah, something like that. We sort of met at the bar."

"Cool, now we can get the fuck out of here. Let's go get some Coney then chill at my baby's crib," Mekco said. Everyone was down and quickly got up from the table.

"Erica, why don't you go ahead and ride with P, and Mekco can ride with me since he didn't drive here," Nicole suggested.

Erica couldn't control the face that she made. He was cool so far, but she wasn't all too sure about riding with him by herself.

"Damn, baby girl. I'm not gonna bite your ass," Pierre said, laughing.

Even Erica had to laugh at P's joke. At first glance, you would have thought that he was a mean dude and it would have broken his face to smile. He reminded her of a character out of an urban book that she had snuck and read growing up. He looked rough around the edges, but he really was a big goofball. Since he hung out with Mekco, she sort of figured out what type of lifestyle he was living. Erica never saw anything, but Nicole always talked about his dealings in the streets.

Although she had just met him and he was cool to be around, she could never see herself being in a serious relationship with someone like him. First of all, she knew her daddy would take one look at him and have a heart attack seeing him come pick her up for a date. Second, he looked like the type to have a large fan base, and she wasn't about all that drama.

Nicole nudged Erica on her side and whispered, "Girl, you'll be okay. We'll be right behind y'all."

Erica allowed Pierre to take her hand and lead her to his black Denali truck. Being a gentleman, he opened her door and helped her climb in. He then took that moment to sneak a little touch under her dress.

"Watch it!" Erica yelled as she took her seat.

P smiled. "My bad, shawty, but you can't blame a nigga for trying. You did just have all that ass in my face." Her smile showed him that she wasn't pissed, so he knew he still had a chance with her.

P drove off after clicking his seat belt. By Erica being shy and shit, he knew it was his job to start up a conversation. Waiting for her would have taken a lifetime, and he clearly didn't have long, seeing that he just got out of jail. He had already wasted six years that he couldn't get back. He wondered why she was so quiet now when, before she found out who he was, she had been full of conversation.

"So, Erica, what do you do? What you got going on in your life?" he asked.

Erica began to giggle. "If I tell you, you better not laugh at me."

"Why would I laugh at you, shawty?"

"I'm a PK and a student at OCC," Erica said, damn near whispering.

"So umm, what's so funny about that? Shit, the way I see it, you're in school trying to better yourself. And what the hell is a fucking PK?" he asked, confused.

"See, this is where the laughing comes in at," Erica jokingly said before continuing their conversation. "A PK is short for 'preacher's kid.' Have you ever heard of that before?"

"I mean, yeah, but I never actually paid them any attention before. When I did go as a child, the preacher's kids stayed away from me. I was the troublemaker. Shit, I haven't been to church in years," Pierre admitted.

Erica didn't know what to say after that statement. She had spent her life around nothing but churchgoers, so this was something new for her. This was going to be a strike against him—not in her book, but in her daddy's.

"Ay, ma, don't look at me like that. Shit, I'm not Satan or one of his ho-ass helpers. I'm just not easily fooled, and I question everything."

That made Erica laugh. "You are so silly, and I didn't say all that. If I thought you were some type of devil worshipper I wouldn't be riding with you. I'm just always around people from my father's church, that's it. My whole life revolves around school and church."

"So what the hell you doing at a club? And I saw your li'l ass take a couple of shots. Plus, when I first saw you at the bar, you were fucked up. Today ain't first Sunday. What you celebrating?"

"Oh, my gosh, you are too much. But anyway, I was just happy to get out of the house, that's it. Whenever I get a chance to hang, I make sure I enjoy myself," she answered.

Pierre pulled into the parking lot of IHOP. They had agreed on Coney, but since they were follow-

ing him, Pierre went to get what he wanted. Once
he was out of the truck, he went over to the passenger side and helped Erica climb out.

"Damn, you short as hell," P said, laughing.

"Whatever. This is just a big ol' truck."

"Real bosses drive trucks like this. You riding
with a boss right now, shawty."

Erica looked around but didn't see Nicole and
Mekco anywhere. Pierre noticed a look of worry
on her face and decided to ease her mind. He
wanted her to be able to trust him even though
they just met. She was cool, a good girl, but cool.
Maybe it was time to switch his type up, or maybe
she was just someone to play with. After this night
only time would tell where he wanted her to be in
his life.

"Come on, let's go inside and get a table. I know
you don't wanna stand out here waiting for them
fools to roll up." Before she could even protest
what he wanted, P took Erica's hand and led her
inside the building.

They grabbed a table toward the back. "Go
ahead and order something to eat. You might
wanna try something greasy to soak up that liquor.
I know your ass gotta be at church in the morning.
Don't want Pops trippin' on you," P said.

Erica smiled as she looked at the menu. She
usually would just order some chicken wings and
fries, but tonight she was kind of scared to eat in

front of P. It was sort of silly, but she was scared of pigging out or smacking on her food in front of him.

"Man, don't worry about it. I'll order you something 'cause I see you gonna play with that menu all night like you don't know what they sell."

Not saying a word, she just looked down shyly.

Fifteen minutes passed, and the waitress brought them their food. Nicole and Mekco still hadn't made it to the restaurant, and Erica was getting worried. She pulled out her phone before announcing, "I'm about to call Nicole and see where she at."

"Ay, ma, put that phone away. Aren't you cool chilling with me? Shit, let them muthafuckas miss out on all the fun."

Erica bit down on a fry. "Yeah, you right."

They ate quietly for a little while. "I have a question for you, Mr. P," Erica said, breaking the silence.

"What's up?"

"Well, you asked me what I did, so what do you do?"

"Honestly, right now I don't do shit. I'm actually trying to get back on my feet and get used to living my life again."

"So, what does getting used to living your life again mean?" Erica asked. She wasn't sure where he was going with this conversation, but he was an interesting person, and she wanted to get to know him a little better.

P sat there feeling lost by her question. He wasn't sure if she was ready to know his background, seeing that they had just met and all. There was a look in her eyes that showed her innocence, but they also said that she deserved the truth. P wasn't sure what she was doing to him, but he started to feel like he owed her nothing but the truth. He sat up in his seat.

"Look, a few years ago I used to run the streets and was into illegal activities. Honestly, I took the wrap for some shit me and some of my homies were into, and I just got out from doing six years. I was locked up, having another muthafucka run my life and shit. So that's what I mean by getting used to life again."

Erica didn't make a sound. She didn't know what to say. She had never been around a criminal as far as she knew. She asked a question and he answered honestly, so she had no choice but to respect that. How could she be mad at that? He didn't have to tell her anything, but the fact that he was quick to tell her the truth made her want to get to know him better. She wasn't sure what the Big Man upstairs was doing bringing him into her life, but he had her full attention.

"So, what are your plans now that you're free and have been given a second chance at life?" Erica questioned after giving thought to what he said.

Looking into her eyes, P let the truth flow out of his mouth as if he had been practicing his speech. "To be honest, I was thinking about coming home and taking my spot back as the leader of the Detroit Brick Boyz. I got money saved up, so I don't have to touch shit this time around, but I don't wanna come out stepping on my bro's feet. He's been holding things down for the last six years, and I don't know how he would feel stepping back down."

"Oh," Erica said. She silently wished she hadn't asked him something so personal. She had many conversations with Nicole about how Mekco was running things and how he was the man now. From what she could tell, Mekco liked his job. Erica didn't think he would like the idea of stepping back down after so long.

Pierre and Erica didn't know each other for real, and he was opening up to her like they were old friends. Noticing how open he was with his conversation and how surprised she looked, Pierre swallowed his food and tried to ease the conversation. "My bad, shawty. Maybe that was too much to lay on you at one time, but I've always been a man who told the truth. Well, except when I go to court. I tell those crackers whatever to make sure I'm good."

They both burst out into laughter. Just as he'd planned, his jokes had a way of breaking some of the tension from the table. Erica was back to laughing and smiling.

"That's okay, P. I asked, didn't I?" Erica innocently said as she drank her glass of water.

P chewed on his chicken wings as he decided on what to say next. He wasn't trying to scare her, but at the same time he wanted her to know what she was getting herself into if they were to become friends. "You know what surprised me?"

With a confused look on her face, Erica looked up from her plate and asked, "What?"

"We're sitting here getting to know each other, and you never backtracked and asked me my real name. You out here with someone you just met and only know me by the name P."

By now Erica was getting nervous. Not knowing where he was going with this whole serial killer thing, she grabbed her purse and started to get up. She didn't care if she had to call her dad. She was gonna make it home safely that night.

P grabbed her arm, laughing that she was ready to run up out of the restaurant. "Girl, sit down. I was just playing with you. I'm sorry if you ain't find that joke funny."

Erica slowly took her seat. She wasn't sure what was making her stay, but she didn't find his joke funny at all. The look on her face told him that she wasn't for all of his games. He pulled out his wallet.

"Here, baby girl. I see you don't trust me now. Here goes my ID. My real name is Pierre. You can hold on to it until I get you home."

Erica studied his ID. There it was—his name, Pierre Miller, address, and all. "I didn't like that joke at all. There's too much stuff going for you to be playing like that, Pierre. Every day on the news, there's always some dead body popping up around Detroit." As Erica spoke her opinion about his stupid joke, she took her phone out and snapped pictures of his ID.

"What are you learning in church?" Pierre asked, straight off the topic.

"What do you mean by that? I've been in church my whole life, so I'm not understanding where you're going with this conversation."

Shaking his head, Pierre gave her a crazy grin. "Look, I'm pretty sure your father preached about how if you put your faith in the Lord, you shouldn't worry about things. He will protect you and shit."

Looking past his choice of words, Erica couldn't help but speak up. "My father is a good pastor, and yes, he has preached about that and more. So where are you going with this?"

"I'm just saying you got the Lord on your side. So why did my joke scare you so much? Either you a believer or you not and just faking the funk," Pierre said with a straight face.

Erica didn't know how to handle what he said. He was somewhat right, but she wasn't about to go against her father's word. "For someone who don't go to church, you sure do talk as if you know everything, Mr. Miller."

"Hey, you can't be all in public calling my name out like that, shawty. That's why I didn't tell you my shit at the club," he said, changing the subject with a smirk on his face.

Pierre didn't go to church now, but when he was a child, his grandma kept him in church every Sunday and on Wednesdays for Bible study. Once he turned 12, his grandma became ill, and he became rebellious. She had become too old to fuss and fight with the grandchild she was raising. He soon stopped going, and there wasn't nothing that she could do about it. Pierre watched his grandma go to church every chance she got until she passed away. That did something to the 13-year-old boy who had nobody but her. He questioned the Lord daily on why He had to take his granny away. He never got over her death, and since he never got an answer, he never spoke to the Lord again.

After his grandma died, Pierre lived with local drug dealers, and that was the start of his career. By the time he turned 16, he was so gone into this drug game that there was no turning back. He and Mekco had a crew and their own blocks that they ran.

Along with Mekco there were some other guys, named Face, Tony, and Li'l Trey, who were all members of their crew. They called themselves the Detroit Brick Boyz, and that was exactly what they did. They were no longer li'l dope boys. They pushed bricks all around Detroit and the surrounding areas. For the three years Pierre ran the team, he made sure he stacked his money and that everyone on his team ate just as good as him. P was a good leader. His only problem was he was too much of a hothead. He was the type to kill a muthafucka and didn't give a fuck about asking questions. When he finally turned 19, he ended up adding more niggas to the crew because they had more areas to cover, and that was when shit went south.

Some members on his team got sloppy, and he ended up doing six years behind their shit. He wasn't sure who it was, but someone had been running their mouth. As a result, he took the wrap. For the past six years, he did his time in peace without mentioning anybody's name. Now that he was out, he wanted to claim his position as leader and also find out who the snake was who got him knocked.

"What's wrong, Pierre?" Erica asked, taking him out of the daze.

"Shit, just lost in my thoughts. Ay, what time you gotta be in? I'm not trying to get you in trouble or anything," P said.

"I'm staying over at Nicole's house this weekend. I have to wait for her so I can get in her house. Am I'm boring you?"

Shaking his head at her question, he answered honestly, "Nah, ma, I'm not bored with you. I'm actually enjoying your company. I never met anyone like you before. You're different, but I'm not bored with you."

Erica giggled. "I thought I was boring you since you asked what time I had to be home. I have a question for you."

"What's up? I just might have an answer for you."

Adjusting in her seat, she asked, "What type of females are you used to, since you say I'm so different?"

"Shit, you know, the type of hoes who would be mad if I brought them here after the club and not somewhere to dick them down. When I was out in these streets before, I had hoes lined up begging for me to fuck them and begging for money or some shit. So yeah, you are way different from anybody, and don't think that I'm complaining either. I really like you, Erica. You seem to be down to earth. Maybe if I had someone like you by my side, I wouldn't wanna be out here in the streets."

Blushing, Erica sat there not knowing what to say next. He had said everything right, but she knew her father would just die if he saw her with him. Besides making her laugh, Erica liked how Pierre spoke the truth. As they sat there talking, whatever she asked, he spoke up and answered each question. He wasn't trying to cover up anything from his past or what he wanted his future to be like.

Erica looked down at her phone and saw that it was going on 3:00 a.m. "Dang it, I have to call Nicole. It's getting late, and lucky me, I have Sunday school at eight," she said, pulling her phone out again.

This time P didn't stop her. He understood that she had things to do in the morning, even though he was enjoying her company and felt like he could stare at her all night if he could.

"This is just crazy!" Erica said sort of loudly, placing her phone back in her purse.

P looked her way and was now concerned. "What's going on, shawty? Are you good?"

"Not really. Nicole is not answering her phone. This girl is always bull crapping knowing I need to get to her place. There is no way I can go home at this time of morning. My dad would flip out."

Pierre took his phone out and dialed Mekco's number. He hung up and called it back right after not getting an answer the first time. "Damn, bro not answering either."

Pierre then pulled out the money for their food and some extra for a tip. "Come on, let's get you out of here."

Erica stood up to follow Pierre's lead. She wasn't sure what his plan was, but for some reason she followed him. After getting to know him a little better, she felt like he wasn't the type to cause her any harm. If anything, he would prevent any harm that came her way.

P drove off and headed downtown toward his condo. He had to admit Mekco did a good job picking out a place that he would love. He had a great view that overlooked the river, and he could see over into Canada. The place was furnished really nice. It was supposed to be a bachelor pad, but it was fixed up too nice. *He must have had a bitch put this shit together.*

P thought the first day out he would have been happy laid in some wet pussy, but meeting Erica was just as good. He could tell she wasn't one of the females he was used to dealing with, but she held his attention past the bedroom. That night he was okay with not fucking. He thought of it as having just found a new friend.

"Umm, maybe I should have asked this before, but where are we going?" Erica asked.

"Look, Erica, it's getting late, and neither of our people are answering their phone. We can go back to my place, and you can get you some sleep."

"Your place?" she questioned.

"Shit, it's either my place or I can take you home to your daddy and let him deal with your tipsy ass. Which one do you want?"

Erica didn't say anything after weighing her options. She knew if she was going to go home, her dad would trip and it would mess up any chances she had of having any type of freedom. She sat back in her seat and enjoyed the rest of the ride. She prayed she wasn't the female in a movie who the audience was screaming at for being dumb. She didn't know P like that and could only pray that she wasn't making a big mistake.

Chapter 2

Pierre drove in silence, knowing she was over in the passenger seat worried. He laughed to himself knowing that he really wasn't on no bullshit. He wasn't trying to pressure her into anything because he knew she wasn't even that type of female. Erica was different, and that was what made him want to get to know her better.

Finally reaching their destination, P killed the ignition and hopped out of the truck. He then went over to her side and helped her get out. "Come on, girl. I've been telling you I wasn't gonna bite your ass."

Once they got into his place, Erica looked around and noticed where she was. "Wow, this is so crazy."

"What are you talking about, girl?"

"A few weeks ago, Mekco had Nicole decorate this place, and I helped her put everything together. So I hope you like it."

"Hell yeah, y'all did a good job hooking my place up. I might have to pay you," Pierre said, laughing. He looked over to Erica and saw sleepiness all over her face. "Look, I see you about to pass out, so you can go ahead and get the bedroom. I'll crash on the couch."

"Thank you, Pierre," Erica said as she took her heels off and made her way toward the bedroom.

Pierre turned on the seventy-five-inch TV that covered most of one wall in the living room. He turned on the news and undressed down to his boxers. It was his first night out and he was stuck on the couch. He had to laugh to himself as he pulled a sheet out of the linen closet and got comfortable on the couch. He knew if he and Erica hit it off, he was gonna have to get used to this type of shit. She was a good girl, and he was gonna have to respect that.

It didn't take Erica any time to fall asleep in Pierre's king-size bed. One thing she couldn't understand was why he needed such a big bed for only him. Before falling asleep, she dialed Nicole's number one last time only to get the same result: no answer. She was gonna kill Nicole the next day at church. Erica hated how she was so caught up in Mekco.

Rolling over and opening her eyes, Erica didn't recognize where she was. It was still dark outside, but she could tell the sun was going to rise pretty soon. Looking down at the time on her phone, she saw that it was 6:30 a.m. Wasting no time, she dialed Nicole's number, and this time she got an answer.

"Boo, I am so sorry. Please don't kill me," Nicole whined into the phone, still sounding half asleep.

"Nicole, where are you?" Erica asked, trying not to go off.

"I'm at home, Erica. Where are you?"

Messing with her, she joked, "I'm at IHOP waiting on you." After a short pause, she giggled, then said, "Nah, I'm just playing. I'll be there soon."

Before Nicole could ask any questions, Erica ended their phone conversation. She climbed out of the bed and went into the bathroom. She remembered the extra hygiene items that they put in the hall closet, so she helped herself to a toothbrush and facecloth.

After taking care of her business, she went into the living room to wake up P. "Hey, Pierre, I hate to wake you, but I need to get going. My Sundays start early, remember?"

Pierre pulled the cover off his face and just stared at her for a minute. He had to remember who she was and why the hell he was being woken up so early. Him waking up with someone standing over him wasn't something that he was used to. That shit happened once when he was locked up, and he damn near killed a nigga. After that, everybody knew he wasn't to be fucked with.

"Damn, Erica. My bad, girl."

As he got off the couch, Erica could help but notice his morning wood. She tried not to stare, but with a small grin on her face, she softly said, "Good morning."

"Good morning," he replied, fixing his dick in his shorts. He saw her looking, but he didn't want to be the reason for her to end up in hell right along with his wild ass. He then made his way to the bathroom.

He walked out of the bathroom and came back into the living room. "Look, I'm still kind of fucked up, but I know you got to get the hell out of here, so take this and put some gas in my shit," he ordered, passing her his truck keys and placing a bill in her hand.

"Are you serious? You gonna let me drive your truck? How are you gonna get around until I get out of church?" she questioned.

"About the time you get out of church, I'll just be getting up. Plus, this is my way of seeing you again," he had to honestly admit.

"Thank you, I really appreciate it. My dad would kill me if I'm late," she said, putting her heels back on.

Pierre took this moment to give her a hug. "You be careful and take care of my baby," he said, laughing.

"I will, silly."

***

After her second try, Erica finally was able to climb in the truck. She drove straight to Nicole's house so she could get ready for church. When she finally parked Pierre's truck and locked it up, she called Nicole to buzz her in.

"Girl, I'm gonna kill you. Matter of fact, let me hurry and get ready for church. Just remember, after church it's over for you," Erica yelled as she walked into the apartment.

"I see you're still grouchy this morning. That could only mean P didn't put the D on you the right way," Nicole teased.

Erica didn't find anything funny and was quick to defend herself. "Look, girl, don't even play with me like that. You know I don't play like that."

"I'm sorry, boo. That was a bad joke. But what happened between y'all last night anyway?" Nicole asked, following Erica to the guest bedroom.

"No, before you ask me any questions, where were you last night? You left me hanging with Pierre."

Nicole noticed how her friend was calling him by his real name and not his street name. "So it's Pierre now?" Nicole teased.

"Whatever, girl," Erica said while making her way into the bathroom.

Nicole followed her. "So after church we definitely gotta talk. And you better not leave anything out."

"Okay, now let me get ready," Erica yelled before slamming the door in Nicole's face.

"Wake up, nigga. What's good with you?" Mekco asked P through the phone.

"Dawg, where the fuck you and your girl disappear to last night?"

Mekco laughed before answering, "Man, I thought if we got ghost, you and shawty could get to know each other a li'l better. If you know what I mean."

Pierre sat up on the couch. "Ay, nigga, she cool and all, but she not like that. She's really a good girl."

"Yeah, whatever. They all good until they get piped down. I'm gonna swing by around noon. We gotta get you plugged back in. I already called the fellas. Welcome back home, my baby," Mekco said.

Mekco and P ended their conversation after chopping it up for a few more minutes. The fellas had decided to hook up in a few hours to discuss some major business moves. There was money out there to be made, and they were about to get it all the Detroit Brick Boyz way.

Since Mekco had been running the streets for the last six years, he managed to build the proper empire. He never touched anything illegal, and he had invested most of his dirty money, making it clean money. Mekco had always been behind the scenes of the Detroit Brick Boyz. For years he was the one trying to show his bro how to handle things, but P was such a hothead and loved the attention. That was why his ass got knocked, being too damn flashy and making muthafuckas envy him. Once P started getting too much attention, niggas started to envy him, and shit got too hot for the crew. Mekco, on the other hand, was low-key with his shit. Not only did he have it set up that he didn't have to touch shit, but his crew ate better than any other team out. Now that P was back out, he was gonna have to learn the ropes.

Erica walked through the church, collecting any trash or pamphlets that were left behind. This was something that she did every Sunday while her dad sat in his office after service. She was trying her best to hurry up and get her job done. For one, she was dead tired, and on top of that, she wanted to call Pierre so she could return his car. Seeing him again wouldn't have been a problem either.

Walking out of his office, Pastor Collins watched his daughter work. "Erica, I'm glad that you're still here because I have a few more things for you to do right afterward."

Erica smacked her lips hearing her dad say that. She was ready to go and get her day started after a long nap. Plus, she wanted to meet up with Nicole for dinner and discuss what went down the night before.

"Dad, I did have plans to meet up with Nicole after service. Do you remember I'm staying at her house?" Erica said with an attitude.

"Erica, don't give me that attitude. God is King, and He is the leader over our life. Do you know what that means? That means He is my boss, and I'm your boss. You should know by now that you have to listen to me in order to make it to those golden gates to meet our King."

"Yes, Father," Erica said, rolling her eyes without letting her father see her being disrespectful. No matter what she said, he always found a way to turn her words around as if she were disobeying the Lord.

"Now that we are on the same page, I need you to make twenty copies of these sheets for the students. Do you remember vacation Bible study starts soon? I would like for everything to be well put together for our lovely teachers who are working with us this summer," Pastor Collins said as he passed her the small stack of papers.

"Thanks, Dad. I'll get them done. Even though it doesn't start for another two weeks," she said, still with a slight attitude.

Pastor Collins walked toward the office, not liking his daughter's attitude. "Next time you will get here on time and will not be struggling to stay awake during service. And if you keep up with the attitude, I will make sure you won't see Nicole's house all summer. Try me if you want."

Pastor Collins walked out of his office feeling good for punishing his daughter. She knew better than to arrive at church late. Then on top of that she was nodding off during service. She had completely embarrassed him in front of his fellow congregation.

Pastor Collins was told before that he was too hard on his daughter, but he never saw it like that. He really just wanted what was best for her. Erica's mother had passed away when Erica was just 12 years old. Just like any other child who lost a parent, Erica took it hard. She cried every day, begging for her mom to return. Instead of Pastor Collins being there to comfort his daughter or tell her that everything was gonna be okay, he felt like she was somehow going against everything that she had learned in church. He once overheard her asking God why He took her mom from her, and it upset him. He watched his daughter question her faith in the Lord. For her punishment, he made sure to tie her down to everything that was going on with the church. He was gonna make her a true believer again. He made it so she barely had any time to do normal things that a teen was into. He was determined to get her back on the right path.

Nicole's mother would sometimes step in and get Erica whenever Nicole would start to discuss how much she missed having Erica around or whatever the latest news was on how Pastor Collins was keeping Erica locked up like a prisoner. Even now that Erica was 21 and grown, he still tried to control her every move. She had to give him a speech about her being grown now and needing some type of freedom. Besides church and school, he loosened up and allowed her to stay over at Nicole's house some days. At first, he didn't like the idea because Nicole was no longer living under her mom's roof. But after taking someone's advice of letting her have some type of freedom before he completely lost her to the streets, he pushed his pride to the side and allowed her to spend time with her friend. When Erica wasn't in his eyesight, he asked the Lord to lead her in the right direction.

Chapter 3

"Anyway, girl, you know I love me some Mekco, and I missed him so much. I couldn't help but give him the best sex ever last night," Nicole said, stuffing her face with a taco.

Erica shook her head. "So you being in love is the reason I was left alone with a stranger until this morning? Girl, you lucky I love you, because you deserve a beating, but since I don't have a life, I'll settle for one of your wild stories."

"Okay, boo. You know how we get down, so no judgment."

Erica giggled, "Now you know I don't judge you."

Nicole started her story. "So when Mekco and I went to my car, I told him to follow P's truck, because I was buzzing and wanted to relax. Girl, he helped me get in the car, and next thing I knew he had his head buried in between my legs. I swear, that man does something to my body that I can't even begin to explain," Nicole went on with a huge smile on her face.

Erica sat there with a slight smile on her face. She wasn't sexually active yet, but she loved hearing Nicole's sex stories. Sometimes she secretly wished that she was the one who could feel what Nicole claimed gave her life.

"I guess after that you still couldn't call me or just make it to the restaurant."

"Erica, you know if I had made it, your ass wouldn't be here right now soaking up my story. Just go ahead and admit it. You love that your best friend has a bomb-ass sex life, and you don't mind listening to my nasty stories," Nicole teased.

The best friends shared a laugh.

Erica had to admit to herself that she loved listening to Nicole's nasty sex stories. When she was growing up, her father taught her that sex was for married folks only. He had it implanted in her head that she was going to wait until she was married before she made that major decision in her life of giving up her virginity. Her husband was the only one who would be able to explore her body.

Being curious, Erica spoke up after being deep in her personal thoughts. "So what happened next?" she asked, with full excitement.

"Girl, we didn't even make it out of the parking lot. I ended up riding him right there. Once we were done, he drove straight to his house and did it all over again until we passed out. But enough of me. What happened between you and P last night?" Nicole questioned.

"Well, since you wanna know so bad, me and Pierre went straight to the restaurant to eat like we all planned. We talked and got to know each other better. I tried calling you a couple of times because I wasn't able to get in your apartment. Since you were out being a THOT, I had to stay at his house. There wasn't no way I was going home at no dang three in the morning."

Nicole interrupted her story. "So you telling me he didn't even try to kiss you or anything?"

Erica wore a straight face. "No, girl. He was a perfect gentleman. He also let me sleep in his bed, and he took the couch. Then he gave me the keys to his truck so I could make it to service this morning."

Nicole was stunned by P's actions. "Wait a minute. You mean to tell me that you stayed at that nigga's house, slept in his bed, and you two didn't do nothing? Plus he let you drive his car? Now that shit could only mean one thing, boo."

Confused, Erica looked over to her friend. "And what is that, crazy girl?"

"That means he was impressed by you. He didn't try to hit 'cause he saw how you carried yourself and respected that. Girl, he let you drive his car and he just met you. That nigga want you bad. Anyway, have you talked to him today?" Nicole asked.

Erica was kind of happy to hear her say that. She secretly thought it meant he wasn't interested and was just being nice since he was stuck with her. Then she slowly replayed their conversation over in her head and remembered that he did say he was digging her. She wasn't sure if he was serious or just trying to run a game on her.

"After church I did call him so I could return his car, but I didn't get an answer. Since then, I texted him and asked him what time he wanted me to bring his ride back to him. He just texted back and told me he was busy handling business, so he'll hit me up later," Erica said, answering all of her friend's questions.

Nicole stared at her friend with a huge smile on her face. She was happy for her friend. Not much happened between P and Erica, but in Nicole's mind that was a sign that he liked her, and by the way Erica blushed when talking about P, she knew her friend liked him too.

Still full of excitement, Nicole yelled out, "OMG, just think about this. We could be each other's bridesmaids. Or maybe we could do a double wedding with matching colors. We gonna be the shit, best friends marrying best friends."

"Come on, Nicole, chill out with all that talk. I honestly can't even say Pierre and I are even friends, so I'm not seeing all that crap you just said. Don't try to rush anything," Erica said before picking her mess up from the table and walking off to the kitchen.

Mekco stood at the head of the table with ten other major playas of his team. After everyone welcomed P back to the crew, Mekco was ready to handle business.

"As y'all niggas know, P is back and will take the position as my right-hand man. If I'm not around, y'all muthafuckas can hit him up with any problems, which we shouldn't have. Anyway, he will handle shit accordingly," Mekco told his crew.

P looked around to see if anyone's face showed a sign of hatred. Most of the niggas knew him, but there were a few fresh faces in the crowd. He really wasn't worried and was ready to do a nigga dirty. It had been too long since he had to show a nigga he wasn't the one to play with.

"Okay look, Li'l Trey, I need you and Face to go to Cameron's spot tonight and pick up that package from him. He should already have it ready, so in and out," Mekco ordered.

"Ay, boss, them niggas over there on the east side be testing me. Every time I gotta go that way them niggas be posted. I think they up to something," Face spoke up.

"My nigga, you scared?" Brandon asked.

"Nah, nigga, I'm not scared, but I know how Mekco said he didn't want any extra attention on us. That's why I been ain't smoke me a nigga. You know I don't give a fuck about killing a nigga," Face said, boosting his own ego.

Mekco turned his attention toward P. "Ay, right hand, how would you handle this?"

"Shit, flex on them niggas, and let them know who you with. Niggas should already know not to fuck with a Brick Boy. If they jump, pop they ass and get the fuck on."

Everyone sat around the table laughing and geeking P up after his statement. They liked his way of thinking, but Mekco didn't say a word. Secretly he thought P was still a hothead and that was why he did those six years. The sad part about it was he still hadn't learned shit over the years. All that hot shit wasn't good for business.

"So now that we got this shit taken care of, I can go see my wife. She was texting me all fucking day. I put it on her ass last night, so I already know what her li'l freaky ass wants," Mekco said as he rolled up a blunt.

P didn't say much as they walked to Mekco's car and got in. He had been thinking about Erica and also getting his position back, but he wasn't sure how to bring that shit up to his homeboy. He usually was the strong-minded one between the two, but seeing how Mekco was handling things, he just wasn't sure how things would work out. Mekco had the team believing that they could do whatever without having to kill a muthafucka, but P knew better. He knew that when push came to shove, niggas feared bullets, not words.

"Ay, dawg, I still can't believe you let Erica ride off with your whip and you ain't get no pussy from her last night. Jail must have turned you soft or something."

"Fuck you, nigga. You talking all that shit, but you the one who tried to hook me up with a fucking pastor's daughter. You knew I wasn't getting any pussy my first night out. Bitch ass set me up," P joked.

"Ay, bro, my girl all into that church shit too. You just gotta know how to fuck her mind before you actually get the pussy. Shit, my bitch turned the fuck out. Her freaky ass would let me fuck in the church if that's what I wanted to do."

"Nigga, where we on our way to, anyway?" Pierre asked, trying not to laugh at his bro. He knew Erica wasn't cut like most females, and talking about it was pointless, so he changed the subject.

Pierre was digging Erica, but he wasn't about to jump in the ring with the Lord to get a chance with her. If push came to shove, he'd just go backward to one of his old hoes until something new popped up. They always loved jumping on his dick whenever they saw him, and he was pretty sure that word was out that he had been released.

"My nigga, I'm about to pull up to Nicole's crib, and you know her homegirl gonna be there. Now you can get your truck and stop using me as a fucking Uber driver."

P chuckled at his friend's joke. "Man, fuck you, bitch. We rode to two places together and you talking major shit."

The rest of the ride went smooth. They smoked a blunt, and Mekco put his homie up on all the latest rap music that had come out and taken over the radio. Pierre sat back, still thinking about Erica. She was beautiful and smart, and he liked that she wasn't a rat like the girls from his past. At the end of the day, she was a preacher's kid, and he knew it was gonna be too much work to get to her the way he wanted her.

Before they reached the house, he had decided to wash his hands of the thought of even trying to deal with her. She was way outta his league. A preacher's kid with a Brick Boy would never work. Just the thought of it made him laugh to himself. He had to be tripping to ever think she would consider even looking at him like that.

She was beautiful and had a bright future ahead of herself, and he was straight out of jail with plans to continue doing the same shit that got him locked up before. His body was covered in tattoos, each with a hood story to tell, so there was no way she would pick him to be who she brought home to meet her pops.

***

"Hey, baby!" Nicole yelled as she allowed Mekco and P into her apartment.

"What's up, baby?" Mekco asked while wrapping his arms around her waist and gripping her ass.

Once they let each other go, Nicole looked up at P. "What's up, P? Thanks for taking care of my girl last night."

"Shit, no problem," he responded.

Mekco was giving Nicole a strange look, and she knew what time it was. "So, P, you can have a seat in the living room. Me and your bro have to go talk about something."

Mekco gave his boy a look, letting him know to just chill for a minute. P watched them walk down the hallway and disappear in one of the bedrooms. He walked into the living room and instantly smiled at the image that was in front of him. All that hand washing was now down the drain. Her beauty had his mind gone.

Erica sat on the couch with a schoolbook in her lap and a highlighter hanging out of her mouth. For a few seconds he watched her read and then run her highlighter over some words. She wore some black leggings with a T-shirt. Her hair was up in a messy bun, nothing special, but that sight was sexy as hell to him.

Feeling like she was being watched, Erica slowly lifted her head and turned toward the doorway.

"Oh, my Gawd, you just scared me. How long have you been watching me?"

"My bad, shawty. I wasn't trying to scare you. I just saw you working hard and didn't know how to enter the room without interrupting you," P said, being honest as usual.

"It's okay. I was just wrapping up. Finals are coming up, so I just did a little bit of studying. You can come in and chill if you still want to."

Pierre tried not to smile as he walked over to the couch. Erica dug in her purse and handed him his truck keys. "Here, and thanks again for allowing me to drive your truck. I filled the tank back up like you asked. I was still late for service, but I made it because of you."

"No problem. That's the least I could do. Especially since you were with me, it was only right. Plus, I already told you that was my way of seeing you again."

Erica began to blush. Knowing how her last relationship ended, she prayed that Pierre wasn't just trying to run game on her. After her ex, Raymond, broke her heart, she tried to stay away from relationships and just focus on herself. But here she was soaking up every word that flew out of Pierre's mouth.

Mekco and Nicole wasted no time rushing to her room and stripping each other down, then jumping into her queen-size pillow-top bed.

"Damn, daddy," Nicole moaned out as her lover slurped up every ounce of passion juice that flowed out of her center.

"Open them damn legs, girl, and stop pushing me away," Mekco hollered.

Mekco had his tongue go to work on her clit while one finger slid in and out of her juice box, making his mouth fill up with even more of her sweet juices. He must have been doing something right, because after so long, she started trying to push his face away and run from his tongue game, when at first she was pushing his whole face deeper in her.

"Okay, baby, I'm about to cum," Nicole yelled as she tried her hardest to stop Mekco from snatching her soul.

Mekco didn't ease up, not one bit. He continued to eat away, causing Nicole to wrap her legs around his neck when they began to shake. She tried to use that moment to put her weak legs down, but Mekco was hip to the game. He hurried and used his arm to pin her legs down. He still wasn't easing up on shit. She had been sending him all types of messages saying how horny she was and was ready for him to come see her. He was only doing what she begged for.

As she released all her juices, Mekco made sure to lick her dry with no problem. She felt so refreshed at that moment. She giggled as he finally put her legs down to wipe his mouth off on his T-shirt.

"Damn, girl, with your water-fountain ass," he said, laughing and digging in his pocket to get his condom.

Nicole secretly rolled her eyes. She felt like they should have been at the point in their relationship where he should be fucking her without condoms. She was so in love that she wanted to have all that man's babies.

She couldn't even catch her breath well enough before she was begging him to put it in. "Come on, baby. Hurry up and come fuck me," she demanded.

"I got you. Hold up, baby," Mekco replied as he rolled a Magnum over the monster that swung between his legs

He caught Nicole staring and couldn't help but grin. He came over that day to play no games. His plans were to fuck the shit out of her, putting her ass straight to sleep.

She tensed up a little as he slid his dick into her wet opening. It was crazy how she stayed begging for the dick and she couldn't even take it all. When they first started fucking, he started off with just fucking her with half, and that drove her crazy. But over the time of them being together, she was now taking it all and occasionally she allowed him to enter her in her other hole. She was his personal li'l freak, but he loved her ass.

Pierre and Erica tried to have a conversation about an episode of the TV show that was on, but it was hard to stay focused with all the moaning, grunting, and just hearing the headboard bang against that apartment's thin walls.

"Ay, shawty, you wanna get the fuck out of here? Your girl got a nice crib and all, but I'm not into listening to other muthafuckas fucking and shit. That's just not my thing."

Erica jumped up, giggling. Nicole and Mekco were always going at it. She quickly put her shoes on and grabbed her cross-body bag from the coffee table. "I'm ready. I wasn't sure how much more of that I was gonna be able to take. Usually when I'm over and get tired of hearing them two, I go in the hallway to study or read a book."

Pierre placed her hand in his as they rode the elevator down to the garage. Erica didn't protest his move, but she did put her head down as she blushed for the whole ride down. That let him know that she liked him but was shy.

Once they reached the garage, Pierre looked around for his truck. "Where you park my whip?" he asked, not seeing it parked anywhere.

"Come on, it's over here. Since I was late for church this morning, my dad made me stay after, and by the time I got here, all the good parking spaces were gone. So I had to park all the way back here."

"It's cool, as long as my shit is still in one piece," he said, following her between the other cars.

"So what are you trying to say, I can't drive? You sure were quick to hand me your keys before knowing if I could drive."

"You right. I don't know what made me trust you," he mentioned with a slight grin on his face.

"Anyway, there go your baby all in one piece."

Pierre helped her into his truck. "Man, how tall are you anyway?"

Erica laughed, "Don't start with that short crap. I'm happy to be five feet five. You're just a darn giant," she joked.

Pierre jogged over to the driver's side of the truck. Erica looked over toward Pierre. "So where are we going?"

"Shit, I don't know. I just know that I didn't wanna sit up in that apartment and hear no more of that bullshit. They were in there fucking like wild animals."

Erica couldn't hold in her laughter. He had looked so thuggish and so mean, but Pierre was so goofy.

"If you're hungry, we could go eat. Like I said, it really doesn't matter to me what we do."

"Dang, we just ate some tacos. You came a little too late. So umm, what else did you have in mind?"

"Fuck it, let's just ride out. I've been locked up for so long unable to do what the hell I want. We could just chill. You cool with that?"

Erica didn't have anything else to do, so spending time with Pierre wasn't a bad idea. She quickly said yes and sat back to buckle up her seat belt. The ride was somewhat awkward. They were both from two different worlds, but somehow their differences were like a strong magnet that pulled them closer.

After driving for a while, they finally pulled up to a liquor store. "I need to grab something from here. Do you want something?" Pierre asked.

"Yeah."

Pierre helped her out of the truck, and then they walked in the store hand in hand as if they were a couple. Pierre stayed up front getting some blunts while she went to the cooler in the back to get a bottle of water. After a minute she walked up front, holding her water and a big bag of plain potato chips.

As she placed the items on the counter for the cashier to bag up, Pierre started to get annoyed. There were two dusty-ass niggas staring at Erica just a little too hard, and he was ready to go back to the old him. He tried to ignore them, but then the dumb niggas started mumbling shit.

"Damn, look at that bitch. She bad as fuck," the guy in the red shirt said.

Then the taller dude in a black shirt added his two cents. "Man, I swear I'll fuck the shit out of that bitch and fuck around and get that bitch pregnant." They both started to laugh.

Pierre couldn't believe them li'l bum-ass niggas even thought they had a chance with someone like her. Then, on top of that, they were being very disrespectful. Pierre looked up to see if Erica had heard them, but she was digging in her purse while the cashier helped someone at the lottery register.

"Ay, li'l niggas," Pierre called out, trying to get the guys' attention. But what he wasn't expecting was for Erica to turn back and look his way. He just looked at her, playing shit off. He couldn't let her see what he was up to.

The cashier telling her the total took her attention off Pierre for a second. The guys were still looking his way, wondering what the hell he wanted. Pierre walked up behind Erica and gave the cashier the money for her stuff.

"What's up?" the guy with the red shirt said, trying to be hard.

Pierre whispered to Erica to get his change as he turned around to address the guys. Without saying a word, not wanting to draw too much attention to himself, Pierre lifted the side of his shirt up. They quickly took away all that tough shit, seeing his gun and the tattoo on his hand that represented what crew he was with.

"My bad, nigga. We didn't know," the tough guy in the red said.

"We good?" the other one asked with his hands up, surrendering.

Pierre grabbed Erica's bag and her hand with his other hand. He walked out of the store laughing at them niggas who had just bitched up in the store.

"Thanks for buying my stuff. My card is in here somewhere in this stupid bag," Erica said, buckling her seat belt.

"It's all good, shawty. I do know how to be a gentleman. There's more to me than being a thug," he said, laughing.

Erica started laughing. "Okay, Mr. Miller, that's good to know."

Finally making it to their destination, Pierre parked and pulled out a bag of weed and the blunts that he bought from the store. Something told him to look up. When he did, he saw Erica's innocent eyes staring at him.

"Damn, I'm sorry. It's a habit."

Erica didn't want to seem uptight and have him feeling like his every move was being watched and judged, so she changed the subject. "Wow, I haven't been down here in years. I really like it down here the most when it's dark and they turn all the lights on. Downtown Detroit was always beautiful at night," Erica said, looking around, full of excitement.

Pierre was happy that he had picked a place that she would enjoy. The two found an empty bench that was facing the beautiful blue water on the riverwalk. Pierre started to think that she must have been so tired the night before that she didn't even notice the view of the lights from his crib.

"Yeah, before I got knocked, I used to come out here and chill. Looking at the water helped me clear my mind."

Listening to him talk, Erica could tell that there was a deeper side to him than just a drug dealer. And the side that he was showing now was who she wanted to get to know better.

Picking the conversation back up, Erica started talking again. "My father's church does a walk for cancer down here every year, but I haven't been out here in a few years." She really wasn't trying to cry in front of him and have him thinking that she was a big crybaby, but this conversation had started bringing up old memories of her mother.

Pierre found himself watching her body movement as she talked, and it wasn't hard to see how she was no longer the same person who had started the conversation. Something was definitely wrong with her. "You all right, shawty?"

Not sure what to say, Erica got up from the bench and walked over toward the rail that separated her from the water. She allowed a few tears to drop. Pierre wasn't sure what he had said to upset her, but he didn't wanna be the reason for her to be crying. He let her have her privacy at first, but after a few minutes, he got up to make sure she was okay.

As he leaned on the rail facing her, he slowly lifted her head up and used his finger to wipe away her tears. "I'm not sure what's going on, but I'm here if you need someone to talk to."

Erica didn't respond at first. She just looked back down at the water while trying to calm herself down. For a moment they both just stood there speechless. He stood there watching her. There was something about her that touched a soft spot in his heart that he thought he had lost, but it made him wanna be there to make her feel better.

Finally looking back up, Erica softly started to apologize. "I'm sorry. I'm usually not a big crybaby. I'm not sure what came over me."

Through her apology he could sense that she knew what was bothering her deep down inside, but she wasn't ready to talk about it. He also hated how she felt like she owed him an apology for showing her feelings.

"Nah, ma, it's okay. You don't owe me shit. You only human. But on some real shit, I'm here if you ever wanna talk."

Erica felt like he was being sincere about what he was saying. "Thank you, Pierre. I really appreciate it," she said just above a whisper.

Something was going through Pierre's mind, and he just had to act on his feelings. He pulled Erica closer toward him. He then placed a soft kiss on her lips. After that little peck, Erica pulled back.

She wasn't expecting that, but she wasn't mad at him either. Pierre's mind was racing. He wasn't sure if he had made a mistake with her or what. She was so shy and quiet, sometimes it was hard to tell what she was thinking.

The two stood face-to-face just looking at each other. "My bad, shawty, I—"

Before he could even finish his sentence, the magnet between them turned back on, and their lips became one again. That very moment, it felt like the world came to a standstill for just them. Not only were their friends trying to push them together, but it also seemed like the universe was working hard too.

Chapter 4

Erica was at an all-time high. In the past, she had snuck around and had li'l boyfriends, but those relationships only lasted for about a good three months. At first she thought what they had was real, but then the guys started demanding sex, and Erica wasn't ready for all that. She was heartbroken for a while until she realized that they were fools and she actually was better without them in her life.

Their kiss slowly came to an end, and Erica couldn't hide her feelings. Her beautiful brown skin lit up from her blushing so much. The smile on her face made Pierre feel good for making the decision to kiss her.

"I hope I wasn't out of line for doing that, shawty," P said, breaking the silence between them.

At first Erica was stuck with her words. She didn't know how to tell him she enjoyed it without looking fast. Soon, the words flowed out of her mouth. "Actually, you weren't out of line. I really enjoyed that kiss," she finally admitted.

"Good, 'cause you're too beautiful to be crying and shit, and I'm feeling that smile you're rocking right now."

Both were locked into the moment as he kept his arms wrapped around her. The view of the water was beautiful and helped ease their minds.

Erica was so caught up in her thoughts that she didn't even feel Pierre release her. "Ay, it's getting late. What time you gotta be at the crib?" he asked, taking her out of her thoughts.

Although she was grown, it was embarrassing to have someone ask her what time she had to be at home as if she were 16 years old. Just the thought of being treated like a baby upset her.

"I'm staying at Nicole's house this week. You know I'm not a baby, right?" she dryly asked.

"My bad. Once you told me who your dad was, I had to accept the fact that your daddy worked for the Lord. So you ready to roll out or what? We could go get something to eat or whatever you want to do."

Thinking about the real reason she loved downtown, she replied, "Is it okay if we stay a little while longer? I really want to see the lights when the sun goes down completely."

That was when Pierre thought about what she said when they first arrived. She did mention how much she loved the lights down there. "Yeah, we can stay. Like I said before, it's whatever you want."

Pierre placed himself back behind Erica. He placed soft kisses on her neck that sent shocks through her body. She loved the vibe his body was sending her body.

"You were right. The view is beautiful once it gets to be nighttime. It's been years since I've been down here, and I haven't been home long enough to see it from my room."

"Yeah, I love it. When I was younger, I was the kid who loved sleeping on the floor around the Christmas tree just to be around all the bright lights. Right now, I have lights hanging around my room, and I'm grown." She laughed after admitting one of her embarrassing secrets. She couldn't believe that she had just shared that with him. That right there just might have been another sign that she really liked Pierre.

Of course Pierre's silly self started to laugh at her confession. "Wow, I guess we all have something that we love that takes us back to our childhood."

"I'm glad you feel that way. Now I know I won't be judged by you. Are you gonna tell me what you hold on to from your childhood?" she asked, curious about his answer.

"Shit, I'm not about to embarrass myself. I'm having too much fun laughing at you," he teased.

Erica playfully hit him on his chest.

"Don't break your li'l-ass hand," he continued to tease.

After more conversation and laughs, Erica felt good to be able to talk to someone other than Nicole and her dad. When talking to her dad, she couldn't get into everything because he was so strict, and every conversation turned into them talking about the Lord. Then with Nicole, she would listen, but somehow their conversation always turned into them talking about Mekco and how good his sex was. Pierre was so chill and silly at the same time that it made it easy for her to deal with.

Soon after, they decided they had no other choice but to leave the riverwalk. Out of nowhere it started pouring. Pierre grabbed Erica and hurried to his truck.

"Come on, girl, before all that chocolate melts," he joked.

As they finally reached the car and Pierre unlocked the doors, Erica had to remind him that chocolate as perfect as hers didn't melt in the rain. Of course he chuckled before he got in the car.

"Okay, so what now?" she asked, curious to see what the plan was. They both were soaking wet from the storm.

"I hate getting rained on, but I'm hungry. I want to go eat, so let's change into something dry, then head back out," he suggested.

"I'm down, but first I have to call Nicole so she can let me in. My bag is at her house."

Erica pulled out her phone and dialed Nicole's number. After a couple of rings, Erica hung up.

Nicole heard Erica's ringtone go off on her phone on her nightstand. She had a feeling that she was calling so that she could get in.

After their third round, she had gone to the kitchen to get some water and noticed P and Erica were gone. She was happy that her friend was gaining another friend.

"Damn, Mekco, that's Erica calling. They must be back. Let me get up and get the phone."

"Man, they good. That nigga got his own place to take her to. Lie your ass back down," Mekco ordered.

Nicole lay back on his chest and closed her eyes, trying to doze off like nothing happened.

"I swear I'm gonna replace her as my bestie. She don't never answer her phone when I need her to," Erica said, sliding her phone back into her purse.

"Let me call this nigga Mekco," Pierre said, pulling out his phone and calling his bro.

After a few rings, he hung the phone up. "That nigga not answering his phone either. Them muthafuckas probably still fucking or passed out from dehydration, 'cause I know they dry as hell."

Erica laughed, then asked, "So what now? I can't get in the house and I'm wet. We can't go out like this."

"Just put your seat belt back on. I got an idea. You just got to work with me."

"Work with you, huh? And what exactly did you have in mind?" Erica asked. So far, he hadn't done anything that would put her in harm's way or put her in a position that would make her uncomfortable or make her step out of character, so she wasn't too worried. She just wondered what he was thinking about.

"I know we are still in the phase of getting to know each other, but just know that I will never do anything to hurt you on purpose or make you be who you're not when you're around me. You're a good girl, and I understand that that's actually what I like about you," Pierre admitted once he saw Erica's face show some sign of worry.

Erica sat back in her seat and let him take over the plans for the rest of the night.

After driving for a hot minute, they ended up back downtown, but at Pierre's place this time. If it were anyone else, Erica would have panicked, but something in her was telling her to trust Pierre. Yeah, she had just met him, and if he were gonna be a grimy dude, he would have shown her that side of him already.

"Let me get you something dry to slip on. You're soaking wet, and I'd hate for you to fuck around and catch a damn cold," he said as he walked toward his bedroom.

Erica followed him to the back with her arms folded up, blocking her C-cup breasts. She was still a little shy around him, and the wet white T-shirt she had on showed off her hard nipples.

He couldn't help but grin. He had already peeped them before she tried to cover them up. Even though he wasn't used to dealing with shy females like her, he had to admit that her innocence was turning him on even more.

At first something was telling him it would be best to leave her alone, but he found himself liking her. He fought with himself, going back and forth on his feelings about her. He was a man fresh out of jail, and he had needs that she wasn't ready to handle. It was crazy that he knew this but still wanted her to himself.

"Hey, here goes a T-shirt you can stick on while your clothes dry. Once you're done changing, come out here and we can decide on what we're gonna eat," Pierre ordered before walking out of his room.

Erica stood there for a minute. She was lost in her thoughts. She had only known Pierre for two days and here she was about to spend another night at his house. From what she could tell, Nicole and Mekco were pushing them together, but she heard from the horse's mouth how he got down before getting locked up. She wasn't anything like the females he was used to dealing with. When it all boiled down, she was left thinking that she was out of his league.

Peeling the wet clothes off her moist skin, Erica stared at her reflection in the mirror. She admired her brown skin and long black hair. She was her mother's twin except for the large hips that Mrs. Collins had.

Pierre had just remembered to bring Erica a towel. As he walked back to his room, he caught her standing in front of the mirror. He was stuck in his tracks as he saw her wearing nothing but some black boy shorts. She was sexy as fuck before, but without any clothes he was having a hard time trying not to reach out and touch her.

"Damn," he mumbled, but not low enough.

Erica jumped at the sound of his voice. "You scared me."

"My bad, shawty. I brought you a towel to dry off with," he said, handing her the towel.

As she took the towel and hurried to wrap it around her, her shyness took over, and she was stuck staring at the carpet.

"No need to be shy. You're beautiful with a nice body," he admitted as he licked his lips.

The combination of his deep voice telling her how beautiful she was and the way his eyes pierced a hole through her body left Erica in a trance as Pierre walked closer toward her. If it weren't for her being saved, she would have allowed the passionate kiss that they shared to go a little further.

With his hands roaming all over her body and his mouth hungrily sucking on her lips, Erica could feel her heart pounding faster than usual. Now, she hadn't gone all the way before because of the whole "saving herself for marriage" thing. She had made out before, but this time was a little different. Before, she always stopped her boyfriends, but with Pierre, she wanted him to keep his hands on her.

Pierre slid his hands in her boy shorts and cupped her ass. It wasn't one of those stupid phat asses, but it did hold a little weight. Either way he liked it.

"Wait, Pierre," Erica whispered, stepping out of his grip.

Breathing faster than normal, Pierre pecked her lips one last time. He wasn't ready to stop and hated that she was. "What's up, ma?"

Being honest, Erica had to admit how she really was feeling. "Look, Pierre, that felt good, but I'm not ready for all that right now."

Pierre stood there with a dumb look on his face. He wasn't sure what her problem was. She was just all into everything, and just like that she turned cold. She wasn't sure what to say after his face told her that he was confused, but she was too. They both were at a loss for words at that moment.

Hearing her phone ring took both of their minds off of what was really going on. Erica walked over toward the dresser and picked up her phone. She grinned seeing that it was Nicole calling.

"Hey, what are you doing? I called you earlier."

"My bad, boo. You know when my baby is around, I be too busy to answer the phone," Nicole said as she looked over to the other side of the bed where Mekco lay knocked out.

"Well, I'm glad that you could squeeze me into your busy schedule. I swear if it weren't for Pierre, I'd be stuck out in the rain."

"Girl, whatever. Anyway, you on your way back to the apartment or you good with Pierre?" Nicole asked her friend.

Erica looked at the disappointment on Pierre's face and knew that she had messed up her chance with him. It was fun while it lasted, but she just wasn't ready to move forward, especially after only knowing him for two days. He was smooth, but not that damn smooth.

"I guess I'll see you in a little bit," Erica said before hanging up the phone.

Hearing her say that she was going back to Nicole's place, Pierre knew it was gonna be a wrap for anything that he had planned. He wasn't gonna rush or beg for no pussy, but he did enjoy her company. With the hoes from his past, he just fucked and sent them on their way, but he enjoyed chilling with Erica. Plus, it felt good to be able to be himself around her. He would crack all his jokes and she would be right there laughing at each one, being silly right along with him. She was someone different from the rest.

Pierre didn't say a word as he walked out of the room. She had clearly made her mind up on what she wanted to do for the rest of the night. The way he looked at it was they just met and weren't in any type of relationship, so there wasn't any point in being mad.

Pierre took a seat on his couch. Since his clothes were also wet, he had changed into a pair of hoop shorts and a T-shirt. He grabbed the remote and flipped through the channels. He wasn't sure what he wanted to watch. He just wanted to take his mind off Erica. It probably would have worked if she didn't come out of the room with nothing on but the T-shirt that he had given her to wear.

"Here go my wet clothes."

Pierre got up from the couch and took the clothes from her hand. He then went to the back to place her clothes in the dryer. Erica took a seat on the couch and tucked her shirt under her thighs.

"Your clothes should be ready in about twenty minutes," Pierre said, taking a seat on the other couch.

They sat in silence for a while. Erica's thoughts started to get the best of her, and she had no choice but to speak her mind. "Pierre, are you mad at me now?" she bluntly asked.

Pierre turned the TV down and looked over toward her on the other couch. "Look, Erica, to be honest, I'm not mad at you. We cool, shawty. We both were just caught up in the moment."

Erica could sense that he was upset even though he didn't say it. She sat there for a minute blaming herself and wondering if she was leading him on. "Look, I'm sorry for leading you on. I do like you, but I just—"

Before she could finish her sentence, Pierre cut her off. "Look, ma, like I said before, we good. You don't owe me shit, so stop apologizing for being you." Pierre gave her a little grin to show her that they were still friends. "I heard you on the phone with your girl. Do you wanna go back to her place or chill with me for a while tonight?"

"I can chill here for a while, but I did tell her I was coming back over there," Erica mumbled.

"Okay. I'll order us a pizza or something, and we can find a movie to get into. After that I can take you back to Nicole's crib."

Erica didn't say a word. He knew what it was, and at the end of the day, he was no different from the next guy.

After two hours of awkwardness in his crib, they finally pulled up to Nicole's apartment. Pierre felt some type of way, but he still walked her inside of the building and made sure she got in okay. As they stood outside of Nicole's door, Pierre gave her a friendly hug.

"You got my number. Use it when you wanna get away and chill."

Erica said, "Okay," before opening the door so she could go in.

After a long, hot shower, she went into the guest room that she'd made hers and climbed into the bed. She lay with the thought of Pierre on her mind. She liked him, and he was cool, but the way he acted when she wouldn't give it up made her question her taste in guys. She knew what she wanted out of life, but now she also questioned if she was a big tease.

After lying there for a while, she finally started to doze off when the bedroom door opened. Erica sat up only to find Nicole standing there. "What's up, boo? Are you still mad at me?" Nicole asked, hopping in the bed with her best friend.

"No, girl, I'm not mad at you, but I'm kind of disappointed in myself," Erica admitted.

Nicole sat back up. "What the hell happened? What did you do? Did you finally give it up?"

Erica sat up in the bed and popped Nicole in the head. "No, girl, I didn't give anything up. Why is that the first thing that came to your mind?"

Nicole giggled. "Okay, I'm gonna calm down and let you talk then."

Erica put her serious face on so Nicole would know that she wasn't playing. "So I've been chilling with Pierre all day, which you should know because you wouldn't answer your phone for me. Anyway, we were cool, chilling and having a good time. We ended up back at his house and we kissed. I had a feeling that he wanted to go further, but I froze up. I think he is mad at me now. Nicole, is there something wrong with me? I mean, at my age, should I be ready for sex or what?"

"Ugh, bitch, let me get you straight right now. First of all, age doesn't matter. If you're not ready, then that's that. If he can't understand and respect how you feel, then fuck that nigga. Second, ain't shit wrong with you saving yourself for the right person. I wish I could start over with my sex life and only have one body count. Third, I'm sorry for pushing you closer toward his sorry ass. Do you forgive me, boo?"

Erica giggled at her friend before answering, "Yes, I forgive your crazy self. I just thought he was gonna be different from the others. I was really starting to like him, too. He was so sweet and chill at first. Pierre really had me fooled," she admitted.

"It's okay, boo. There will be somebody out there for you," Nicole said before climbing out of the bed and leaving the room.

Erica replayed the day over in her mind while trying to go to sleep. Even after talking to her bestie, she still felt some type of way. She felt stupid for falling for his nice-guy routine, and then she blamed herself even more because she did allow him to get comfortable with touching and kissing her. She was at fault for leading him on.

Instead of going home, Pierre pulled up to a bar that he used to visit before getting knocked. He had a lot on his mind, and a few drinks and pussy were all he needed at that moment. He took a seat at the bar and ordered a double shot of Hennessy and a beer.

After shit went south with Erica, he realized that when he said he was gonna wash his hands of her the night before, he should have kept his word. She was still young and wasn't ready for the life that he was living.

It was clear that her dad still ran her life and probably threw God in her face every time she didn't do as he wanted her to do. She was cool, and Pierre had enjoyed her company while it lasted, but he had to pull back from her. The fact that he was trying to forget about her and just chill and have a few drinks but couldn't get her off his mind said a lot. He had caught feelings no matter how many times he said he was done with her. Pierre wasn't used to females turning him down like that, and the simple fact that she did only intrigued him more.

"I know that's not P over there," Jessica said to her friend Michelle.

Michelle turned around, then quickly turned back toward her friend. "Yeah, bitch, that's him. I wonder when he got out."

Jessica didn't even bother to respond. She stood up and fixed her dress. "I'll be back."

Michelle watched as her friend walked over toward P.

"Hey, P, long time no see. What's up with you?"

P turned his attention to Jessica. He looked at her, then remembered that he used to fuck with her before getting knocked. "What's up, ma? What's good with ya?"

"Shit, just here chilling with my homegirl Michelle. We trying to catch a body if you know what I mean," she said with nothing but lust in her eyes.

"Yeah, I know what you talking about. This ain't my first time meeting you. So what's the ticket?" he asked. At this point he was desperate and didn't care if he had to pay for it.

Jessica smiled before saying, "You know it's usually two hundred dollars, but tonight I'm with my girl, so it's gonna cost ya double."

P finished off his shot, then drank his beer halfway down before telling her to come on. As he walked out toward the door, Jessica went back to her table and told her friend that they had a job for the night.

The plan was for them to follow him back to his place, but he changed his mind and led them to a hotel. He didn't know them bitches like that, and bringing them to his crib would have been stupid. After he fucked the friends, he didn't want them hoes popping back up, stalking him and shit. He just hoped that he could take his mind off Erica long enough to enjoy the company of the hoes following him to the room.

The next morning, Mekco got up and showered. He had to meet up with Li'l Trey and Face to collect some bread from them. He looked at Nicole and saw that she was still knocked out. He grinned just thinking about how he put it on her the night before. He thought about waking her up before he left, but then she would have begged him to stay a little longer, and he couldn't afford to be late to collect his money.

Once he got in the car, he called P. "What's up, nigga? You still asleep or what?"

"Nah, nigga, I'm up. You know a nigga still used to getting up early as hell. I'm still on that jail-house alarm system," P admitted.

Mekco laughed before asking, "Ay, you still with shawty?"

"Hell nah. I dropped her ass off last night. Let me tell you this now—don't ever try to hook me up with no chicks. I'm fresh out of jail and was trying to get my dick wet, not fucking babysit no bitch so you and your girl can fuck with a fucking audience."

Hearing him say that only made Mekco laugh hard. "Dog, I wasn't trying to make you babysit. You know me and my girl don't give a fuck about who's around. But I swear I thought she was cool."

P ended the conversation by simply saying, "Fuck her. I'm doing me from here on out."

Chapter 5

Erica found herself thinking about Pierre from time to time. It then hit her that they hadn't talked in three long weeks. Although she had only been around him for two days, she thought that she had made a friend. Seeing that he hadn't reached out since the night she turned him down, she then realized that maybe she had dodged a bullet.

Lately her mind went back and forth, causing her to have mixed feelings about Pierre. She often found herself questioning if she was crazy for even thinking about him.

"Ay, boo, you okay?" Nicole asked as she walked into the pastor's office.

Erica snapped out of her thoughts and looked away from the papers she was copying. "Yeah, I'm good. Just trying to finish up this stuff for my dad. Since I will be at your house for the weekend, he got me making copies for Sunday's service. That way I don't have to come down here on Saturday to work."

"Okay, so do you need any help or are you good?" Nicole asked as she took a seat in front of the desk.

"I'm almost done. I'm so ready to go. Bible study ran extra long tonight."

Nicole laughed. "Did you notice Bible study always ends late when you coming to my house afterward?"

Both girls laughed before Erica spoke up. "Shut up before my daddy hears you."

"Girl, bye. He's gone already. You know I don't enter this office if he is still around. Anyway, I think he been getting fresh with my mama."

Erica put the stack of papers down and looked at her friend strangely. "Girl, don't play with me like that. Why would you even think that?" she asked. She wasn't mad, but she wanted all the tea.

"'Cause my mom was cooking dinner before service, and she said she had invited him over for dinner. When I asked her if she had dessert, too, she just looked at me and laughed."

Erica shook her head. "Your mom cooking dinner for them too don't mean she trying to get fresh. Is that really what you're getting out of everything?" Erica said, still laughing at the thought of her dad getting a girlfriend.

"So what do you think about that? I mean, are you mad about it?"

"Nicole, to be honest, I'm not mad at all. Maybe if he had a friend, he'd get off my back."

Both girls laughed before Nicole said, "We gonna be sisters for real now if they get married."

After locking up the building and the church gates, they jumped into Nicole's car and made their way to her apartment.

Erica sat on her bed at Nicole's house studying for finals. The following week she was taking her finals, and she wanted to make sure everything that she learned that semester was implanted in her head.

Nicole had just gotten off the phone with Mekco, and she was ready to go have some fun. She entered the guest bedroom and flopped down on the bed. Erica put her book down and turned toward her. "What is it? What do you want, Nicole?" she asked.

"There's this party tonight, and I think we should go have a little fun. You down?"

"I have finals next week. Do you not see me studying?"

"Please, come have fun with me. I'll be your best friend for life, and we could be sisters forever," Nicole said, laughing.

Erica laughed at her before standing up from the bed. "Man, what are you wearing?"

Nicole jumped up with a huge smile on her face. "Thanks, boo."

"Whatever."

"I'm not sure what I'm wearing. Let me go search my closet. Please find something cute and be ready in the next two hours." Just like that, Nicole disappeared out of the room.

Erica opened up the closet and stared at all of the clothes that she secretly bought behind her daddy's back and kept at Nicole's house. She pulled out a black dress that she thought would look good on her. After a second thought she put it back. She wanted to have fun without having fools thinking she was ready to go home with them. She then pulled out a pair of skinny jeans and a black cropped top.

"This will do just fine," she said to herself.

After showering and getting dressed, she stood in the mirror flat ironing her hair. She always liked her hair up in a messy bun, but that night she wanted to change her looks just a little.

"Okay, bitch, I see you," Nicole said, walking into the room and admiring her best friend's beauty.

"Must you be so loud?" she joked with Nicole.

"Whatever. We look good as hell. Let me put my lip gloss on, and then we can leave. I heard this party is about to be off the fucking hook."

"I'm glad I did wear pants. You didn't tell me this was a house party. I hope the cops don't get called and we gotta run out like a bunch of wild animals," Erica teased.

Nicole smacked her lips. "Ugh, come on now. Don't start all that shit. We just got here. Please let's have a good time," Nicole said as they climbed out of her car.

Erica didn't bother to say anything. She just walked in the house with Nicole. As she entered the house, she was impressed by how big and nicely decorated it was. It was like a mini mansion. "Dang, whose house is this?"

"Girl, this house belongs to a nigga named Cross. He was the original leader of the Detroit Brick Boyz back when Mekco was a young boy. He's the one who put most of these niggas on. If I'm not mistaken, if it weren't for him, Mekco's daddy would have never had a chance to run the streets with P's dad when they were growing up."

Erica took in the info, but her stomach felt funny once Pierre's name was mentioned. She repeatedly tried telling herself that it didn't matter if she ever saw him again, but now she was back thinking about him.

"Come on, boo, let's go get a drink," Nicole suggested, grabbing Erica's hand and leading her toward the bar. Nicole ordered them both a Long Island iced tea. "Let's start with something weak. We in white folks' land and gotta drive back home safe," she said, laughing.

The girls had to walk toward the back to find a table. As they walked through the crowd, they heard someone say, "Bring your ass here, girl."

Not knowing who was talking, both girls looked up, and there stood Mekco. Nicole jumped up with a grin on her face. "Hey, baby, it took you long enough to get here."

"Man, we've been here for a minute now. Where the fuck you been?" Mekco asked, picking up her cup and taking a sip. "Nicole, why you drinking this bullshit? It's an open bar, and this is what you got?"

Mekco then took a seat, and Nicole sat on his lap. The homeboys he came with were rude like him and didn't speak to Erica as they took a seat at their table.

"Hey, rude asses, this is my girl Erica. Now speak," she ordered.

Face, Brandon, Cory, and Brian all looked Erica's way and said hey. She said hey back and turned her attention toward her phone. She wasn't interested in chatting with any of the dudes at the table. In her opinion, they all were probably after one thing, and she wasn't providing what they needed.

As they all sat around the table drinking and talking about crap that didn't impress Erica not one bit, she excused herself and walked away.

Sometimes she secretly envied Nicole because she was dating a boss and all of his homeboys respected her, but at the same time she hated how Nicole could get around Mekco. She became a whole other person at times. It was like Mekco controlled her with his sex or something.

Erica found a bathroom on the second floor since there was a long line at the one on the first floor.

"I'm just curious why y'all would come sit at this table and not speak to my girl? That probably made her feel uncomfortable," Nicole asked the members of the Detroit Brick Boyz.

At first nobody said a word. They just looked off as if she hadn't just asked a question. Mekco then took a sip of her drink. "Leave these niggas alone, Nicole. They were given orders not to say shit to her."

Nicole couldn't help but laugh. "By who and why?" she asked, trying not to laugh too loud.

"I did, muthafucka," Mekco said loud enough for everyone at the table to hear.

Nicole gave her lover a weird look.

He gave her a kiss on her forehead before saying, "Stop being so nosy, baby."

As Erica walked out of the bathroom, she couldn't help but notice the nice painting on the wall. The guy they called Cross had good taste, she thought. All of his paintings were gorgeous, but there was one that caught her eye. She stood in front of a painting of a beautiful woman. She admired the raw beauty the lady held. The lady had a very dark complexion, but it glowed as if the sun was shining right on her body.

"You're just as beautiful if not more."

Erica turned around and was surprised to see Pierre standing there leaning on the wall.

"Thank you," Erica shyly responded.

Pierre didn't say shit else as he walked closer toward her and cradled her in his arms. For his own personal reasons, he had kept his distance from her, but he really missed the hell out of her. He wasn't a bit surprised when she wrapped her arms around him. He then pulled back a little to look her in her eyes.

"I missed your short ass," he said, laughing.

She giggled a little before he grabbed her face and kissed her. As they shared that kiss, Erica felt lost in her thoughts. She had been telling herself to forget about him because he wasn't the right person for her, but the first time she ran into him she allowed him to tongue her down in a stranger's hallway.

"Come here. I need to talk to you for a minute," Pierre whispered as he pulled her into one of the bedrooms.

She couldn't deny that there were still feelings for him that didn't leave, and with those feelings she allowed him to take her into the room without a fight. She stood there, waiting for him to say something. "What is it?" she asked.

Pierre didn't know what he was gonna say. He just really wanted her to himself. He then drank the last bit of his drink before holding her back in his arms. This time he held her a little longer while she allowed his hands to roam all over her body. Erica didn't stop him. She was enjoying his touch and all the kissing and sucking on her neck and lips.

"Pierre, wait a minute," Erica managed to say after finally pushing him away.

"Come on, shorty, don't be like that. Just let me hold you for a minute," he said sluggishly.

"Pierre, you're drunk. Go lie down and chill for a minute," she ordered as she walked him over toward the bed.

Pierre sat down, then pulled her down on his lap.

"Pierre, let me go get you some water or something," she said, trying to unwrap his arms from around her.

"Nah, don't leave me. I need you right now," he half-ass mumbled as he lay back in the bed. Pierre held on to Erica with a tight grip. He knew that he wasn't drunk, but something wasn't right with his drink.

Erica sat there, not sure what to do. She knew he was drunk, and from the looks of things, he wasn't gonna let her leave that room anytime soon. "Look, we're at someone's house. You can't just climb in these people's beds. Get up so I can at least drive you home."

Pierre lay there faded. Since he had been out of jail, he drank every night, and this was his first time feeling like that. If he didn't know shit else in the world, he knew he wanted Erica to be by his side.

Erica dug inside of his pants pocket and pulled out his keys. "Pierre, I'm about to take you home, okay?" she yelled, but he didn't respond.

"Dang," she said as she thought about how she was supposed to get him to his truck. She then pulled out her phone and called Nicole.

"What's up? Where the hell did you disappear to?" Nicole asked.

Erica explained how she was in a room upstairs and she needed help with getting Pierre to his truck.

"Girl, fuck that nigga. Leave his ass up there, and let him sleep that shit off. Plus, you don't fuck with him like that anyway," Nicole yelled, making Mekco look at her funny.

"Man, what the fuck is wrong with you?" Mekco asked.

"Nothing, baby. Stop being nosy," she said, feeding him the same line he'd fed her earlier.

Mekco wasn't buying that shit at all. He snatched her phone right out of her hand. "Hello, who is this?"

"Hey, this is Erica. Mekco, I'm upstairs with Pierre, and he is drunk. I need help getting him to his truck so I can take him home."

"All right, we're on our way," he said. He could tell that she was scared. After getting their exact location, Mekco hung the phone up. He gave Nicole a dirty look. "So you really told her to leave my bro up there fucked up like that? I swear, girl, you a fucking trip."

"I'm sorry daddy, but he did hurt my girl's feelings, and I was just looking out for her," Nicole said as she placed kisses on his lips to calm him down. She hated when he was mad at her.

He looked around and spotted Brandon and Brian. He told Nicole to get up so he could get up and help his bro. Nicole watched as he walked up to his boys, said a few words, then took off with them, going up the stairs. Nicole was being nosy and followed.

Once they got to the room, they saw Pierre knocked out, but somehow he still managed to hold on to Erica.

"Damn, what you do to my bro?" Mekco said jokingly.

"Whatever. Pierre just drank too much like a fool," Erica said as she tried to get up again, but just like the times before, Pierre held a grip on her that prevented her from leaving his side.

"This nigga bugging," Mekco said as he snatched Pierre's arm from around Erica.

She then stood up and went over toward the dresser where Nicole was standing.

"Girl, you done put some type of voodoo on that nigga. He wasn't playing about you leaving with anybody else but him tonight," Nicole whispered in her ear. She knew Mekco would be talking shit if she had said that shit out loud. Both girls laughed at her joke.

"I just pray he will be okay," Erica mumbled to her friend.

"Boo, he drunk, not dead. That man will be fine," Nicole mumbled back.

"Y'all niggas help me put this nigga in his truck," Mekco ordered the other members of his crew.

Nicole giggled as she watched the guys damn near drag his ass down the stairs and outside. Erica had his keys, so she walked off and pulled up closer toward the house, just to make their job easier.

The crew laid him in the back seat, then shut the door.

"Ay, Erica, we're gonna follow you back to his house and get him in the house. Nicole, you ride with your girl," Mekco said before he and his boys jumped in the car.

"Girl, you know I was trying not to say anything, but what the hell are you doing? One minute you don't want to deal with him because you found out he only wanted to hit it. Now tonight we at a party full of niggas with bread and you locked in a room with him playing 'Captain Save a Nigga' and shit. What's up with that?"

"Nicole, I don't know. There's just something about him that I can't shake. Just look at him back there. He really needed me tonight. I couldn't just leave him like that. When you flaked on me not once but twice to get busy with Mekco, he was there making sure I was good. I'm just returning the favor," Erica tried to explain to her best friend.

"Yeah, okay, whatever, girl," was all Nicole could say before turning her attention back to her phone. She knew her girl was feeling P, and at first, she was okay with it, but after he showed his true colors, she wasn't sure if she wanted her friend with a guy like that. At the end of the day, she only wanted to protect her friend's feelings.

Once they pulled up to Pierre's place, everyone got out of their rides to play their roles. Erica used Pierre's keys to let them in.

"Damn, this nigga heavy as hell. Where you want this nigga?" Brandon asked, looking at Erica.

"Umm, just put him back there in his bedroom," Erica said, pointing toward the back of the house. There was only one bedroom, so they shouldn't have had a problem finding his room.

"So, your li'l friend is home now. Are you going back to the party or what?" Nicole asked.

She was starting to get on Erica's nerves. It was crazy how quick she was to forget that her relationship with Mekco wasn't always perfect.

"Come on now, Nicole, let me just make sure he's all right."

"Come on, Nicole. Let's get the fuck outta here," Mekco ordered as his boys started to walk away.

Nicole looked back to see if Erica was gonna get up to leave with her. Erica turned her head, then looked down, burning a hole in the floor. She didn't wanna leave Pierre, but she didn't want her friend to feel like she was being stupid for staying by his side.

"Ay, Erica, make sure my nigga good. Call us in the morning with an update on how he is doing," Mekco ordered.

Erica started to notice how he never asked people to do anything. He just gave orders. Even though she wasn't one of his workers, she said okay before everyone walked out.

After making sure the door was locked, she went into the kitchen to get Pierre a bottle of water. She then went into the bathroom to get some aspirin out of the medicine cabinet. She knew if he woke up with a headache, he was gonna need these items. She had gotten used to taking care of Nicole when she had hangovers.

As she walked in the room, Pierre started moving around in the bed. She placed the water bottle and pills on the nightstand. Since they had left the light on, she could see that he had started to sweat. Being a good friend, she took off his shoes, then took his clothes off. Once she was done helping him out, she went toward the door to turn the lights off and return to the couch.

After grabbing a sheet out of the linen closet and lying down on the couch, Erica stripped down to her bra and panties. She let the night's events replay through her mind before she ended up falling asleep herself. She knew the next day she was gonna have to deal with Nicole's attitude because she stayed the night with Pierre, and she'd need all her energy to battle her ass.

"Bro, why the hell you trying to fuck up my nigga's shit?" Mekco asked Nicole.

"What are you talking about? I wasn't trying to mess up anything, bro," she said, calling herself mocking him. She hated when he called her that like she was one of his niggas.

"Look, everybody could see that your girl was feeling P, and that nigga is definitely feeling her ass. He even told me that shit himself. So why is your li'l ass trying to block that shit?"

"That nigga not feeling shit, 'cause if he were, he wouldn't have played her when she ain't give it up. Then his trifling ass had the nerve to ignore her for three weeks. I was the one trying to tell her that there wasn't nothing wrong with her but it was his no-good ass," Nicole said, now raising her voice.

"Stay the fuck out they business. Your ass is always running that fucking mouth. I talked to that nigga about what happened, and he got his reasons why he stopped fucking with her."

Not listening and still running her mouth, Nicole asked, "So why he trying to fuck with her now?"

"Shut the fuck up and mind your business like I said," Mekco demanded.

He didn't even have to yell for Nicole to know that he was serious. His tone held enough power. Nicole knew better than to talk back or to make him upset, so she sat back in her seat and didn't say shit else. Since they had been together, Mekco was quick to put Nicole in her place. She also knew that a man with his status was wanted by any bitch trying to get a quick come-up. With that being said, she played her role. Being replaced wasn't an option in her book.

As they stopped at a red light, Nicole took that moment to rub on his print through his jeans. Anything sexual usually put him in a good space. Him not even paying her any attention made her mad, so she did it again. This time he pushed her hand off.

"Man, leave me alone. Don't you see me driving?"

"I'm sorry. Let's just go to your house and have some fun makeup sex," she suggested, hoping sex would fix whatever problem they were having.

"Nah, bro, I'm good."

Nicole tried to hold her composure the rest of the ride home. Him turning her down could only mean one thing and that was that he was tired of her shit. Once he pulled up to her apartment, she looked out the window and saw Brian park her car and start making his way toward them.

"Get out of my shit. I might be back later," Mekco coldly said.

Trying not to cry in front of Brian, she grabbed her keys, then ran into her building. Mekco had a way of always hurting her feelings, but there wasn't any way she was about to let him go.

As she climbed in the bed, she wrapped herself up in her sheet and cradled herself to sleep. Nicole had always been so strong-minded, but loving Mekco had become her weakness.

Sitting up on the couch, Erica grabbed her phone and looked at the time. It was 2:20 a.m. After using the bathroom, she cracked Pierre's bedroom door open and stepped in just to see how he was doing. He was still asleep, so she turned around to leave. She didn't want to wake him.

"Erica," Pierre called out.

She slowly walked back to the bed to see why he was calling her. "What is it? I didn't mean to wake you. I was just trying to see if you were all right now."

"Can you hand me that water, then come lie with me?" he asked.

"Man, Pierre, you better not throw up on me or we gonna have a problem," she said, secretly smiling at his request.

Erica grabbed the bottle of water off the night-stand and turned the lamp on before opening the water bottle up for him. Pierre drank the water down to the middle all while staring at her. He couldn't help but wonder what the hell she had on under the sheet that was wrapped around her body.

"Man, I'm good," he told her.

"Go ahead and lie back down. Don't try to pretend like you weren't just pissy drunk."

"I wasn't drunk. But fuck all that. Bring your sexy ass over here."

Erica walked closer toward the bed and just stood next to him. Pierre grabbed the sheet, but before it fell off her, she grabbed it tighter. Pierre laughed at her.

"Man, stop acting all shy and shit. I'm not on no bullshit, shorty. Open that shit up and let me get a li'l peek."

She knew she was playing with fire dealing with Pierre, but she slowly opened the sheet, then quickly closed it back up. "Okay, you got your peek. Now I'm about to go back to the couch."

It surprised her when she turned around to leave and he jumped up, grabbing her. She thought he would have been too sick to move that fast.

"Dang, Pierre!" she said, laughing.

He also laughed as her sheet dropped to the floor. She was enjoying his touch, but she thought it was crazy how, no matter how much time had just passed, they were back doing the same thing that caused a problem between them before. "Pierre, stop for a minute. I have to tell you something."

"What is it?"

"Remember what I told you the last time I was here? Well, I still feel the same way. I don't want you to get mad again and think I'm trying to play games with you. I mean, I like how you make me feel when we kiss or when you touch my body, but that's the furthest I'm willing to go," she honestly told him.

"Okay, shorty, I appreciate the honesty, and just to let you know, I'm not trying to rush shit with you."

The two shared another kiss before Pierre stopped. "Damn, my fucking head hurting like a muthafucka," he said, sitting back down on the bed. He had jumped up too fast, making shit worse.

"Here, Mr. Drunk," she said, handing him the aspirin from the nightstand. She then took a seat next to him.

He popped two of the pills. "Erica, stop saying I was drunk. I swear I wasn't drunk. I think that bitch making drinks put something in my cup."

"Really?"

"Hell yeah! Think about it. I was cool at first. Then something just hit me once I drank that last little bit that was in my cup. I've been drunk before and never felt like I was about to stop breathing. That's why I didn't want you to leave my side."

Pierre lay back down, hoping that his headache would go away soon. Everyone thought he was drunk, but he knew after a few shots he wouldn't have been like that. Some shit wasn't right, and he was gonna get to the bottom of that shit, but for right now he just wanted to cuddle with Erica. He had missed her company more than anything.

Erica thought it was all about sex, but truthfully, he pulled away because he was scared of hurting her or getting her caught up in his shit. He told himself that he could just forget about her, but once he saw her step into the party, he knew he had to have her in his life. While every other female at that party wore little dresses and walked around half naked trying to get a nigga's attention, Erica walked in with a pair of jeans and a shirt on. She stole the show in his eyes.

While Pierre lay back in the bed, Erica stood there weighing her options. He said he wasn't on no bullshit, so lying there wouldn't do her any harm. Since they both had an understanding, she went ahead and climbed in the bed with him. She laid her head on his chest, thinking about how she was just so mad at him before. After seeing him at the party and listening to him tell her how beautiful she was, nothing else really mattered.

Pierre knew he couldn't have his way with her, but that didn't stop him from allowing his hands to feel all over her body. Her skin was as smooth as a baby's bottom, and just her scent drove him crazy. "Damn, ma, this shit feels so good."

Erica sat up.

"Man, what's wrong now, E?" he asked.

"Nothing, Pierre. Maybe I should go back to the couch."

"Nah, ma, you good. I told you I wasn't on no bullshit."

"I'm just not used to all of this. And it's just all new to me," she admitted.

"Look, I'm not trying to pressure you into anything or make you feel uncomfortable. It's just when you around, it's hard for me to keep my hands to myself. If I'm making you feel funny, I'll stop. Well, I'll at least try to."

Ignoring the grin on his face, Erica lay back down next to Pierre. She closed her eyes, hoping that she could go back to sleep. Pierre wrapped his arms around her and kissed her neck.

"Pierre!"

"Man, I said I'll try, and I failed."

They both laughed. She knew he couldn't help it, so instead of complaining, she just lay there. Before they knew it, they both were knocked out.

5:00 a.m. crept around, and Mekco used his key to enter Nicole's apartment. When he walked to the back and entered her room, he saw that she was knocked out.

She had gotten on his nerves so bad earlier that he had to hurt her feelings and break her down so she could remember that he was the one running shit. He knew she could be so insecure at times and worried that he was gonna leave her, but truthfully, he loved her. He just wanted her to learn how to keep her mouth closed and mind her own business.

"Man, go back to whatever bitch's house you just came from," Nicole yelled out to Mekco as he climbed into bed with her.

"Chill with all that shit. I wasn't with no bitch."

"Whatever. I'm so tired of your ass trying to play me like a fool."

"What the fuck you bitching about? I wasn't with a bitch. You know I love your crazy ass. What the fuck can another bitch do for me?"

"Just leave me alone and go back to wherever you was at."

Nicole was pissing Mekco off. He wasn't even lying to her. He really wasn't with nobody. He was so pissed at her earlier that he went straight home and ended up falling asleep on the couch. When he woke up, he knew he had pissed her off, so he got up and came back to her house.

"Man, you tripping, but fuck it. I'm about to go back to the crib. I don't have to take this shit from you."

Nicole watched as he climbed out of the bed and put his pants on. She really didn't want him to leave. With every item that he put back on, her heart broke a little more. She lay there silently crying as he walked toward the door. She loved him with everything in her, but she was tired of his shit.

Before he reached the door, she turned around to look away from him. She didn't think she could handle seeing him actually walk out on her. Once she heard the door slam, she broke down crying.

Mekco couldn't bring himself to really leave her. He stood at the door listening to her cry. He hated hearing that shit, especially when he was the cause of it all. He took his clothes back off, then slowly walked toward the bed. She was so into her feelings, crying and shit, that she didn't even hear him in the room with her.

Nicole jumped as she felt someone enter her bed and wrap his arms around her. Mekco had scared her, but she was happy that he didn't leave.

"Baby, stop all that crying. I love your crazy ass, and I swear I wasn't with a bitch. I was knocked out in the crib. When I woke up and noticed you weren't with me, I came here to be with you."

Nicole turned around to face him. He couldn't help but to kiss his baby. That little kiss was all that they needed to start their lovemaking session.

"You still want me to leave you the fuck alone?" Mekco asked while releasing her body from his mouth.

"No, daddy," Nicole moaned out with her eyes closed and her legs wrapped around Mekco's neck.

Erica didn't know how, but she woke up to Pierre's head resting on her breast and her arms wrapped around him. She slowly climbed out of the bed, trying not to wake him, and went into the bathroom. She was surprised that her toothbrush was still in the medicine cabinet. After taking care of her business, she went into the kitchen.

Looking through the fridge, she shook her head, noticing that he didn't have anything to eat for breakfast. "How is he living like this?"

Erica got dressed, then picked up his keys. She needed to make a quick stop at the market.

She wasn't sure how he was gonna feel once he woke up, but she figured that he was gonna want something on his stomach. At first, she was just grabbing breakfast food. Then she had decided to just grab whatever she thought he needed. It didn't make any sense that he had been home for over a month now and still didn't have anything in his fridge or cabinets.

After unloading the car and putting away the groceries, Erica made her way around the kitchen and started cooking breakfast for them. As time passed and the food was just about done, she poured them some orange juice and started to fix the plates. As soon as she was about to walk out of the kitchen to wake Pierre up, he appeared in the doorway.

"Damn, you got it smelling good as hell in here. You trying to make a nigga marry your ass or something?"

"Whatever. Just sit down and eat. Anyway, how are you feeling?"

"I'm good. I told your li'l ass I wasn't drunk last night, and I think that bitch put something in my drink."

"So what are you gonna do now?"

"Shit, if I see her, I might murk her ass," he said like it wasn't nothing.

"Pierre," Erica yelled.

He started laughing. "My bad. Shit, I don't know. What should I do since you didn't approve of my real answer?"

"Maybe you should go to the emergency room and see what was given to you just in case you have a reaction or something."

"Niggas like me don't go to the hospital unless we about to die," he explained.

Erica decided not to even try to finish that conversation. Him mentioning dying wasn't something she wanted to talk about.

After eating, she started washing the dishes that they used.

"Leave that shit there, I got it. You did hook breakfast up."

"I got it, Pierre. You just need to go lie down somewhere. You might not wanna go to the hospital, but I don't think it's a good idea for you to be up so much."

Pierre gave her a sneaky grin. "You know if I gotta stay in the bed all day, that means you gonna be right in that muthafucka with me."

"And how do you figure that?"

"Shit, 'cause I'm gonna be in bed all day. How are you gonna get around?"

She then picked his keys up off the counter behind her. "The same way I got to the market this morning."

"Who gave you permission to drive my shit?"

"I gave myself permission. Now what?" she said, laughing.

Pierre walked out of the kitchen laughing, then returned to his bed. He had been so caught up in how good the food was earlier that he didn't even question where the food had come from.

Once Erica was done cleaning the kitchen, she found herself with only her underclothes on, lying in the bed and watching movies with Pierre. He made her happy and kept a smile on her face. She was thinking that maybe it was a good thing to give him a second chance.

It wasn't long before they were back kissing each other.

Laughing, he asked, "How the hell your short ass be getting in my truck?"

"Man, stop laughing at me. I got in it. That's all that matters."

Pierre wanted to crack another joke, but as he looked down and stared into her eyes, he couldn't do anything else but kiss her again.

Erica pulled back to stop the last kiss. "Pierre, can I ask you a serious question?"

Pierre sat up in bed. He could tell whatever she was about to say was heavy on her mind. "What's up, baby?"

The sound of him calling her baby made a smile pop up on her face. "Pierre, what are we doing?"

"What you mean?"

"I mean, what are we doing? What's this thing that's going on between us?"

"Man, we doing us."

She continued to question him. "And what does that mean?"

"Damn, you got a lot of questions."

Erica gave him a funky look, letting him know that she wasn't in the mood to joke around with him.

"I'm just playing, E. Fix your face. You sitting here looking like you ready to kill my ass," he said, trying to lighten the moment. Seeing that she still wasn't playing with his ass, he got serious. "Look, on the real, I don't know what we doing right now. I just know that I like it and I'm not ready for it to stop. If you feel me too, just let the shit play out."

Erica didn't even have a chance to respond. Before she could open her mouth to talk, they were back to making out. She didn't want to rush things with him because she really liked him, but she also didn't want to continue catching feelings for someone who wasn't trying to move forward. Erica was scared of messing up her chance with him, so she allowed his explanation of what was going on between them fly. It wasn't gonna be long before she brought the situation back up.

Pierre was feeling Erica, and he knew that she would have made the perfect woman for him, but he had his reasons for not laying everything out on the table. First, he knew she was a good girl, and he was scared to be the first guy to hurt her. He didn't have plans to hurt her, but he knew he wasn't used to fucking around with chicks like her. She still had her innocence and was still a good girl. On the other hand, he was a street nigga and nothing more than that. Then knowing who her pops was, Pierre knew he would never accept a nigga like him in his daughter's life.

The two lay there holding each other. They both were caught up in their personal thoughts.

Brian and Brandon sat around that Thursday afternoon smoking blunt after blunt while playing on Brandon's game system.

"You know what, nigga? You and your bitch Tiffany is some fuckups," Brian said as he passed the blunt.

"Man, that wasn't me. That was that bitch. I told her a few days ago how shit was supposed to go down. I guess she didn't use enough to take that nigga P out."

"Right. Tiffany's dumb ass was always a little on the slow side. I didn't wanna tell you that shit before 'cause that's your girl, and I know your pussy ass was all in love and shit," Brian said in a joking way, but he was serious as hell.

Brandon laughed before responding, "Bitch, fuck you. Anyway, we gotta take care of that nigga P. Ain't no way we gonna allow him to come out and shit on us like that. We've been putting in too much work for that nigga Mekco for him to just look over us like that. That nigga was supposed to be left slumped."

"Bro, I feel you, but pass that blunt, mutha-fucka. I hate niggas who give out twenty-minutes speeches while holding my weed. Fuck it. Let's just go with plan B," Brian suggested while holding his hand out, waiting for Brandon to pass the blunt.

Brian passed the blunt while thinking about how they were gonna cross P together. He really wanted to cross everybody and be the leader. At the end of the day, Mekco was gonna have to go too.

Over the last six years, stepbrothers Brian and Brandon sat back and watched Mekco take over the streets. Now they couldn't lie, he was doing a good job and he made sure everybody on his team was eating good. Mekco had built the perfect operation, and they figured that once he and P were out of the way, they wouldn't have too much work to do.

The day Mekco held the meeting for the crew and announced that some workers were getting promoted, they felt like it was their turn to run some shit. Mekco left them with the shitty boo-boo face when Mekco announced P was being released and getting placed right back on top. The brothers pretended everything was okay but were pissed. That bitch move that Mekco pulled only made them wanna kill everybody. Dropping those two muthafuckas was in their plans now just so they could get their chance to shine.

Chapter 6

"So, I really ain't seen a bitch since Wednesday night. What did I do so special to have your ass ringing my bell this Friday morning?" Nicole teased as she opened the door for Erica.

Erica was feeling so high off the time that she had spent with Pierre that she couldn't do anything but smile. The last couple of days were everything, and she didn't do anything but lie up in Pierre's arms.

"I miss you, boo," Erica said, trying to change the topic.

"Whatever. You wasn't even thinking about my ass. I couldn't even get a phone call letting me know if you were good."

Erica and Nicole mugged each other for a minute before finally breaking down and giving each other a hug. "I'm sorry if I had you worried, Nicole."

"It's okay. Come sit your ass down and tell me what happened. And don't leave out any details," Nicole ordered.

Erica and Nicole took a seat on the couch and started their story time. Nicole sat there yawning, acting like Erica's story was boring her. "So for two days you left me worried about your ass just to kiss a nigga and eat. Girl, I'm ready to kill myself from boredom."

"Nicole!"

"What? That nigga probably over there with a major buildup or blue balls," Nicole said, laughing.

"You too much, girl. We have an understanding and are on the same page now."

"Yeah, okay, boo. I'm happy for you," Nicole finally admitted.

Erica was happy to hear her best friend say that. It was good that Nicole had a change of heart. "So you're not mad that I'm back cool with him?"

"Nah, I'm not mad. I mean if it were me, I couldn't deal with a nigga who wasn't ready for titles in a relationship or whatever you call it, but you grown. If you're straight with it, then I got your back. Just be careful."

Nicole had to act like things didn't bother her, knowing Mekco would fuck her up if she got in the middle of his boy's shit. She wanted to protect her friend but do it without pissing her man off.

"Thank you, Nicole. I really do love you."

"I love you too. So what's our plan for the weekend? I wanna go out," Nicole said, standing up and twerking.

Both girls started laughing. "I have finals next week. My plans are to study all weekend and go to church Sunday."

"Ugh, you lame. I love you and am happy you're in college, but I guess I'll just chill by myself 'cause Mekco is taking care of some business," Nicole said, trying to sound sad.

Erica laughed at her before saying, "Okay, cry-baby. I'll see what I can do. Just let me knock out a few hours of work."

Nicole went into her room and climbed in the bed. She wanted to go out, even though her body was killing her from all the makeup sex that she shared with Mekco over the last couple of days. His dick stayed buried deep in her pussy even after she was sore. But she would do anything that he wanted her to do. Making him happy by any means was her job, and she tried her best to do it right.

Erica sat on the couch going over her notes. She couldn't wait for finals to be over the following week. She just prayed her dad would allow her to stay over at Nicole's house for the summer.

Erica was caught up in her textbook when she felt her phone vibrate. She looked down and saw that she had a text message from Pierre. She couldn't help but smile.

Mr. Miller: Hey, beautiful. Wyd?

Erica: Hey, I'm studying for my finals next week. Praying I get an A+ in all my classes.

Mr. Miller: Shit, your daddy works for God. I'm pretty sure he can pull some strings.

Erica: Lol, you so darn silly. Wyd?

Mr. Miller: About to take care of some business.

Me: Okay then. I miss you.

Mr. Miller: Yeah, I know. I seem to have that impression on people.

Me: LOL whatever.

Mr. Miller: The next time I see you I might have something for you. Anyway, I'm gonna hit you back up a li'l later.

Erica put the phone down, smiling hard. Pierre really was winning her over. She was happy that she gave him a second chance to act right. Nicole had a point about the whole title thing, but for right now she was just happy that they had some type of understanding. He knew she wasn't ready for sex, and he respected that.

"Damn, dog, what the fuck got you cheesing so hard like that? Yo' girl must be sending your punk ass some pictures of that holy pussy," Mekco teased.

P laughed at Mekco's joke, then got serious. "Man, chill the fuck out. E's not like that. She's a good girl."

"Anyway, sensitive nigga, we about to meet up with them niggas Brandon and Brian. We gotta get them ready to make this drive later today."

"Cool. I'm just glad I don't have to make those trips anymore. I used to hate when Cross had me doing that shit. His payments were good, but I used to be shitting bricks when I first started. I went from shitting bricks to moving them bitches."

P and Mekco laughed as they pulled up to one of their stash houses. Mekco was glad to see their car already in the driveway. Usually Face would be making the run, but he had been on some other shit lately, so instead, Mekco had Brandon and Brian doing Face's job. It was a step down, but the way Mekco saw it, they were all on the same team, and as long as the job got done, it shouldn't matter who did it.

"What up? Y'all niggas ready to do this shit?" Mekco asked as he and P stepped into the house.

Mekco looked around and couldn't believe his eyes. The fellas had the spot dirty as hell. There were old pizza boxes, liquor bottles, and empty chicken boxes everywhere.

"I was gonna let you niggas chill until it was time to roll out, but it's so fucking nasty in this bitch, y'all need to clean up. How the fuck y'all working in this bitch? Y'all muthafuckas trifling as fuck."

Brian shook his head. He was pissed at the way Mekco was talking to him and his brother. Since that nigga P had gotten out, that nigga Mekco had been on some other shit. Brandon had noticed how that nigga was ordering them around more than before. When Brian and Brandon linked up and discussed his actions, they had come to the conclusion that he was just showing off for P knowing that P really didn't fuck with them like that. Yeah, he had been making sure the pockets were straight, and his whole operation was flawless, but his ego had grown too big. He started to act like a little bitch when his little buddy came back.

"Man, you are bugging. Why don't you make those li'l niggas come and clean this shit up? Making this run is beneath my job, so you know cleaning this bitch up really is not about to get done by me," Brandon barked.

P was cracking up at Brandon, who had somehow grown balls over the years. "Mekco, I see you still don't have your workers in check. Muthafuckas running their mouth and shit like a bitch telling you what the fuck they ain't gonna do and shit."

Brandon jumped up from the dirty off-white couch. "What's that shit you saying over there, nigga?"

P stepped a little closer toward Brandon. "I fucking said you over here bitching and shit when you need to go grab a fucking broom, bitch."

Brandon stood there breathing hard, and everyone in the room could clearly see that he was bothered. Brandon had gotten so used to bragging about what crew he was in and playing that tough role that he almost forgot that he was a soft type of nigga. He forgot how P got down back in the day. P had a body count in the double digits, and Brandon was all mouth.

"What's up, nigga?" P asked before spitting on the hardwood floor. He hadn't fought in a minute, and he enjoyed being disrespectful to niggas.

Brandon stood there pissed, still breathing hard but speechless. In his mind he had so much to say, but couldn't nothing come out. He was scared.

"It's all good, P. We cool. There ain't no problems this way," Brian said, finally speaking up for his brother.

P wasn't trying to hear that shit and took this moment to embarrass him a little more. "You over there huffing and puffing, ready to blow this nasty-ass house down, when you need to save that energy to clean this filthy-ass house up, my nigga."

Mekco stood there laughing at the two. He knew P was a fool, but at the same time he needed for everyone in his crew to get along. There was money to be made, and them trying to kill each other was only gonna be a distraction. "Ay, P, let's go make sure these niggas' car is packed up right." Before Mekco walked out of the house, he picked up the bag on the couch. He knew it was his money for the month and couldn't wait to get home to count it up.

"Yeah, let's get the fuck out of here. This bitch looks like it's infested with bed bugs and shit," P said before walking out the door.

The whole time P was bullying Brandon, his brother Brian sat there looking stupid. Toward the end, he did try to stop the confrontation. He didn't want Brandon to fuck up plan B. He also knew going toe-to-toe with P was the wrong move. He remembered the old P. That nigga could be heartless at times. It had pissed them off more that Mekco didn't say shit to the nigga. He just stood there laughing with his stupid ass. That was one of the reasons why they were about to do both of them niggas dirty. It was time for the brothers to finally get their shine.

"Ay, why the fuck you do that nigga like that? Had that nigga about to cry and shit," Mekco asked as they climbed back in his ride. He wanted to ask him back at the house, but he knew that would have only provoked P to cut up even more.

"Man, fuck that nigga Brandon and his bitch-ass brother Brian. You know I never liked them niggas. Ain't shit changed but the fucking year."

Mekco didn't even bother to respond as he turned his attention back to the road. He really wasn't in the mood to deal with P's bullshit. Yeah, P was funny, but at the same time Mekco saw that he was still the same hothead who had gotten locked up years ago. He was still on the same shit and still holding a grudge. He never grew the fuck up.

Mekco drove back to his crib. He had to split up some dough that he had collected from Face, Brandon, and Brian. Face had dropped the bag off the day before Cross's party and had gotten ghost. Mekco wondered what was going on.

Once they entered the house, they went straight to the basement. Now Mekco didn't have the average basement. One side was sectioned off and set up like his office, and the other side was the entertainment area. It had a bar, a pool table, and some tables and chairs.

"Damn, I see you doing your damn thing. This shit nice as hell," P said, admiring Mekco's house.

"Yeah. It ain't on Cross's level, but it's straight."

P took a seat at the office desk and watched as Mekco opened up his safe, pulling out a backpack. They sat at the desk with the money counter and watched as the numbers increased.

After completing Face's bag, Mekco sat there with a smile spread across his face. "Man, this is the fucking good life right here. Got all this money and a bad bitch as my wife. I don't give a fuck about shit else."

"I hear that, my nigga."

Mekco pulled out a couple of stacks from the brothers' bag. He was ready to count their shit up so he could pay his workers and then go see his girl. Mekco took the rubber band off the first stack, then placed it on the counter. "What the fuck!" he yelled as he jumped up from his seat. "Ay, P, I know you just got out, but do you think you ready to bite down on some niggas?"

P pulled out his piece. "Nigga, I stay ready. Let's go."

Now Mekco really wasn't into all that killing shit unless it was mandatory to do so. He tried to keep his team low-key, but he wasn't about to tolerate muthafuckas stealing from the team.

P sat there with a devilish grin on his face. "You got me geeked up now. Let's go put some work in."

Mekco grabbed the black bag that he had taken from the brothers and dumped the contents out on the table. He started slipping through the stacks, wanting to cry. Each rubber band had a few hundred-dollar bills at the front and back, but the middle was all cut-up newspaper.

"Fuck, look at this shit, nigga!" Mekco yelled out.

"Bro, you slipping. How the fuck you pick up your bread and not check that shit before you leave the spot?" P asked, not believing that his homie could be so stupid.

"I never had a problem with them niggas before. They were on top of shit," Mekco said, defending himself for his bad judgment.

P stood up from the desk. "Man, what the fuck? Let's go take care of this shit now before them niggas leave town with those bricks," he ordered.

Mekco put the money from Face back into the safe and took out his gun. "I'm about to kill these niggas."

P shook his head at Mekco as they walked out to the car. "Nigga, you got too damn soft with these niggas, being friendly and shit. They got so used to you just taking the money or just dropping it off. They knew your ass wasn't gonna check that shit."

Mekco drove off in his thoughts. It was a damn shame how being locked up didn't change P or at least calm him down a little, but Mekco was happy to have his wild ass on his side right now.

"I just fucked up. I just gave them all them fucking bricks to move. I know I'm about to hear that nigga Cross's mouth about this shit."

"Fuck that shit, bro. Bring Cross them niggas' heads so he'll know you ain't on no bullshit," P suggested.

Mekco knew he had fucked up. Not only did they steal his money, but he had just loaded their ride up with some bricks. These niggas just got an easy come-up. He was beyond pissed and saw red. He now looked at things the way his best friend looked at things.

Mekco pulled out his cell and dialed Brandon's number. He wasn't a bit surprised when he didn't get an answer. He then tried Brian's number and was surprised he answered.

"Yeah, what's up?" Brian said into the phone.

Mekco was pissed and wasn't in the mood to chitchat, so he cut straight to the point. "Where the fuck my money at?"

Brian had put his phone on speaker so that his brother could hear the conversation between them. "Dog, you took your bag with you. What the fuck you talking about?" Brian said, acting stupid like he didn't sit up the night before helping his brother and Tiffany cut up the paper.

"Look, stop fucking playing with me. Where the fuck my bread at?"

Mekco then heard Brandon speak into the phone. "Bitch-ass nigga, fuck you. This is our fucking bread and work. Y'all niggas swear y'all fucking bosses, but you just got finessed out of all y'all shit."

The phone then went dead as Mekco pulled back into the stash house's driveway. "They car gone. I know these niggas went ghost already," Mekco said to P.

"What we gonna do now?" P asked.

Mekco shook his head. He couldn't believe this shit had happened. "Shit, from the look of things, these niggas already dipped. So I'm gonna have to pay the workers out of my pocket."

"Bro, let's pull up to them bitch-ass niggas' mama's house. Call them back, and let's see how many bullets she can take until they pull up with that bread."

They both looked at each other and laughed. "Boy, you still crazy as fuck, I see."

"Hell yeah. Ain't shit changed about me but my fucking age," P said, rolling a blunt up.

"Here's some shit to relax your mind," P said as he passed the blunt to Mekco.

As Mekco drove around the city, he and P passed the blunt back and forth. P wasn't sure what the big boss man's next move was gonna be, but he was ready to call it a night if they weren't about to murk a muthafucka. He was thinking about going out and finding him some entertainment for the night.

"Ay, take me to my car so I can get home."

"Hold up. Let's ride out to Face's crib. I want to put him up on game just in case he runs into one of them niggas," Mekco mumbled.

"Let's go."

It took them only fifteen minutes to get to Face's house. Mekco parked in front of the house. After the third knock, Destiny opened the door.

"Hey, Mekco and P, what's up?" she asked.

They both greeted her while she let them into the house that she shared with her three kids and their father, Face. Now, Face was only 25, but he had the most kids out of the squad. When he hooked up with Destiny, they moved quickly and ended up with stairstep kids.

"Ay, Des, where that nigga Face at?" Mekco asked.

"You haven't heard?" she said, looking at them, confused.

"Heard what?" P questioned.

"His dad had a heart attack, and he has been up at the hospital for the last couple of days. I thought he might have told you."

Mekco was confused and wondered why he didn't say shit. "Nah, he didn't say anything to us, but okay. Des, we about to head out. Do y'all need anything?"

"No, we're good."

Destiny let them out, then locked the door behind Face's homeboys. She then sat back on the couch to continue watching TV.

Mekco and P stood outside in front of the house. They needed to get an understanding before they went their separate ways.

"Why do you think he didn't say anything to us?" P asked.

"I don't know, man. We all know how much his dad means to him."

The ride back to Mekco's house was quiet. Both guys were caught up in their own thoughts. Between the bullshit that Brandon and Brian had pulled and Face's pops being in the hospital, there was just too much going on at once.

As they pulled up to his crib, P jumped out of the ride. "Ay, hit my line if something comes up."

Mekco simply said, "Yeah, okay, man, and I'm gonna hit Face up. I'll holler at you later."

Mekco was about to try to get in touch with Face while P was about to go find some pussy to get into. He had been caked up with Erica for the last couple of days, and even though they were crushing on each other, it was too soon to be thinking about hitting that. He had no choice but to respect her and her decision to wait. That didn't mean he couldn't go fuck somebody else.

Mekco lay across his bed deep in his thoughts. He had a nice crib, but he was so used to Nicole's ass being around that he barely stayed there. He spent most of his time at her crib laid up with her. Being at his place without her around was always boring, but at times like this he needed to be alone so he could clear his mind.

Pulling out his phone, he dialed Face's number. After the third ring, Face finally answered the phone.

"What's good?"

"Man, shit all bad right now. My pops is in the hospital, and things are not looking too good for him. I haven't even been home in the last couple of days, man."

Mekco could hear the pain in Face's voice. Mr. Perry was all that Face had growing up once his mom had died from a drug overdose. "Ay, bro, I'm sorry to hear about your pops. I hope he pulls through."

"Thanks. I'm so fucked up behind this shit. I'm scared to leave here, man. I just keep thinking like he might pass away while I'm gone," Face admitted to his childhood friend.

Mekco felt bad for Face, but at the end of the day, his money was still short. "Look, I hate that you're going through this right now, but I need to ask you something."

"What's up, my baby?" Face asked. He had switched his emotions, seeing that Mekco was ready to talk about some business.

"Have you heard from Brandon and Brian today?"

"Hell nah, my nigga. I really been solo dolo since my pops been in this bitch."

"I'm about to put you on game now. Them niggas ran off with the money from this month and the bricks that go to that nigga Biggz. If them niggas hit you up, act stupid and try to meet up with them somewhere. Just call me and let me know. I gotta get at them ASAP."

Face couldn't believe what he was hearing. P had always said them brothers were some bitches and couldn't be trusted. "Yeah, I got you, bro."

"Cool, and I hope your pops pulls through. That nigga used to beat my ass when I was younger, but he was cool as fuck and kept us on our toes."

They both reminisced about old times and laughed before ending the call.

Brandon and Brian rode through the city, happy that they were finally about to leave the cold streets of Detroit. They knew Mekco probably already had a hit on their heads, so they had no choice but to dip.

"Ay, I think we still have time to go get Tiffany, man. She's gonna be pissed when she notices I left her ass," Brandon said.

"Bro, her slow ass gonna be straight. We don't need her tagging along anyway. We got all this money and dope. What the hell you want her stupid ass for? We got what the bad bitches want."

Brandon didn't say anything else. He knew Tiffany wasn't the prettiest or smartest girl in the world, but he had grown to love her. Now she had helped them out a few times, and Brian just wanted to say fuck her and basically fuck how his brother felt about her.

"Don't tell me you over there about to cry over that bitch. Bro, get your shit together," Brian ordered.

"Nah, I'm good. I just think that if we weren't gonna take her with us, then we should have at least broken her off with something."

"So what the fuck you want me to do, drive back, risk our lives, and pay her? Fuck that. We gone. Just look at it like this: next time she'll know to get her money up front," he said, laughing.

Brandon shook his head. He couldn't believe that he had followed along with his brother's plan. He sat back in the passenger seat and closed his eyes. Before going to sleep he said a silent prayer that they could get away with the stunt they just pulled off.

P opened his eyes and looked over to his night-stand to see what time it was. The clock read 10:30 p.m., so he knew it was time to get up and hit the bar up. He was in desperate need of some wet wet.

Once he showered and got dressed, he jumped in his truck and drove to his favorite bar. Just like any other night, the atmosphere was just right. It wasn't empty or too full. One thing P hated was a crowded place. Some people just couldn't be trusted.

He was seated, minding his business, when he noticed a familiar face. He was about to have a good night after all. There was nothing like putting in work after dealing with bullshit all day.

He walked over to the young lady and took a seat right next to her. "How are you doing tonight?"

The young lady looked up from her phone and gave him a smile. "I'm good. How about you?"

"I'm good," he responded.

"So you gonna buy me a drink since you're over here in my face?" she bluntly asked.

"Damn, shorty, can a nigga get your name and a fucking conversation first?"

"Oh, I'm sorry about that. I've been having a bad day, but my name is Tiffany."

P smiled. "Okay, Tiffany. That's a cute name. What are you drinking?"

Tiffany wasn't a real drinker, so she didn't have a favorite. She sat there for a minute before saying anything. P saw that she was lost, so to save her the embarrassment, he took over. "Don't worry, you can drink what I'm drinking on." He then went to the bar and ordered a few double shots of Patrón.

When he got back to the table, Tiffany was hesitant to drink the shots. She wasn't sure if she really wanted to get drunk with this man or just go home and wait for her boyfriend to call her back. She had a feeling that he might have wanted some pussy for the drinks. Too bad she didn't know he wanted more than that.

"Come on, girl. Whatever got you bothered can't be that bad."

After twenty minutes of talking and more drinking, the two walked out of the bar. Running into her wasn't in his original plan, but he had no problem making her part of it. He helped her get into his truck before slowly walking over to the driver's door. He took his time getting in so he could text Mekco.

P: I got that nigga Brandon's bitch right now. Give me an hour, and I'll let you know where to meet me.

Bro: Yeah, okay.

While talking to Tiffany, she fucked around and started talking about how her boyfriend left her and shit. After so many drinks, P had put it together that Tiffany was Brandon's girlfriend. At first, he thought he was just gonna torture her and find out why the fuck she had put something in his drink at Cross's party, but learning who she fucked with explained it all.

P pulled up to a cheap hotel and got them a room. As they walked into the room, she started to undress. All that boyfriend talk she was doing didn't mean shit once she got that liquor in her system and they got behind closed doors. That bitch was ready to take pipe.

Tiffany wasn't the type he usually would fuck with, but since he had to play with her all night, she had blocked any bitch he really wanted that night. He stood by the dresser slowly undressing.

He was about to fuck her, then call Mekco. She was about to pay for the shit her ho-ass nigga did.

P slid the rubber down his dick while watching her play with her pussy. That liquor had turned her into a freak. He then climbed on top of her and pushed himself into her. She went crazy as he went in and out of her wet pussy. He was killing her shit and wasn't even trying.

P had just busted his nut and climbed off her. He went straight in the bathroom to flush the rubber and wash his dick off. When he walked back in the room, Tiffany was looking at him weird.

"So, are we staying here tonight or what?" she asked.

P started laughing at her, hurting her already-bruised feelings. "You don't even know my fucking name, and I don't have time to be laid up with you."

"So are you gonna tell me your name or what?" she asked, feeling foolish.

"We fucked already. What you need it for," he coldly said.

She sat up in the bed and then went into the bathroom to clean herself up, feeling shitty. Her buzz had worn off, and she just was ready to go home and get in the bed at this point. He texted Mekco, then chilled, waiting for her to get dressed so they could leave. Now if he didn't have further plans with her, he would have just left and let her find her own ride, but they needed her for info.

She walked out of the bathroom, buttoning her pants up. "You know you have some good dick, but you're a complete asshole."

P didn't even respond to the bullshit that she let fly out of her mouth. Nine times out of ten she was gonna end up in a ditch by sunrise. Letting her talk shit was the least he could do for the dingy-ass bitch.

Mekco ended up texting P a location. "Come on, let's go."

As P drove off, Tiffany started telling him where she stayed. He drove as if he were listening. Too bad she wasn't gonna make it home that night. He pulled up to one of their older stash houses. The house was barely used, so they didn't have to worry about shit.

"Come on, get out!" P ordered.

Tiffany looked around, worried. "Where are we at?" she asked.

"Just get out the fucking truck!" he yelled.

Tiffany didn't move. She was scared. She was really hating herself right now. P noticed how shook she was and knew she wasn't gonna move on her own, so he opened his door and stepped out of the truck. She thought he was about to shut his door and go over to her side, but instead he grabbed a handful of her braids and dragged her out of the truck from his side.

As she started to scream, he put his gun in her mouth.

"Bitch, shut the fuck up before I smoke your dumb ass," he whispered in her ear.

Tiffany was so scared that she pissed on herself.

"Nasty bitch," he said as he dragged her into the garage.

Once the door started to shut, the lights clicked on, and Tiffany started looking around. "Oh, my God, Mekco," she said after seeing him standing in the corner posted like a fucking stop sign.

"Ay, bitch, where the fuck your nigga at with my bread?" Mekco asked.

Tiffany started crying. Her mom always told her about dealing with guys like Brandon. They were nothing but trouble was what she would say. "Please, Mekco, please don't kill me. I swear I don't know where he is. I've been calling him all day, and he won't answer my calls."

Mekco questioned her, and with each question she cried and begged for her life.

P finally spoke up. "Do you remember me, Tiffany?"

"You looked familiar. That's why I left the bar with you."

"Just answer this question: why did your nigga have you put something in my drink when you were bartending at Cross's party?"

At first, she didn't say anything. She just looked at him funny. She now knew where she recognized him from. "I'm sorry. Brian told me to do it. I'm so sorry. Please just let me go home," she cried.

Mekco grabbed her cell from her and dialed Brandon's cell.

All the driving that the brothers had done that day had made them tired, so they got a room to relax for the night.

Brandon was asleep when his phone started going off. Brian was still up, so he grabbed it and saw that it was Tiffany calling. He shook his head, but he still answered it. He was about to act like his brother and just cut her loose.

"What's up?" Brian said into the phone, acting like Brandon.

Although she had a gun pointed at the back of her head, Tiffany tried to act normal. "Hello, Brandon. Where are you?" Tiffany asked.

"Look, bitch, thanks for helping us out and shit, but we gone already. We no longer need your help."

Mekco shook his head. He started to feel sorry for her. Them niggas used her, and now she was about to die because of them fools.

"Please, Brandon," she cried before Mekco started to talk through the speakerphone.

"Ay, Brandon, we got your bitch, and if y'all don't bring me my shit, I'm gonna kill her."

Brian started to laugh. "Fuck you and that bitch. Do what you gotta do, bitch."

P looked at Mekco. Mekco gave him the go and it was on. P and Mekco shot Tiffany up, making sure to end her life. The way they looked at it, she was gonna end up doing the shit on her own after hearing what her boyfriend had just said over the phone.

Brian didn't even flinch. He hung the phone up and went back to watching the game that was on TV. He didn't give a fuck. They weren't going back to Detroit, so Brandon would never find out about her.

Mekco called the cleanup crew and walked up the street to his car. P jumped in his ride and headed home. He just wanted to jump in the shower again and take his ass to sleep.

Mekco drove straight to Nicole's house. He had been stressed all day and just needed her to hold him after this major loss he just took. When he entered her bedroom, she was knocked out, so he jumped in the shower and then climbed in the bed.

As much as he loved fucking her, it felt good just to hold her that night. She was his everything, and just hearing that nigga say fuck his girl knowing she was gonna be killed was fucked up. He prayed he never got his girl caught up in a situation like that. He knew he would save her life in a heartbeat even if that meant getting killed himself. Just thinking about it made him hold her tighter and plant kisses on her.

P slept like a baby right after his shower. Tiffany was his first kill since he had been out, and he knew he now had the juice. He was ready to body anybody who got in his way.

Chapter 7

The next morning, Nicole opened her eyes and was surprised to see Mekco knocked out next to her. The night before, she was supposed to go out with Erica, but Mekco had told her to stay in. She had been with him long enough to not ask questions, so she stayed in with her girl. They danced around the house drinking wine and listening to their music. Best friends having fun at the crib was better than anything.

She placed a kiss on his big lips before climbing out of the bed. She frowned as she went into the bathroom and saw his dirty clothes on the floor. When she picked up his shirt, she saw small spots on the front. She was hip to the game by now. Going into the kitchen, she grabbed a garbage bag for the clothes. When she returned to her bedroom, she hit him with the bag.

"Stupid ass!" she yelled.

With his eyes barely open, he yelled, "What the fuck is your problem, girl? Don't you see I was asleep?"

"Get your ass up, Mekco. How can you be so careless and stupid? You know Erica is here, and you left this bullshit in the fucking bathroom," she yelled.

Hearing her say that woke him all the way up. "Damn, baby, I'm sorry. My bad. I was so tired I really forgot."

"Mekco, you got to be more careful. She wouldn't say shit, but she still doesn't need to be mixed up in this shit."

Getting out of the bed and giving her a hug, he tried to calm her down. "My bad, baby. Slip some clothes on and go get rid of it for me please."

She was still a little pissed and asked, "Why can't you do it?"

He looked down at his dick. His monster was at full attention. "You want me going outside like this?"

She looked down with a grin. "Okay, baby, I got it. Just have that ass in the bed and ready for me when I get back."

Nicole giggled before slipping on some clothes to take the trash out. Her love for Mekco had her so gone that she looked past the fact that he was out committing crimes and she was helping to cover it up.

When she returned, she was mad to see Mekco fully dressed. "Really? This is how you gonna try to play me?"

"Baby, I gotta go, ma," he said, pulling a shoebox out from the closet.

Nicole stood with her arms folded. She was in the mood to feel him inside her.

"Baby, don't be like that. Face just called me. His dad just died. I need to go check on my boy."

Nicole's whole face changed. "Oh, my God, Mekco. I wanna go with you. His dad was cool."

"Man, get dressed and hurry the fuck up," he firmly said so she would know he wasn't playing with her slow ass.

Once Nicole was ready, she went into Erica's room. "Ay, I'm about to ride out with Mekco. Are you gonna be straight here by yourself?"

"Yeah, now leave me alone. I got a headache out of this world."

Nicole got up to leave the room. "I'll see you later."

Without even looking up, Erica said, "Bye, girl."

That Saturday went by quickly. Nicole had stayed with Mekco all day with Face and the rest of the crew. Erica stayed in bed for most of the day. When she finally got up, she ate, then pulled out her notebook to study. She couldn't wait for the following week to be over with.

Feeling her phone vibrate, she looked down and saw that it was Pierre calling. She was happy he was calling but waited until the fourth ring so he wouldn't know that she had secretly been waiting on his call.

"Hey, Mr. Miller," she said softly into the phone.

"Hey, what's good? What you doing?"

"Nothing much."

"Look, I wanna see you. Can I come swoop you right quick?" Pierre asked even though he knew the answer already.

"You wanna see me, huh? All right. I'm still at Nicole's house, so come get me."

That was all he needed to hear before hanging up the phone. Erica got up to get ready. It was in the afternoon, and she was still in her nightclothes.

She ended up putting on a pair of black capris and a black-and-white T-shirt. As she walked into the living room, Pierre was calling, saying he was downstairs. She hurried and put on her shoes, then left the apartment.

Pierre leaned against the car and waited for her to walk out of the building. He grinned as he saw her walk out the door. Erica walked straight to him with a big smile on her face.

"What you smiling for, girl?" he teased as he gave her a hug.

"I guess I'm happy to see you. What we about to do?"

If P could say what was on his mind, she probably would have gone back in the house, so he didn't say shit. He opened the car door for her. "Get in."

"Wait, Pierre, whose car is this?" she asked.

"It's mine. Now get in so we can ride out."

Erica looked at the all-black Camaro before getting in, and she was very impressed. "Can I drive?"

"Hell nah. I still can't believe I was letting your little ass drive my truck," he said as he jumped in the driver's seat.

Erica sat back in her seat and didn't say anything else during the ride.

"Damn, girl, you spoiled as hell, I see."

"Why do you say that, Mr. Miller?" she asked as if she never heard those words before.

"'Cause any other time you would be talking my ear off and shit, but I told your li'l ass no and you quiet as fuck. That's a sign of being a brat."

"Whatever, Mr. Miller," she said with a slight attitude. She knew she was somewhat spoiled, and she was pissed about not being able to drive his new car. She had gotten used to him telling her yes.

"So I guess you're mad and just gonna keep calling me Mr. Miller. I been asked you not to do that. Man, you a trip," he said as he pulled into a store parking lot.

He went into the store and quickly returned. When he got to the car, he opened the passenger door and told her to move over. A huge smile crossed her face, and she quickly slid over. P took his seat, then turned his attention to her. "Here go the keys."

"Thank you, Pierre," she said as she took the keys from him. And just like that she was calling him by his name and wore a smile on her face.

"Damn, I should have told you to grab your church clothes so you could spend the night with me."

"I didn't know I was staying the night, but I'll have Nicole bring me some later."

"Good. That's exactly what I wanted to hear, baby," Pierre said, then sat back in his seat.

Entering Pierre's house, Erica took her shoes off at the door like every other time she visited. "E, you know you don't have to do that. It's not like I have carpet through this muthafucka," Pierre said, laughing.

"It's a habit. I do this everywhere I go," she said as she straddled his lap on the couch.

Pierre gazed into her eyes with a grin on his face. "Man, E, I swear you so fucking beautiful," Pierre said as he kissed her on her full lips.

Being caught up in his kisses and the sucking on her neck, Erica could barely mumble out, "Thank you." Pierre had Erica so turned on just by his kisses and the soft touches that he placed on her body.

Pierre's phone ringing broke their make-out session. As good as it felt, he was somewhat glad because his dick was rock hard, and she was sitting right on it. He knew any minute she was gonna jump off him anyway. He let her slide off his lap so he could answer it.

"What up, bro?"

"Yeah, I took care of that."

Mekco had called him to make sure after he left Face's house that he had gotten rid of his truck and copped something new. He didn't want anything tracing back to him.

Pierre placed his phone on the table.

"Everything okay?" Erica asked.

"Yeah, baby. Stop being nosy. I'll be right back." Pierre got up and went into his bedroom.

He sat on the bed trying to get his dick to stop thinking about fucking Erica. He had to be a fool to think that he could chill with her sexy ass without getting hard, and Tiffany's wack-ass pussy didn't do him any good. He lusted after Erica, but in more than one way. He didn't just wanna fuck her. He also wanted her to be his. He loved being around her. She was so smart and beautiful. Plus, she never asked for shit even though she knew she could get whatever she wanted. He was falling hard, but there was one problem he would have to deal with, and that was the no-sex thing. How could he make her his and still be fucking with random bitches just to fill in for what she wasn't ready to do? After having nothing but his hands for six straight years, he wasn't sure if he could do that shit anymore.

He sat there weighing his options. He needed to get his mind together. As he looked up, he saw Erica standing there just staring at him.

"Hey, you sure you okay?" she softly asked.

"Yeah, I'm good. Got a lot on my mind right now, but it ain't shit I can't handle," he said, playing it off.

Erica took a seat next to him. "So is there anything I can help you with?"

He chuckled to himself. She just didn't know what she was asking. It took everything in him to tell her no.

"So what are we about to get into for the rest of the day?"

"Ay, something came up, and I'm gonna have to drop you back off at Nicole's house."

A little while later, walking out of the room and entering the living room, Pierre saw the sad look on her face, but he knew he couldn't give in to it. "You ready?"

"Yeah, I already called Nicole, and she just got there, so I'm good."

As they walked to the car, he opened the door for her, then went over to his side and got in. "Look, E, I'm not trying to hurt your feelings or anything like that, and I'm not sure how to explain this shit I'm feeling right now. I just know that you're not ready to be with a guy like me, and I don't know how to handle someone like you without breaking your heart."

Tears filled her eyes. He was really calling it quits before it really even started. "Just take me to Nicole's house," was all she could say before her tears rolled down her cheeks.

Pierre felt bad for making her cry and hurting her feelings, but he knew that it would have been worse if he kept her around. She didn't even know that he was saving her from the monster that was running wild through him.

Not sure what to say, he started the car and started driving toward Nicole's apartment. Erica didn't wanna say anything to him. He was pissed and hurt all at once. She stayed on social media, scrolling through her timeline and not really caring what the people were talking about, just trying not to cry.

P felt bad and saw that she was upset. He placed his hand on her thigh just like he would have done any other time. "E, please don't be like that, okay? I'm doing you a favor. Trust me."

"Stop playing with me and just get me to where I need to go," she ordered with lots of attitude.

The rest of the ride was quiet. Neither wanted to be without each other, but they both had to learn how to handle each other's ways.

Finally making it to Nicole's building, he parked his car in front like always. Usually he would get out and open the door for Erica, but when he got out this time, she opened her own door and started walking off. Pierre walked faster to catch up with her.

Grabbing her arm and turning her around, he yelled, "Man, what the fuck is your problem? I said I was just looking out for you. You acting like we were really together and I just broke up with your ass." As soon as those words came out, he regretted it. They didn't have a title, but there was something there. "My bad, E."

"It's cool. You're right. We weren't together for real." With that being said, she snatched her arm away from him and walked away.

P wanted to stop her and explain why he wanted to call it quits, but he decided that it would be best if he just let her go. Erica had his heart in her hand, and he didn't know how to handle it. He stood there watching her disappear into the apartment door.

Erica went straight in the room that she called her own. She could hear that Nicole was busy with Mekco, so she undressed, put on her nightclothes, and climbed back into her bed. Pulling the cover over her face, she broke down and cried her eyes out.

The next morning, she got up to get ready for church. She prayed that the day would go by quickly so she could go home and just be by herself. The feelings that she had grown for Pierre had gotten the best of her, and she just couldn't deal.

After service, Erica cleaned up the aisles just like always. She was so happy that the service flew by and didn't run over.

"You're almost done?" Nicole asked as she walked out of the restroom.

Erica looked up at her friend. "Yeah, but you know I would have been done sooner if you had helped me out."

"Whatever, girl. Are you feeling okay? You don't seem like yourself today."

"Not really, but I'll talk to you once we get in the car."

"Man, I'm so mad you have to go home, but after this week you will be all mine for the summer," Nicole said while playing around.

Erica barely gave her a smile, and that was how she knew that something was definitely wrong with her friend.

While Nicole drove Erica home, Erica explained what happened between her and Pierre.

"Hell nah. I wonder why he is playing games with you like that. I'm gonna fucking stab his funky ass as soon as I see him."

"He just kept saying it was for my own good and he was trying to protect me. I don't understand what that meant. He then said it was best for me if we didn't move forward and just quit whatever was going on between us. This is the exact reason why I usually stay to myself. I hate when people play with my feelings like that," she said, now crying.

"Damn, Erica, I hate that you are hurting like this. I swear I hate his ass. I'm gonna call him and go off on his punk ass."

"It's okay. You don't have to do all that," Erica said, trying to calm her friend down.

Nicole pulled up in front of Pastor Collins's house. "Oh, my fucking Gawd, you love that nigga?" she asked full of excitement.

Erica didn't deny or confirm that she loved him, but deep down inside she knew that she did. And it hurt her more knowing that he didn't want her.

"Is that why you don't want me to call him?"

Erica still didn't say anything. At that moment she was hurt and embarrassed.

Once Nicole pulled up to Erica's house, Erica opened her door. "Okay, Nicole, I gotta go, but I'll call you later."

"Bye, boo. Just remember, if you change your mind and want me to beat him up, I will."

Erica walked on the porch laughing, but she had a feeling that, once she settled in, she was gonna end up crying again.

Nicole waited until Erica got in the house safely before driving off. It took everything in her not to call Mekco and go off on him just because his bro was on some bullshit. She drove home and decided not to trip but only because she could see that her friend still had feelings for that clown.

***

Later that night, Erica sat at the dinner table with her dad. Dinnertime in their household had always been awkward. Erica really couldn't talk to her dad about anything that had to do with her life because he only could comprehend what was printed in the Bible.

After clearing his throat, Mr. Collins put his fork down and started talking. "Erica, I've been looking at you since you got home, and I've been trying to figure out what that mark is on your neck."

Looking up from her plate, Erica gave him a weird look. "What are you talking about, Dad?" she asked, pulling out her phone and turning the camera app on. Her heart dropped as she stared at the passion mark that Pierre left on her neck.

"I know that is not one of those hickey things boys leave on girls to prove that they got between a young lady's legs. Come on, baby girl, all the preaching and teaching I've been doing only for you to still end up sneaking around with these boys who only want one thing?"

"Dad, calm down. I'm still a virgin," Erica said, defending herself.

"I highly doubt that now," Mr. Collins coldly said.

Halfway lying through her teeth, Erica quickly said, "Dad, you going a little too far. I burned myself straightening my hair this morning."

Pastor Collins stood up from the table and walked over to his daughter. He then snatched her up from the chair. He was pissed and knew she had lied. "Look here, little girl, you better stop playing games with me, okay? I'm not a fool, and I can feel the devil running wild in you. Since you are out doing what you want, you can just forget about being with Nicole for the summer. All that is over. I just knew that she was a bad influence on you."

"What do you mean all that is over? Did you forget that I am grown? You cannot stop me from having her as a friend!" Erica yelled back.

The way she was acting, Pastor knew there had to be a guy in her life. "That girl is loose, and I didn't raise you to be like her. I know what's best for Erica. If it's the last thing that I do, I will pray that my King will help take the ho out of you."

That was the first time in her life Erica had heard her dad use a bad word, and it hurt her down to the core that he was using it toward her, calling her out of her name.

"I'm not a ho!" she yelled back, not noticing that she had just cursed back at him.

Pastor's eyes got big, and he was filled with rage right before he slapped the right side of her face.

"I can't believe you just did that!" she screamed as she grabbed her face and ran into her bedroom. The way her face stung, she knew there was gonna be a bruise on her.

The pastor couldn't believe how out of control everything had gotten between the two. He had never flipped out on her like that. He was ashamed of his behavior but knew he couldn't allow her to embarrass him. He went into his prayer closet and locked the door. He was gonna ask the Lord to forgive him and to remove his daughter's sinful ways.

After calming down Erica grabbed her phone and called the only person who would forever have her back. She needed to leave that house. There was no way she was gonna stay there with her dad acting up. She dialed Nicole's number.

"What's up? Why you not sleeping? You've been driving me crazy about these damn finals."

"Nicole, I need you to come get me now. I really need you."

Nicole could hear the pain in Erica's voice and could also tell that she had been crying. "Say no more. I'm on my way."

It took Nicole no time to pull up and see Erica already on the porch with her backpack. Erica jumped in the car, and before she could say hi or even thank her friend for coming to get her, she said, "Please get me away from here."

"What the hell is going on?" Nicole questioned as she drove off.

"I can't stay there. Nicole, that man has lost his freaking mind. I can't believe he hit me," she cried.

"Wait a minute. Who hit you?" Nicole asked, making sure she heard her correctly.

"My daddy hit me. He saw a hickey on my neck from Pierre and flipped out on me. I can't believe he called me a ho and slapped me."

"Girl, you lying. Pastor didn't do that for real. Damn, he is a completely different man at home." Nicole couldn't believe that he was capable of doing something like that. And then that Erica said he had cussed was crazy. At the same time, she never cussed either, so when she did, Nicole knew she was telling the truth.

"I'm so serious. I never saw him so upset like that."

"Well, you know you are always welcome at my place. Shit, it's like you already live there anyway."

When they finally made it inside of Nicole's apartment, she followed Erica into the bathroom. They looked into the mirror to check out Erica's face. And just like she said, his handprint was there.

"Damn, boo, Pastor wasn't playing."

Erica didn't respond. She walked out of the bathroom and went into the room that she called her own. Of course Nicole followed. "What you about to do?"

"I'm about to just go to bed. I still gotta go to school in the morning."

"All right, boo. Good night."

Nicole went to her room, undressed, then climbed back in the bed with Mekco.

"Your girl okay?" he asked.

"Nah, her dad flipped out on her, called her a ho, and hit her."

Mekco was surprised. "Damn, that's fucked up. What he do all that for?"

"'Cause your ho-ass friend left a hickey on her neck," she replied with an attitude.

"That nigga P gonna be pissed and wanna hurt that man if he finds out."

"Fuck P. He hurt her too. I told you what happened."

"Yeah, but anyway my nigga got his reasons. Let's just leave their shit alone."

Nicole couldn't let that slide. "What was his reason to hurt her like that? Go ahead and make some shit up."

"That's that man's business. Now get up here and ride this dick."

Nicole climbed on top of Mekco and did as she was told. She rode him until they both came and were tired. Afterward, they cuddled up under each other. Mekco was the first to fall asleep. Nicole was up smiling and just thinking about how they had finally fucked without using a rubber. She prayed that one time would give her that baby she wanted from him.

The next morning, Erica got up and got ready for class. It was her last week of school for three months, and she was happy. Once she was finished getting dressed and fixing her hair, she went into the living room to put her shoes on to leave. She jumped as she walked in the room and saw Pierre on the couch.

"Hey, you ready?"

At first, she wasn't gonna respond, but she couldn't help herself. "For what?"

"I came to take you to school."

"I'm good. I have a ride."

"Look, E, don't be like that. I'm trying to help your ass out," P said, pissed that she was so fucking stubborn and beautiful at the same time.

"Why don't you help me by staying away from me?" she said as she walked out the door.

Before walking out himself, Pierre mumbled, "Damn, I fucked up with her."

Once Pierre got downstairs, he looked around and didn't see Erica. She was nowhere in sight. "Damn," was all he could say before getting into his car and driving off.

Erica had jumped in the back seat of her Uber ride. Even if she hadn't already requested a ride, she wouldn't have gotten in the car with P anyway. She was tired of playing his game. He was too old not to know what he wanted.

That morning, Mekco had texted P, letting him know what was going on with Erica. Since P really loved her, he got up early to take her to school. P knew he had hurt her, but he still wanted to be nice to her. He loved her, and that was why it was so hard for him. He had never really loved a girl before. When he was younger, his grandma had warned him that one day a female was gonna come into his life and gain hold of his heart. And since she'd been dead, he never let a female get too close to him until now.

Chapter 8

That week seemed to go by fast for Erica. She had been so stressed out over the different twists and turns in her life, but she somehow managed to pass every final with a 90 percent or better. It surprised her that her dad only texted her once, and that was to ask her not to tell anyone from the church what was going on between them. She didn't respond even though she didn't plan on telling anyone other than Nicole her business. It was now Friday night, and Nicole had talked her into going out to celebrate her success. At first Erica didn't want to do anything, but after enough begging, she gave in.

Nicole walked into the room wearing a hot pink fitted dress and some heels. "Are you almost ready, Erica?"

Erica, who was wearing a dress similar to her friend's but in black, turned around and said, "Yeah, I'm ready. Let's go."

They made it to the club in twenty minutes. Once they got in, Nicole pointed to an empty table toward the back. "Come on. Let's get that table over there before someone else grabs it." They worked their way toward the table and took a seat.

"So what are we drinking tonight?" Nicole asked over the music.

"Me and my niggas about to grab a couple of bottles for everyone," Mekco said, standing behind them.

Erica gave Nicole a funny look. "Really, Nicole?"

Mekco walked off to the bar to get their drinks. He could tell by her attitude that Nicole didn't tell Erica that he was coming right along with his team.

"I'm sorry, boo. You know once I told Mekco we were going out to celebrate, he invited himself," Nicole explained.

"As long as his li'l friend is not here, I'm good."

"Whatever. You know that's your boo. I don't see why y'all be playing these games with each other."

Erica looked at her friend strangely. She didn't understand the sudden change in her attitude about Pierre. She was just talking about how she wanted to cut him up.

Mekco came back with two bottles, and a couple of his boys had bottles in their hands. "Congratulations on passing all your finals," he said, handing her one of the bottles.

"Thanks, Mekco."

"Hey, everyone or the ones who don't know, this is my best friend, Erica."

Most of them said hi or just nodded their heads. Mekco's boys were entertaining some other bitches around the table and really weren't paying her any attention.

Erica and Nicole talked to each other. "Girl, you all right? Are you having a good time?" Nicole asked.

"Yes, girl, I'm okay. Thanks for pushing me to come out. Drinks were what I needed to ease my mind."

They both giggled. There really wasn't anything funny, but the drinks were getting the best of them. Everyone at the table talked and laughed, just having a good time. Mekco leaned over to whisper something in Nicole's ear. Erica wasn't sure what he had said, but she had a feeling it was something nasty when Nicole's face lit up. She then jumped up and whispered in Erica's ear, telling her that she would be right back.

Erica sat there for a minute just looking around. That was when it hit her that if she didn't have Nicole, she wouldn't have anybody. She then got up from the table to go to the restroom. She was happy that the line wasn't as long as usual.

As she worked her way through the crowd, she felt someone grab her by the arm. She turned around to see that it was one of the guys who had tried to talk to her earlier when they first walked in. "Hey, you Erica, right?"

"Yeah, I'm Erica. Who wants to know?" she said back.

"What's up? I'm Tim."

"Okay, and?"

"Damn, ma, no need for all that attitude. I just wanna dance with your sexy ass. Is that all right?"

Erica weighed her options and figured there wasn't anything wrong with a little dance. She followed him to the dance floor so they could have a little fun. Tim was enjoying dancing with Erica and kept making sure to keep his hands on her ass even after she kept removing them. Once the song was over, she turned to walk away, but he wasn't having that.

"Wait a minute, Erica," he said as he grabbed her arm and pulled her closer toward him. Tim hugged her body with a tight grip as he whispered into her ear, "Fuck that table. Chill over here with me." That was followed by a kiss on her neck.

Still trying to break free from his tight grip, she whispered back in his ear, "I'm good. I'm about to head back over there with my girl now. Let me go please." She then tried to snatch away, but his grip was so tight it was useless to even try.

"Stop acting all stuck-up and shit. You think you too good for a nigga or something?" he asked, squeezing her tighter.

Pierre sat back in the cut watching what was going on. He thought Erica was feeling ol' boy at first and was pissed. He was on his way to snatch her ass from the dance floor and fuck that nigga Tim up. As he walked closer, he saw that Erica was trying to get away from him and wasn't feeling him at all. He still was pissed that she had even entertained him in the first place.

All he saw was red when he saw her begging him to let her go and his bitch ass just holding her like she belonged to him. This nigga was about to learn not to put his hands on nobody's woman. He didn't give a fuck what he told her before. She was his, and that was the end of the story.

"We got a fucking problem over here, my nigga?" Pierre asked. He usually wasn't into all that talking and really wanted to knock the nigga out, but since he held on to Erica so tight, he was sure that she would have been hit in the process.

Tim wasn't a punk about his shit and quickly let Erica go. He then stepped up to Pierre. "Nigga, the problem is you need to mind your own fucking business."

Pierre gave Erica a look that sent a shock through her body. She had never seen him so pissed off before, but she felt like it was only right to step back. A short second after she moved out of the way, Pierre turned into a beast and attacked Tim. Everything happened so fast, and before Erica knew it, she saw more guys jumping in and trying to help Tim. Pierre had Tim on the ground, stomping him. It wasn't long before she saw the members of the Brick Boyz jumping on the guys who were trying to help Tim. It was a big mess, and Erica was scared and worried about Pierre.

Nicole grabbed Erica's hand. "Come on, girl. Let's get the fuck out of here."

The girls ran out of the club right along with the other innocent bystanders. About the time they made it to Nicole's car, there wasn't shit they could do. The parking lot was packed, and it was hard for anybody to move.

"Girl, do you know who the fuck that nigga was Pierre and them was fighting?" Nicole asked as she looked out the window, looking for Mekco to walk out of the club.

"Nicole, all I know is that he said his name was Tim. We danced, and then he started tripping. Next thing I knew, he and Pierre were fighting."

"You okay?"

Erica wasn't sure how she was feeling. That night she saw a side of Pierre that actually scared her. Maybe this was what he was talking about when he said he wanted to protect her from himself. "I guess I'm okay. I just never thought all this would have happened because I danced with that guy," Erica admitted.

"Pierre really do care about you, and he wasn't about to let another nigga step to you."

Erica looked at her friend strangely. "That's not what he said, remember?"

"Erica, that nigga was fighting a dude for dancing with you. Plus, Mekco told me that's what he said, and that's why I haven't stabbed his ass yet."

They both burst into laughter. For that moment they had forgotten all about the drama that they were trying to get away from. The parking lot was starting to thin out, and they were halfway out of the lot when they heard a couple of gunshots going off.

"Fuck, they need to move faster," Nicole yelled as she hit the steering wheel.

Everyone must have been thinking the same thing, because they cleared the fuck out. Everybody was trying to make it home to their loved ones that night.

Nicole drove to her house, hoping that Mekco would make it back to her safely. Erica didn't say anything out loud, but she said a prayer for Pierre. If anything happened to him, it would be all her fault. She got sad thinking about it, and the truth was it would have hurt her because she did love him. She was scared to admit that at first even to herself, but she knew her heart craved him.

Nicole parked her car, and then they made their way into her building. The girls took their shoes off and sat on the couch.

"What now?" Erica asked, still worried.

"We sit here and wait for our men to call or pop up saying they are okay," Nicole mumbled.

They ended up falling asleep on the couch while the TV watched them. Three hours later, Mekco and P walked into Nicole's apartment. Hearing the door slam shut, Nicole jumped up and ran over to Mekco, giving him a big hug.

"Baby, I'm so happy you are okay." She cried in his arms.

"Baby, go get a garbage bag for me," he ordered while walking toward her bedroom.

Pierre stood there staring at Erica, and she couldn't help but stare back. Breaking the silence, she finally spoke up. "Thanks for helping me out, Pierre."

"Go get some clothes and come on," he coldly ordered. After putting in work, he really just wanted to go home, shower, and lie the fuck down.

Erica was confused but went into her room and packed an overnight bag. Pierre waited patiently for her to return. He wasn't sure how tonight was gonna end, but he had decided to be real with her. Seeing another nigga grabbing and touching on her really made him realize he didn't wanna be without her and would kill a muthafucka for trying to step to her the wrong way.

Erica walked back into the living room with her bag. "I'm ready," she said just above a whisper.

Pierre took her by the hand and led her out of the apartment and into his car.

The ride there was quiet. Neither knew what to say to each other, but they did know that they wanted to be with each other. The time that they did spend together was always great even when they just laid up under each other, watching TV.

Entering Pierre's house, Erica took off her shoes and set her bag by the door. P leaned against the wall, looking at her from the opposite side of the room.

"Pierre, I thanked you at Nicole's house. Why did you want me over here?"

Pierre walked in her face, wearing a mug, which caused her to step back. "So you was feeling that nigga or something?"

After seeing how Pierre did the guy in the club, she stood there too scared to answer or move. She wasn't sure if he was pissed at her and wanted to hurt her.

"Answer me!" he yelled.

Erica's emotions got the best of her, and her tears started to fall. "I didn't like him. I just met him. I swear."

Pierre didn't say a word but could see that she was afraid of him. He never wanted to scare her, but once it was turned on, he couldn't help but still be pissed. He tried to calm down, seeing that she was scared and crying.

"Pierre, calm down, please. You're scaring me," she cried out as she held on to his arm.

Her touch alone warmed his heart and helped him control his anger. Pierre looked down at the woman he wanted to love, and he grabbed her face, placing a kiss on her soft lips. They stood in the living room wrapped up in each other's arms, sharing a passionate kiss. Their feelings were on display, and it was clear that they were feeling each other.

Pierre slowly stepped back from Erica. His kiss had her stuck, and she couldn't do anything but stare.

"If you're still scared, I'll take you back to your girl's crib."

"I wanna stay here with you."

Hearing that, he grinned. "All right, cool."

Pierre walked down the hallway as he took his T-shirt off. It had bloodstains on it, but none of them were his. As he went into the bathroom, he turned the shower on. There was something about having another nigga's blood on him that made him feel dirty. Once the water got to the right temperature, he undressed, then got in.

Erica sat on the couch debating whether she was making the right move. She wanted Pierre so bad that she couldn't see herself being without him. He wasn't the tough guy everyone else thought he was. He was cool and lovable whenever they were together. She also loved how he protected her from that guy Tim.

After about ten minutes of weighing her options, she decided to just go with her heart. She walked down the hall and into the bathroom. Her heart was racing, and she was scared, but she knew what she wanted from him.

Feeling the cold breeze hit his wet body, Pierre took his head out from under the showerhead. He was surprised to see Erica standing there buck-naked with the shower door open. He admired her body for a minute before she climbed in.

Although Pierre was enjoying his view, he still had questions. "What the fuck you doing, girl?"

Erica stood under the showerhead with him, nervous like nothing before. She didn't wanna say the wrong thing, so she just kissed him. That little kiss was all that he needed to turn him on. He kissed her back while she allowed his tattooed hands to roam freely all over her wet, smooth skin.

The two stayed in the shower a little longer, kissing and washing each other's bodies. Pierre was enjoying this shower with her, but he wondered what the night was gonna bring them. While holding a handful of ass, he lifted her up and allowed her back to rest on the shower wall. He wanted to stick his dick in her so bad, but he knew she was still a virgin, and it was gonna rip her ass in two if they did it that way for the first time.

Seeing that she was feeling him and wasn't trying to stop him, he held on to her with one hand and opened the shower door with the other one. He carefully carried her to his bed. As he gently laid her wet body down in the middle of the bed, he couldn't help but gaze into her pretty brown eyes.

Staring back at him, Erica wanted so badly to tell him how she really felt about him. She knew somewhere underneath the tattoos and tough skin he also loved her.

"E, if you don't wanna go through with this, you don't have to. I won't be mad at you."

Erica knew how she felt, and she also knew why she followed him into the bathroom that night. "Pierre, I want this. I love you."

Those words were like music to his ears. Kissing her lips, he replied, "I love you too, baby."

Pierre took his time sucking and kissing on every inch of her body. He wanted her first time to be the best. After going back and forth sucking on her hard black nipples, he licked down her stomach, but stopped when he got to her shaved pussy. He took an extra minute to admire what was now his. He couldn't wait to taste her sweetness.

Erica moaned uncontrollably as she placed her hands behind his head. She soon found herself gripping the little hair on his head that he had grown out. "Oh, my God, Pierre, that feels so good."

Pierre grinned as he sucked up the last bit of her juices. He had never tasted someone so sweet as her before. As he climbed back on top of her, he whispered in her ear, "I love you, girl."

Heavily breathing, she mumbled, "I love you too, Pierre."

Pierre let his pole find her opening and slowly worked his way into her. He felt bad as he saw the pain spread across her face. "If you want me to stop, just tell me. I don't wanna hurt you, okay?"

Erica didn't respond. She felt like her insides were on fire, but she didn't want him to stop. As he slid in and out, her eyes got watery, but she lay there trying to handle him like a pro. With every stroke, she dug her nails deeper into his back. Although he hated seeing her cry, there was no way in the world he wanted to stop making love to her. She felt so good, and he had been dreaming of this night since the first time he saw her. Between her loud moans and her tightness, he knew it was only a matter of time before he released into her. It was too good, and he had no plans to pull out of the place that was now his.

"Damn, you mine now, girl."

Erica nodded before they shared more sloppy, wet kisses. Pierre started to pick up his speed as he felt his nut racing to the tip.

"Shit," he yelled over her loud moans.

"Pierre," Erica called out as they came together.

"Goddamn, girl." P then placed another kiss on Erica's lips. "Baby, you all right?" he asked, pulling her into his arms.

"Yes, Pierre, I'm okay. It did hurt a little, but I don't regret doing it."

Erica got comfortable lying on his chest as he held her in his arms. They had finally stopped playing games with each other and with their own feelings.

"You know what, E? I do apologize for hurting you before. I have a lot of demons that I'm battling, and I didn't want you around to get hurt. I don't know what the fuck you did to me, but the more I tried to push your ass away, the more my heart wanted you. And don't be thinking I'm one of these soft-ass niggas out here. I'm still the same ol' nigga. It's just that you make a nigga look at life differently."

Erica giggled. She thought it was cute how he explained how he really was feeling. "I love you, Mr. Miller. And just to let you know I never questioned your gangsta, I saw how you cut into that guy tonight."

"Man, you know I damn near killed that nigga for touching you tonight," he said without a care in the world.

"Pierre!" Erica shouted.

"My bad. You know I'm an honest muthafucka. Let's just dead the whole conversation and go to bed."

Erica didn't want to discuss his violent ways anyway. She knew how honest he could be, so she just closed her eyes so she could get some rest.

Mekco and Nicole cuddled up in the bed holding on to each other. Whenever Mekco had to act out, Nicole always became emotional, and each and every time, she got on Mekco's nerves. Tonight wasn't any different. She cried out about being scared of him getting hurt and never making it back home to her. She even suggested that he stop dealing with the streets. He wasn't trying to hear all that. He was tired and just wanted some sleep.

Luckily for Mekco, he had learned how to handle her ass a while back. He fucked her so good that night that she was knocked out as soon as they both came.

Now he was up looking crazy, thinking about the shit that had just jumped off. Tim was a member of a rival crew, and after they beat his ass that night, he had a feeling that shit was about to get hot for them. He tried to keep the bullshit away from his team, but he knew P was still a hothead and quick to beat a nigga's ass. It was a surprise that he didn't kill him. Mekco didn't want the drama, but at the end of the day, P was more than a friend. That nigga was his muthafucking brother, and he was gonna have his back regardless. Even after the world blew.

***

Saturday, Erica woke up to an empty bed. After finally getting up and making it to the bathroom, she realized that Pierre was in the kitchen.

"I see you up early."

"Yeah, you ain't been here for a minute, and I didn't have any food in this muthafucka. So I got up to get your greedy ass something to eat," he said, laughing.

Erica laughed with him. "Whatever, Pierre. What did you get? Because there's nothing on the stove."

"Look, I don't know how to cook, so I went to Coney Island and got you breakfast."

Erica giggled. "Oh, my gosh, how you grown and don't know how to cook? So what do you think? I'm about to do all the cooking around here?"

"Hell nah, all these restaurants out here. You can take a break sometimes. Besides, I'm a street nigga. I learned how to cook dope to make money. That's all that matters."

Erica gave him a strange look.

"My bad. I just didn't think you would want one of my famous prison cook-ups."

Erica shook her head. Sometimes she wished he didn't say the first thing that popped into his mind.

He saw her look and knew that she couldn't handle his realness. "My bad. I forgot you not used to all that. Don't be mad that I'm an honest nigga."

Before she could reply, Pierre placed a kiss on her lips. They then sat at the table and enjoyed their breakfast.

"What you got up for the day?" he asked.

"Today Nicole wanted me to go shopping with her. Mekco's birthday is coming up, and she wanted to buy him something."

"What time y'all leaving? I wanted you to ride with me right quick."

With a smile on her face, she asked, "Where are we going?"

"Stop being nosy. Just hurry up and eat so we can be out."

After getting dressed, the couple jumped in the car to start their day.

"You know, you should really let me drive," Erica suggested.

"Shit, you not about to be pushing this muthafucka like you did my truck."

"What happened to that truck anyway?" she asked.

"E, you know I don't like to lie to you, and you don't wanna hear my li'l street stories, so just don't worry about it."

"Pierre, what did you do? Nope, never mind. I don't wanna know. I'm just glad you are okay."

"Yeah, too bad for the other muthafucka."

She was back to giving him a weird look.

"I was just playing, baby."

"I wish you wouldn't play like that, Mr. Miller."

"Okay, I'll chill. Just don't be mad at me. I'm trying to be the dude you want in your life, but you know I'm gonna always be a street nigga," he said, holding his hand up and showing off his Brick Boyz tattoo.

Just above a whisper, she mumbled, "Yeah, I know."

"I'm sorry, E. From now on, to make you happy and to keep us cool with each other, I'll leave my street shit on the streets, and when I'm with you, I'll make sure not to piss you off with the truth."

Erica smiled at the fact that he really was trying to do right by her, and she really appreciated it. But she also knew that he wasn't gonna change overnight. "Thank you, baby."

Erica wasn't sure where they were going, but at the end of the day, she didn't really care as long as she was with him. She felt better knowing that she had him all to herself and that he really loved her.

Twenty minutes later they pulled up to a car dealership. "I'll be right back. Let me go holler at my man right quick."

Pierre got out of the car and walked away with a skinny white guy. Erica pulled out her phone to call Nicole. She couldn't wait to tell her that she had finally told P that she had fallen in love with him.

"Hey, boo, what's going on? Pierre not on no bullshit, is he?"

Erica blushed as she answered, "No, he's been great."

"Great, huh?" Nicole asked as she pressed the FaceTime button on her phone. She had to see how her best friend was looking.

Looking at her phone's screen, Erica blushed as she saw Nicole's face pop up. "So, Nicole, guess what?"

"Oh, my fucking gosh! Don't say shit, Erica. I'm so happy for y'all," Nicole yelled.

"Wait, how did you know?"

"Girl, we've been friends for years, and we talk every day. I just knew by the way you were talking. Damn, look at you. You can't even stop smiling. It must have been good as fuck," Nicole said, joking over the phone.

Erica laughed right along with her even though she was embarrassed at first. "Okay, I'll see you later. Pierre about to come back to the car."

"Whatever. Bye."

Pierre came to the car and opened her door. "Ay, come on. Get out."

Erica stepped out of the car. "What's up?"

"Come in here and pick you out a ride."

Erica stopped walking and her mouth dropped. "Are you serious right now? Don't play with me," she said, full of excitement.

"I'm not playing with you. Didn't I tell your ass you weren't about to be driving my shit?" Pierre grabbed her hand, then led her into the dealership.

"You know you don't have to do this just because of last night."

Pierre laughed. "Trust me, that has nothing to do with it. I don't pay for pussy."

This was going to be her first car. Her dad was against buying her a car but made sure she had her license so she could drive the church van whenever he needed her. Over the years she depended on Nicole, a cab, or an Uber to take her everywhere.

Erica looked around the car lot. She wasn't sure what she wanted, but she was happy to finally have her own. "What can I get?"

"What the fuck you want?"

Erica gave him a smile. "I want a car like yours, but red."

"That might be too much of a car for you."

"Boy, the way I was driving yours, I don't think so."

He chuckled. "Hell nah, E. That's a nigga's car. You not getting that. Find you something else."

Erica pouted. "But you said I could get what I wanted."

"G'on somewhere with that spoiled shit. Find something chicks drive."

Erica stood there with her arms folded. She wanted her first car to be the best, and since she had fallen in love with his Challenger, she really wanted one for herself. She pretended like she wasn't gonna move if she didn't get what she wanted. Pierre laughed at her, then started walking toward the door.

"Where are you going?" she yelled.

He turned around and returned to where she was standing. "If you don't want anything, we can go, and I can drop you off at your friend's house."

Getting her act together, she pointed across the room. "I want that over there."

"Ay, Jack, she wants that over there," he said to the salesman he was talking to earlier.

"Okay, Mr. Miller, whatever the wife wants," Jack said, making Erica blush at being called Pierre's wife.

Pierre thought it was cute how she reacted to that. He also thought it wouldn't have been a bad thing to pop a few babies in her. Even the whole married life could be cool, but he knew they weren't ready for all that right now.

After Pierre filled out the necessary paperwork and paid in cash, Erica was now the proud owner of a brand-new 2021 red drop-top BMW.

Erica gave Pierre a kiss as he leaned against her car. "Thank you, baby. I swear I love you so much."

"I love your spoiled ass too. You be careful riding around out here, okay?"

"I will, baby. You don't have to worry about me," she responded.

"One more thing—are you staying at Nicole's house tonight?"

"I don't know. Why, do you want me to come back to your house after our girls' day out?"

With a devilish grin on his face, Pierre quickly answered, "Hell yeah, you already know I want your ass back at the crib with me."

He wanted to tell her that instead of her staying at Nicole's house, she might as well stay at his crib since that was where she would be most of the time now, but he decided not to. He didn't want to seem like he was rushing anything between them.

"I'll see you later then. We're gonna go look for a gift, then go out to eat. I'm just gonna call you when I'm on my way to make sure you are home."

Pierre dug in his pocket. "This is a copy of my house keys, and here goes some shopping money," he said, handing her the keys and a knot of money rolled up in a rubber band.

"Pierre, you don't have to give me this. I have some money," Erica said, trying to give him the money back.

He held his hands up like he was scared to take the money back. "Nah, that's all yours. Go ahead and blow that shit."

"Thank you," she shyly said, placing the items in her purse.

Pierre lifted her head up and kissed her lips. "You my girl now. You ain't never gotta worry about a damn thing. I got you, all right?"

They kissed one last time before they went their separate ways. Pierre had no problem giving Erica the world, and it wasn't only because he loved her. Girls like her deserved the world because they never asked for anything. From day one, Pierre noticed how she wasn't one of those bitches who fucked with a nigga with money and begged for everything. And that was why it was so easy to fall in love with her.

Nicole picked up her phone and saw that it was Erica. "Hey, you outside?"

"Yeah, come on. I have a big surprise."

Nicole grabbed her bag and walked out of her apartment. Seeing Erica leaning on a brand-new car made her scream. "Damn, bitch, I see you."

"You like?" Erica asked, cheesing.

"You already know I do," Nicole said, jumping in the passenger side.

Erica started driving off toward the mall.

"Now, Erica, I know you don't think we are about to ride in silence. You need to be filling me in on you and P. You must have really put it on him last night. You got this nigga buying cars and shit."

"What can I say? He loves me. I'm happy and love him too," Erica softly said.

"Aw. I swear I'm so happy for y'all lovebirds."

For the rest of the ride the two talked about everything from their relationships to how they were gonna spend their summer. Being with Brick Boyz, they didn't have a care in the world.

After walking around the mall for damn near three hours, the girls finally left with their hands full of bags. They both were so tired that they didn't even go out to eat. They both decided to just go home and chill with their men.

Erica pulled up in front of Nicole's apartment. "I'll see you tomorrow at church."

"You still gonna go after what happened between you and your dad?" Nicole asked.

"Yeah. He was wrong, but church is a part of me, and I wouldn't feel right not going. I'm still the same person."

"All right. I'll see you in the morning," Nicole said, getting out of the car and pulling her bags from the back seat.

Erica watched as Nicole disappeared into the building. She then headed to Pierre's house. She was hoping that he wasn't home so she could take a nap before she cooked dinner for them. Entering the apartment, she noticed that the TV in the room was on, so that only meant that he was there. She carried her couple of bags to the back. As she opened the door and walked in the room, she caught Pierre stuffing bundles of money into a bag.

"Damn, girl, I almost forgot I gave you a key. I thought I was about to have to pop a muthafucka," P said, dropping his gun back on the bed.

Erica looked at all the shit on the bed, but instead of pressing the issue, she started taking her clothes off. "I'm tired. Move that stuff so I can take a nap. When I get up, I'll make dinner."

"I'm sorry, baby. I wasn't expecting you home so early. I thought y'all were gonna be chilling all day. Don't be mad at me."

"Baby, I'm not mad at you. To be honest, I knew what you were about before we got serious. I'm just tired. We walked around that dang mall a thousand times," she said, now laughing.

"Okay, cool. That nigga Face is on his way over here to pick this shit up in a few. Then I'll be all yours," P said as he put the gun back in the top drawer of the nightstand.

Pierre cuddled up with Erica and watched TV with her until she dozed off. He thought about how he wanted to be the leader of the Brick Boyz again when he got out, but just passing out money and doing nothing was much easier. Plus, with the type of woman he had on his hands, he knew that his status didn't mean shit to her. She was gonna love him no matter what. He had no problem being second-in-command, especially when he saw how

Mekco had to pay back all that shit that Brandon and Brian had dipped off with. He helped him out not only because that was his day one, but because Mekco made sure that, when he got home, his safe was packed with more bread than a damn bakery.

Someone ringing Pierre's bell woke him up from his nap with his girl. He climbed out of the bed, trying not to wake her up. He got to the intercom and saw on the camera that it was Face. He buzzed his boy in.

"What's up, my baby? How you feeling?" P asked once he stepped into the living room.

Face shook his head. The death of his pops had hit him hard. That man was all he had. "You already know, man. I'm just trying to stay busy to keep my mind right."

"I see. I told you I could have dropped that bread off to you."

"It's all good. Me and the wife were out getting the last-minute stuff for the funeral Monday, so it was no biggie," Face responded.

P handed him over the bag that contained the money. "I'll see you Monday, nigga. Stay safe out here. You know if you need anything, I got your back."

"Yeah, dog, but I'm good. After Monday I'll bounce back to my old self again."

P locked his door behind Face, then returned to the bedroom. He smiled as he watched the most beautiful girl in the world laid out in his bed. He climbed back in the bed, placing his body on top of hers. He started placing small kisses on her lips. As he kissed her from her neck to her breast, she started to wake up.

"Pierre, I'm gonna cook when I get up. I promise," Erica said, still half asleep.

"Just relax and chill, baby. I'm about to eat now."

Because she was still half asleep, she didn't realize what he actually was talking about. Feeling her panties getting pulled off and his mouth buried deep inside her private area, she learned exactly what he meant.

Nicole and Mekco sat in the bed watching TV, feeling good. They were smoking and sipping on some Hennessy. Well, Mekco was smoking. Nicole didn't smoke.

"Mekco, what are we doing for your birthday? You got a couple of weeks, so I know you've been planning some shit."

"I'm not sure yet. You know I just took a lot when Brandon and Brian fucked me over. I'm really thinking about chilling," he said, with his words slurring. His drink was kicking in, and Henny always made him horny.

Nicole was buzzing, but she wasn't like him. She knew that she was gonna have to get up early for service. Seeing that he was nodding off, she climbed out of bed to start cleaning up his mess. Mekco had blunt wrappers everywhere.

"I'll get that shit up in the morning. Get back in the bed with me," Mekco ordered once he felt her remove his cup from her hand.

"Baby, you was just asleep. I'm about to finish getting this stuff up, and then I'll get in the bed myself."

After cleaning up his mess, Nicole climbed in the bed with her love. Sitting on top of Mekco, she whined, "Daddy, get up."

Mekco hesitated to move at first, but just like clockwork, feeling Nicole release his pole from his shorts, his eyes popped open, and his shit was hard.

"Damn, girl, you see a nigga asleep."

"Whatever. When has me being sleepy ever stopped you from fucking me until I woke up? Now get up and fuck me."

Mekco slid his shorts off for her and kicked them on the floor. "Go ahead and do your thing."

Nicole loved when Mekco took control in the bedroom, but she wasn't scared to ride his dick either. After all the time they had been together, she had somehow taught herself how to just take the pain and learn to love it.

He lay back, enjoying Nicole bouncing up and down on his dick. He thought it was cute how she was moving to her own li'l beat in her head. He held a tight grip around her waist.

Mekco had peeped how she wasn't taking it all, and he hated that shit. He liked to be so deep in her shit that he could touch her soul. Mekco flipped Nicole over. Pinning her down on the mattress so he could work his magic, he said, "Your li'l ass think you slick only taking half of my shit. You about to feel this shit."

With that being said, Mekco lifted her legs back, making sure that her toes were touching the headboard. Nicole moaned his name out loudly as she took his deep strokes. He was driving her crazy but in a good way. He always laughed at her, saying she sounded like she was speaking in tongues.

"Man, shut that shit up and take this dick."

She continued to moan out in pleasure, which only made Mekco dig deeper and stroke a little faster. When he could no longer hold it in, he allowed her tight grip around his dick and shot his seeds right in her. He then collapsed on his pillow.

"Damn, baby, that was good," Nicole said, covering her body with the sheet that was on the bed.

"Shit, ain't it always? You know what my fucking name is. But on the real, you know you gonna have to stop all that drinking and all that going-out shit."

Nicole turned his way. She was confused by what he was saying. "Why you say that, Mekco? That's what I do for fun."

"'Cause I love you, and I think I'm ready to give you what the hell you been begging for."

"Are you serious right now? You finally ready to have our baby?" Nicole asked with full excitement. She'd waited so long to hear him say those words. They were magic to her ears.

"Yeah, baby, I think I'm ready now. Don't be acting all surprised either. I've been dicking you down raw lately. Don't think you had me slipping like that."

Nicole giggled but didn't say anything. She was too happy to even reply to his silly self.

Chapter 9

Chanel turned around on her side to wrap her arms around her boyfriend.

"Damn, baby, watch your hands. I told you my body was still sore," he whined.

"I'm sorry. I still think you should have made a police report about the robbery. I just really hate how those criminals did you."

He was tired of her talking about the shit. There wasn't even a robbery for real. He just got his ass beat for playing that tough-guy role.

"It's okay, baby. Just stop talking about the shit. Now get some sleep so you can get up on time for church in the morning."

He was about to get his revenge and have the last laugh. Leaving it all up to him by the end of the summer, every member of the Detroit Brick Boyz was gonna be dead.

Erica got up early to get ready for church. Even though she had been at Pierre's house for the whole weekend, she still was going to attend church. She was still scared to disappoint her dad.

"Ay, where you about to go?" Pierre asked, rolling over.

"Baby, it's Sunday. You already know that means I'm going to church. You wanna go with me?"

"Damn, I thought you loved a nigga."

Erica giggled, "I do love you. What are you talking about?"

"You know if I step in the church, I'm burning the fuck up and going straight to hell. Without passing Go and collecting my two hundred dollars."

Erica walked over toward the bed and sat down next to him. "I wish you'd stop saying crazy stuff like that. The Lord forgives those who ask for His forgiveness."

"I haven't asked for forgiveness, and I'm not sure if I'm done committing sins yet."

Erica gave him a weird look. Sometimes she hated the stuff that came out of his mouth, but he was as real as it got.

Knowing that the look that she gave him only meant that she wasn't happy, he tried to retract his words. "It's just not for me, baby, but you go ahead and have fun. Say a prayer for me. You not taking your ride today?" he asked, noticing her keys on the dresser.

"I told Nicole to come pick me up for church."

Pierre sat up in the bed. "I bought you that car so you wouldn't have to ask anybody for a ride. Take your car, E."

Erica stood by the dresser, shaking her head. The truth was that she was scared of what her dad would say seeing the fancy car.

Pierre thought about why she wouldn't want to drive her car, and then it hit him. It was all about her daddy.

"Look, don't even worry about your daddy. Soon enough he's gonna find out about me anyway. You gotta learn to live for yourself," Pierre said, trying to talk some sense into her.

Erica picked up her phone from the dresser and texted Nicole, telling her that she was gonna drive herself to church. Pierre got up from the bed and gave her a hug before giving her another kiss.

"I'll see you later."

"I love you, E."

"I love you too, Pierre," she said before walking out the door.

Pierre climbed back in the bed. He couldn't believe how Erica had his mind gone. P had never used the word "love" so freely in his life.

Twenty minutes later, Nicole parked her car in the church parking lot. She looked around to see if Erica had made it there yet. She laughed thinking how now that Erica was driving herself to church, she was still late.

Erica was already running late, but when she parked her car, she sat there for a minute thinking about how she hadn't talked to her dad since the week before. She was kind of scared to see her dad for the first time since she left his house. As she reached the church steps, she heard someone calling her name. When she turned around, she saw it was Chanel.

"Hey, Erica," Chanel said cheerfully.

"Good morning, Chanel. I guess we both were running late this morning."

"Yeah, my car was acting up this morning, and my boyfriend just dropped me off," Chanel replied.

As Erica walked toward the front of the church to take her seat, she saw her father standing there talking to the choir director. She then heard him excuse himself to greet his daughter.

"Good morning, my beautiful daughter. I'm so glad you could make it," he said right before giving her a hug.

"I love you, Daddy," she whispered in his ear.

He whispered back in her ear, "I love you too, and I'm so sorry about the way I reacted. I now understand that you are grown and not a baby anymore."

After they released each other, Erica took her seat in the front row next to Nicole and her mom.

During service, Nicole nudged Erica on her side. She then looked toward her mom. Erica laughed to herself as she watched Nicole's mother giving her dad a look that clearly said she wanted him.

"What I tell you?" Nicole whispered in Erica's ear.

Both girls smiled hard, then turned their attention back to the pastor's service.

After service and cleaning up, Erica made sure she locked up the church. Nicole had left her since she was now driving, and her dad went home to warm dinner up for them. Erica had taken up her father on his request to meet him at his house. He wanted to talk to her and just try to make things right between them. He only wanted what was best for his daughter, and he was willing to work things out so she wouldn't walk away from him completely.

They sat at the dinner table praying that things would go better this time than what happened a few weeks ago.

"So, Erica, I heard that you passed all your finals. You know I'm so proud of you," Pastor Collins said, cutting a piece of his fish, then sticking it in his mouth.

"Thanks, Dad."

Erica looked down at her vibrating phone and saw that it was Pierre texting her. She smiled and opened the text message.

Mr. Miller: Wyd?

Erica: At my dad's house having dinner.

Mr. Miller: You going to Nicole's house afterward or you staying there?

Erica: IDK yet. We are trying to make things right between us. I'll call you later.

Erica set her phone back on the table, still smiling from something as simple as a text from the man she loved. Pastor Collins noticed her reaction and couldn't help asking questions.

"So I take it that's the young man who got you wide open?"

"Come on, Dad. Please don't start. We were doing so good."

"I was just asking a simple question. Maybe you should invite him over for dinner next Sunday. Matter of fact, invite him to church. Afterward, we could have dinner," he suggested.

Erica saw how her daddy was trying to act like he was comfortable with her dating, but she wasn't sure about bringing Pierre around anytime soon. She knew her dad would take one look at him and flip out. Pierre wasn't the type of guy her dad painted as the right guy for her, but she loved him.

Erica knew it was only a matter of time before the two met each other. So she looked at her dad with a shy smile on her face. "Okay. I'll invite him over. "

"Well, I can't wait to meet this young fella. Is he the one who bought you the nice car?"

"Yes, Daddy. I picked it out myself. Isn't it pretty?"

"Yeah, it is. It also looks very expensive. I wonder what a person would have to do in order to have a person buy them such a nice ride like that."

That was the last straw for Erica. She knew it would kill her dad to stop being so judgmental. "Dad, I didn't have to do anything. You're talking to me like I'm some type of prostitute or something. Why can't he just love me enough to do something nice for me?"

"I wasn't born last night. Guys these days don't just buy females nice things just because. They only spend money if that young lady gave them something first," Pastor Collins said, trying to get the truth out of his daughter.

"I said what I said. Now can we just finish eating?" Erica asked, irritated.

Once they were done with dinner, Erica cleaned up the kitchen. She was gonna stay there with her dad, but after his performance at the dinner table she decided not to. She only prayed that he didn't try to show his ass when Pierre came to dinner the following Sunday.

Walking into the living room, Erica stood in the doorway for a minute and watched her dad in his favorite La-Z-Boy recliner chair. She loved her dad to death, but she knew it was time for her to live her own life. She wasn't trying to hurt him on purpose. He was just gonna have to learn to respect the fact that she was grown and had a life outside of the church life.

"Daddy, I'm about to head out. I washed and dried all the dishes for you. I'll call you tomorrow to check on you."

"I'll see you Wednesday for Bible study. You be safe out here."

Erica hopped into her car, but before she had a chance to drive off, Nicole called her.

"What's up, Nicole?"

Crying into the phone, Nicole talked hysterically. "Erica, don't go to P's house. Drive straight to my house."

"Nicole, calm down. What's going on? Is everyone okay?" Erica asked as she started her car to go to Nicole's house.

"I'll tell you everything when you get here."

Nicole hung up the phone, leaving Erica more confused than before. She could tell she was upset by the way she was sounding, so she hurried to her house.

Erica called Nicole to buzz her in. She wanted to know what had her so upset. When Erica walked into the apartment, Nicole was on the couch crying her eyes out.

"What's wrong with you, boo?" Erica asked as she took a seat next to her.

Nicole wiped her face and tried to calm down. "You know Mekco's friend Face?"

"Yeah, I ran across him a few times when I was around Pierre," Erica answered honestly.

"Girl, somebody killed him and his girl last night," Nicole said, trying not to cry again.

Erica covered her face. She couldn't believe what she had just heard. The news made her cry also. "That's messed up, and his dad's funeral is in the morning."

"Right. Mekco and P are out now playing detective. They not gonna stop until they find out who is behind this."

The girls sat around talking about what happened to Face. The conversation then turned into Nicole talking about how all of a sudden Mekco was with the whole idea of having a baby.

Erica sat on the couch, cheesing. "I'm so happy for y'all. I can't wait to be an auntie."

"Hold your horses. I'm not pregnant yet. Besides, he just lost one of his best friends. Ain't no telling how he feels now. Face and his girl had three kids, and now they have to stay with their grandma. Just thinking about that makes me not wanna bring a baby in this cold world," Nicole explained to her.

Erica then went on to tell her about her dinner with her dad.

"Pastor is low-key crazy, girl. He knows if P walks into his house, he might try to choke the life out of him." They both had to laugh at that.

"Well, I'm tired, so I'm about to jump in the shower and get in the bed."

"Okay, Erica. I'm about to go lie down myself. I hope Mekco and them are all right out there. I still have to go to Face's dad's funeral tomorrow."

"Me too," Erica sadly said as she walked off.

In the shower, she found herself once again praying for Pierre. She wanted him to return to her unharmed.

After her shower, sleep came easy. As soon as her head hit the pillow, she was knocked out.

"Man, look at all this dough. That shit was lit as hell," Dre said while flipping through the money that they just took from a dead member of the well-known crew the Detroit Brick Boyz.

"Hell yeah, fuck those niggas. I'm gonna have fun taking their whole crew out," Tim said.

"Especially them niggas Pierre and Mekco."

Tim then gave Dre a proud look. "It's my job to let them see everyone in their weak-ass crew die before I finally take them out. I want them niggas to suffer," Tim said as he hit his blunt.

"Did you really have to kill his girl?" Chanel asked. She had known a little of their plan, that someone was gonna die, but she didn't know they were going to kill the guy's baby mama.

"Shut your soft ass up. She would still have been alive if you had tried harder to be friends with Mekco's bitch. I don't understand how you fucked that up," Tim yelled at Chanel.

She didn't want to go back and forth with him, so she carried herself to the room. She hated when he blamed everything on her when things went wrong. He had no idea how hard it was to hang with Nicole and Erica. They thought she was acting funny because she was all into church life, but really she was battling whether she should save their lives or deliver them to Tim and his friends.

Tim knew that Mekco would come running ready to do whatever. *Easy target.*

After Erica and Nicole dissed Chanel, Tim got so mad at her that he broke up with her. Being alone was driving her crazy, and after some time she convinced him to come back. When he did, he had a new plan that didn't involve her.

This time, Tim was determined to bring them all down one by one.

Chapter 10

On this rainy Monday morning, the Brick Boyz were facing a fucked-up task. Today they were burying Face's dad, and it killed them knowing that Face wasn't there to say his final goodbyes to the man who raised him.

Everyone from the hood took it hard because he was such a great guy. As they grew up, he would get in their asses if they fucked up, and feed them afterward. Just seeing their three daughters Jasmine, Chrystal, and Monica cry their eyes out made every thug in the church cry as well. Not only did they lose their grandfather, but they had also lost both of their parents at the same time.

After the repast Erica went to Nicole's house.

The other night, Mekco and P had spent the night out hitting the streets. They were determined to find out who was behind the double homicide. It was hard to understand how two people lost their lives and nobody knew or saw shit. Even Cross had stepped out, showing his face, trying to get some results, and still there were no answers.

The crew was clueless as to who would have done this, and they were gonna lose sleep trying to find out. P had told Mekco that he last saw Face when he came to pick up the bag of money, so whoever killed him just hit a quick come-up. Mekco was pissed once again because it was the beginning of the summer, and he was taking hits left and right. He had been stacking all winter to stunt on niggas all summer, and here he was having to put all his dough in another muthafucka's hand.

The next morning, they went to pay Cross a visit.

Mekco knew the best way to handle his business was to go straight to Cross and tell him the truth about the money. He also knew Cross was gonna get in his ass, but at the end of the day, he had to tell the truth.

Sitting at the round table, Cross poured everyone a shot of Patrón. "Look, I love y'all li'l niggas and been around y'all since before you could even walk, but y'all fucking up big time. How the hell the leader and his right-hand man keep getting finessed by these ho-ass niggas?"

"Look, Cross, I take full responsibility for everything," Mekco spoke up.

Pierre took a sip of his drink, then turned his attention to Cross. "Man, I did pass that money to Face the other day, but I had no idea niggas was about to get at him. I'm gonna get you that bread."

"The way I see it, Mekco, your ass been to fucking up in these streets being too fuckin' nice. Muthafuckas taking you for a fucking joke out here. And, P, I know you just got out and all, but have you been staying out of trouble?"

Laughing at Cross's question, P answered, "Hell yeah, I've been a fucking Boy Scout. That's my story and I'm sticking to it." His joke caused all three men to laugh.

Cross stopped laughing, then got serious. "I know what's wrong with y'all soft niggas. You too busy with y'all head stuff so far up in pussy that you can't even focus on making this money. What the fuck wrong with y'all? I'm pretty sure you know the old saying, 'fuck these hoes not cuff them.'"

"Ay, nigga, you can chill on all that shit. We gonna handle our business and put some niggas to sleep behind it. Plus, we gonna make sure you get your bread back, even if we gotta kill they mama to bring their ass out of hiding," P said, showing Cross that he still had a little fire in him.

Cross sat up in his chair, laughing at P. "Now see, li'l nigga, that's what the fuck I'm talking about. It's about time you brought the old P out. Now, stop telling me what the fuck you gonna do, and show me the shit."

Hearing Cross tell P that only pissed Mekco off more. Mekco saw a little devilish look on P's face. The old P was back, and that only meant he was about to paint the whole city red. Mekco wasn't sure how to take this. He knew how much of a hothead P could be and didn't want his boy to end up back in jail. After a second thought, he said fuck it. He needed that extra force.

Talking to Cross made Mekco wake up. He hadn't become soft because of no pussy. He just got so comfortable having everybody work for him that he lost focus of who he should trust. He was too damn busy trying to make friends, but all that was about to change. Face was gone, and P was always gonna be his bro. Any other nigga was only around for business, nothing more, nothing less.

Since the deaths of Face and Destiny, Pierre had been somewhat distant from Erica. He hadn't really been answering her phone calls and texts. Over time, Erica tried not to worry or let it bother her that Pierre had been distant from her, but when it all boiled down to it, that shit hurt her badly. She wasn't sure what she did wrong, but she wanted to make things right between them. Although she had seen him that Monday at Face's dad's funeral, that wasn't enough for her because he barely said two words to her.

It was two weeks later, on a Wednesday night, and they had just left Bible study.

"Have you heard from P?"

"Nah, girl. I'm actually about to ride out to Pierre's house."

Nicole didn't like her friend feeling hurt. "I wonder what that's all about."

"I knew he was hurt about his friend's death, so I tried to give him space. I just miss him so much and need answers," she sadly responded.

Nicole wasn't sure what to say to her bestie. She knew from Mekco that the crew was going through a lot, but he never told her why P was acting brand new. She didn't want to tell her friend to just forget about him because she knew that would only hurt her, but at the same time if a nigga was ignoring her, she would have played him at his own game.

"Okay, be careful out here. I love you."

Erica gave her a smile. "I love you too."

On her way to Pierre's house, Erica prayed that he was home and could explain why he was acting funny toward her. Then her mind started playing games with her. She started thinking about what her dad said about how guys only wanted girls for sex. Thinking like that only made her cry.

After taking out the keys to his apartment that he had given her a while back, she opened the door and could tell that he wasn't home. She did a walk-through and could see that he had tried to cook but didn't succeed. After taking off her church dress and putting on some relaxing clothes, she began to clean up. To kill even more time, she did his laundry, hoping he would pop up soon.

When 10:00 p.m. rolled around, she decided to just take a shower and go to bed. She had called him three times and was frustrated because the first time he didn't answer, the second call got sent to voicemail, and by the third and final time, he had turned his phone off. She climbed in the bed and could smell his cologne, which only made her cry out for him.

Pierre walked into his place a little after 2:00 a.m. Word had gotten back to them that some east-side niggas were responsible for the murders of Face and his girl. So P, Mekco, and Li'l Trey went to pay them niggas a visit. There were three niggas in the house chilling, and by the time the Brick Boyz left the site, all the niggas were dead. They even picked up the money and drugs they had lying around. Them east-side niggas weren't gonna need it.

Opening the door, he knew that Erica had been by. The smell of cleaning supplies and dryer sheets told him everything. He looked around, and she had even washed his dishes. He smiled thinking about her ass. Lately he had been on some bull-shit, and he knew she was pissed at him. He had planned on hitting her up in a couple of days or after everything was settled.

Stepping into the hot shower water, Pierre started to think about the last time Erica was at his place and the crazy, wild sex in the shower. Just his thoughts alone made him hard, but he had to be strong and keep her away like he was doing.

"Man, what the fuck!" he mumbled as he flicked the bedroom light on and saw Erica knocked out asleep in one of his T-shirts.

Shaking his head, he dried off, then put on his boxers. He stood there for a minute wondering if he should climb in the bed with her or if he should take his ass on the couch. He knew if she felt him in the bed with her, he was gonna have to explain why he went ghost on her. Even though it was for a good reason, he still wasn't ready to talk to her about shit. But then again, he didn't want her to think that he had been playing her and just fucking with her feelings.

Against his better judgment, he turned around and retired to the couch. He just wasn't ready to deal with his feelings, and Erica had the gangsta in him going into hiding. A man who gave a fuck had appeared.

Erica tossed and turned in her sleep. She couldn't seem to sleep peacefully not knowing what she was doing wrong with Pierre. Looking at the time on the clock on his dresser, she saw that it was going on 4:00 a.m., and he still wasn't home. Deep down inside, she knew it was over for them. She cried as she put her clothes on and got ready to go home. She felt like there wasn't any point in even staying around just to hurt even more.

She placed the keys that he had given her on the kitchen counter since she no longer had a need for them. As she entered the living room, she didn't even pay attention that he was lying on the couch.

Pierre heard someone moving around and was ready to pop a muthafucka. As he pretended to be asleep, he pulled his gun from under the couch. As soon as the person came into the living room, he could tell that it was Erica. It was a good thing that she had left the kitchen light on because he was ready to dead whoever was in his house. He was still somewhat fucked up and had forgotten she was even there.

"Where the fuck you going?" he asked as he sat up on the couch.

Hearing his voice made her jump. All this time she was thinking that she was alone, and he was really there. "Nicole's house," she finally answered.

Pierre got up from the couch and walked toward her. He then flicked the light on. "Man, it's four in the fucking morning. Go get back in the bed."

Any other time she would have listened to him, but this time she didn't. "Look, I feel like I'm no longer wanted by you, so there really isn't a point to be here with you. I don't know what I did wrong to you, but I know I don't deserve to be hurt like this," she said, now crying.

Pierre hated seeing her cry because of him and his bullshit. He did try his hardest not to get her mixed up with his ass. Wiping away her tears and staring into her eyes, he tried to calm her down. "Baby, stop crying, please. You didn't do anything wrong. I swear you're perfect."

"Then why don't you want me? I had to do something wrong."

"I do want you. You got my fucking heart, girl!" he yelled.

A part of Erica was happy to hear that, but the other side called it bullshit. His actions were telling her a whole other story. "You don't mean that, Pierre. You've been dodging me for weeks like you were just done with me."

Pierre wrapped his arms around her to show some type of affection. Then he walked her over toward the couch. He sat down, then placed her on his lap, facing him. "Look, E, there's a lot going on right now, and I just really don't think that you would have understood."

"That's bull. You never even tried talking to me to find out what I would understand. Just be honest. You played me. You got what you wanted from me and moved on with your life."

Hearing her say that pissed him off. He pushed Erica to the side of the couch so she could get off his lap. Standing up, he began to yell, "That's what the fuck you think about me? You think I'm some type of ho-ass nigga just out here talking bitches out of their pussy just to have something to do? I'm not that type of nigga, E. I told you before I be out here in a lot of bullshit, and if I push you away for a minute, it's only to keep your dumb ass alive."

Erica sat there crying her eyes out. He was saying one thing, but lately she knew how she had been feeling. She felt neglected by the guy she loved, and she was hurt.

Pierre was pissed, but at the same time he knew she was new to his lifestyle and things could have worked out better if he had talked to her instead of just blocking her.

"E, I'm sorry. I wasn't trying to hurt you in no type of way. Just stop crying, and I'll talk to you for real," Pierre said while pulling her up from the couch.

He pulled her closer so he could kiss her. As they shared a passionate kiss, Pierre picked Erica up and walked her toward his bedroom. "I love you, E. You gotta believe that shit."

Erica didn't respond. She was so wrapped up in her mixed emotions that she wasn't sure what to feel anymore. He placed her in the middle of the bed and began placing kisses all over her beautiful brown skin. Pierre then pulled their clothes off. That night he made love to her as if it were their first time together again.

When it was all over, Pierre held Erica in his arms as she lay on his chest, still placing kisses on her forehead.

"Look, E, I'm not used to giving a fuck about anybody since my grandma died, but when you came around, I knew that I wanted you in my life. I knew that I was taking a chance being with you. I tried to block you out of my life, but that shit didn't work."

"Pierre, I love you, which you should know by now. I just can't take being hurt by you. Every time I called or texted and didn't get a response from you, my heart broke more. What happened so bad that you would just push me away?"

Pierre paused for a moment before answering her question. "I'm just gonna be honest even though I know you hate hearing certain shit."

"I just want the truth, Mr. Miller."

"When that nigga Face and his girl were killed, I thought about how I be grimy in these streets and at any given moment somebody could hurt you just to hurt me. It might sound like bullshit to you, but Face was out with his girl in the fucking car. Now they are both dead and three kids are without a mama and daddy. I wouldn't know what to do if something happened to you because of the shit I was on. I love you so much that I would rather push you away until shit calms down."

Erica somewhat understood what he was saying. He did what he had to do, and she was now feeling better. "Pierre, thank you. I understand. I just wish that you had said something. If you loved me like you say you do, then you would have just let me know what was going on with you. You had me thinking the worst."

"No matter what, I love you and I don't have any plans of stopping. This love shit is something new to me, and I just need to learn how to handle you a little better than what I've been doing," Pierre said, kissing her again.

Erica was happy that she had answers and her man back. She cuddled up under Pierre and soon drifted off to sleep.

The next morning, Pierre woke up to the smell of breakfast being cooked, and it made him happy to have Erica back over. After taking care of his personal hygiene, Pierre went into the kitchen. He stood in the doorway watching the first female he had allowed to hold his heart.

"Good morning, baby," he said, sneaking up behind her, placing a kiss on the right side of her neck.

"Hey, I was just about to make your plate. You showed up just in time, Mr. Miller."

He chuckled hearing her call him by his last name. "Thanks for cooking for a nigga. I swear you're the best."

"You know I got you," Erica said, placing his plate of eggs, grits, bacon, and toast in front of him on the table.

Pierre dug right into his food. He had been so busy running the streets that he hadn't had time to really sit down and eat for real. And even when he did try to cook anything, he just burned the shit. Erica took a seat right next to him and began to eat her breakfast.

"So what do you have planned for today?" she shyly asked.

"Shit, I'm spending my whole day kissing and sucking all over my baby. That's what the hell I got planned," Pierre said, giving her a sneaky grin.

Erica sat there blushing. "Sounds like fun," she said, giggling.

After breakfast, Erica cleaned the kitchen while Pierre went into the living room to use the phone. Pierre called Mekco to see how shit was looking for them.

"Ay, what's up with you?" Pierre asked.

"Shit, I'm chilling with the wife today. Been in these streets for a couple of weeks straight. I'm trying to keep the peace in my household."

"I feel that. I've been fucking up with Erica's ass too, but we good now," Pierre added.

"All right, I'll hit you up if something pops up tonight. Remember, we have to go check in with Cross tomorrow."

"All right, I'll see you there," Pierre said before hanging up.

***

After a much-needed nap, Erica woke up to her phone ringing. She looked at the screen and saw that it was her dad calling. After smacking her lips, she finally answered the phone. "Hey, Daddy, what's up?"

"Hey, my beautiful daughter, you've been dodging me. Have you forgotten about our little dinner date? You know, the one where I'm supposed to meet your little friend?"

"Dad, I'm gonna talk to him, and I'll call you later."

Pierre looked at her strangely as she talked to her dad. Even though he half heard the conversation, he knew she had to be out of her fucking mind thinking he was gonna meet her dad. He just knew that nothing good would come out of meeting him.

"Love you, Daddy."

"Love you too. Now don't forget to call me," Pastor Collins said before hanging up. He badly wanted to meet the young punk who was now taking advantage of his sweet, dear daughter.

"What the fuck you up to, E?"

"So this is the deal. My dad wants to have dinner and meet you. So what do you think about that?"

"Man, I don't know about all that. That man don't wanna meet me for real, and I know one look at me and he gonna flip the fuck out," Pierre explained.

"I'm pretty sure that once he gets used to you, he will like you. You have a good personality. Look at how quick I fell in love with you."

Pierre sat there still with a strange look on his face. He didn't give a fuck what she said. There wasn't no way he was about to sit at a table with a pastor.

"Pierre, please just do this for me. I promise I won't ask for nothing else."

"Come on, you don't ask for shit now, and when I offer to give you shit, you say no. Except for that damn car. So that's not fair at all."

Erica climbed on top of Pierre. "Baby, can you just go? We wouldn't have to stay for long."

Pierre gazed in her eyes and could tell how important this was for her. He was just gonna have to put his feelings to the side and do as she asked. "All right, I'll go to this dinner, but I'm telling you now I'm gonna be myself, and I'm not dressing up."

Erica smiled. "Thanks, baby. I love you, Mr. Miller," she said, placing a kiss on his lips.

Pierre watched as Erica got back on the phone to tell her dad that they were gonna come see him the next day. When she got off the phone, Pierre lay there deep in his thoughts. He really didn't wanna meet her dad, but he knew how important it was for her. That was the only reason he agreed to go. He just hoped her father's opinion of him didn't change the way she felt.

"Pierre, stop looking all crazy, baby. I love you, and that's all that matters. If my dad doesn't like you, that won't change how I feel about you, okay?"

"Yeah, I hear you."

Everything was all set. They were gonna go to Erica's father's house for dinner that Friday, and that Saturday they were gonna go out and celebrate Mekco's birthday.

Mekco really didn't wanna do shit for his birthday, but Nicole had talked him into going out.

"Nicole, I'm telling you this now, after Saturday I bet' not see another drink in your hand. You not about to have my baby all fucked up because you wanna drink all the time."

"Whatever. Mekco, I didn't even drink until I got with your ass. Besides, I'm not even pregnant yet. So until then, I'm gonna drink when I feel like it," Nicole said as she ate her slice of pizza.

"I'm just saying, you have to get your body ready for the baby. Even if you're not pregnant now, you still want your body detoxed from all that shit before you get pregnant."

"All right, dang. You need to stop drinking and smoking, too. How do you expect to deal with a baby and not be in the right state of mind?"

"Damn, fuck that. I'm not about to stop smoking. You got me fucked up," he yelled.

"You have to detox your body for the baby just like you told me, fool," she said, laughing.

"Fuck it. I'll try, but you better be on your shit too," he said, turning his attention back to the basketball game.

Friday night came too fast for Pierre. He was nervous and wanted to back down. Just knowing that it would hurt her, he went ahead and got dressed for the night's event. Erica had already driven to her dad's house to help him out with dinner.

Erica was sweating bullets. She knew her dad was ready to meet Pierre and judge him. She also knew that no matter who she decided to date, her dad would never approve of the guy, so it was best for her to just date who she wanted. At the end of the day, nobody was gonna be right for his baby girl.

Erica started to set the table as she felt her phone vibrate in her pocket. "Hey, baby, where are you?" she asked Pierre.

"I'm pulling up right now. I hope I'm not too late."

"No, you just on time."

"All right. I'm parking now."

Pastor Collins looked at his daughter with a stern look on his face as he heard the doorbell.

"Come on, Dad, don't look like that. He just got here. At least give him a chance," Erica said as she went to open the door for Pierre.

When she opened the door, she was expecting to see him dressed in some jeans and a T-shirt, but he fooled her. He wasn't too fancy, but she could tell that he tried. He was dressed in a white button-up shirt, black pants, and a pair of black designer shoes.

Handing her a rose, Pierre said, "Hey, baby. This for you."

Erica was smiling ear to ear. "Thanks, baby. Now come on, he's waiting for us."

Pierre never was scared of any nigga on the street who he knew was carrying a gun, but tonight a man who carried a Bible scared the shit out of him. He had arrived, and there was no turning back now. It was now time to face his fear.

"Daddy, this is Pierre. Pierre, this is my father, Pastor Collins," Erica said, introducing the two men in her life.

Pierre stuck his hand out to shake his hand, but the pastor wasn't having that. He stared at Pierre with a tight face.

"Daddy, act right please."

"Girl, have you lost your mind? You really brought this thug into my house? You must be smoking whatever the hell he is selling," Pastor Collins yelled.

"Daddy, you don't know anything about him, and you didn't even give him a chance before you started judging him. That's not fair!" Erica cried out.

"Look, E, I told you this wasn't gonna work. I'm about to bounce," Pierre calmly said.

"No, don't leave," she begged.

"Erica, let him go. I can tell that he's not the one for you. I can smell criminal records all on him. I can't believe you could be so dumb as to think this drug dealer could just walk into my house and I'd be cool with it."

Pierre looked at Erica, who was crying now. He so badly wanted to go off on him but knew it would only hurt her more. He didn't wanna be the bad guy, so he just stayed quiet and let him talk his shit. "I'm out, E. Call me later."

"No, Pierre, please."

Pierre wasn't trying to hear shit, but his engine was running. Erica stood in the doorway crying and watching him drive off. At that moment she hated her daddy. He didn't even give Pierre a chance. One look and he went off.

Once Pierre was out of her eyesight, she returned to the dining room. "I hope you're happy now. He's gone."

With a huge smile on his face, he replied, "Yes, I am happy, but still a little disappointed that you picked that guy. He is a monster, and you, someone who grew up in the church, allowed that gangbanger to climb in between your legs. I now look at you differently. You disgust me. I don't even think I can eat my supper now."

Erica was shocked by his mean words toward her, but she was tired of him being disrespectful toward her and the way he treated Pierre.

"Look, Erica, you need to make a choice right now. It's either gonna be me and this household, or that thug guy who'll probably be locked up soon."

"This is an easy choice," she said, wiping her tears away.

Pastor Collins smiled. "I thought you'd see it my way. Now sit down and eat," he ordered.

Erica grabbed her purse and keys. Without saying a word, she walked out of her dad's house.

Pastor Collins watched as his daughter walked out the front door. He didn't say a word. He returned to the dining room, then took his seat. He finished his plate like nothing happened.

Erica drove off in tears because she hated how her dad had acted. Not only did he embarrass her, but she knew that he had made Pierre upset. She called Pierre's phone for the third time and still got no answer.

Once she pulled up to his place, she saw that his car was parked in the parking lot. That made her wonder why he wouldn't answer his phone.

As she got out of her car, Erica tried calling him again. Being so caught up in trying to get ahold of Pierre, she wasn't paying attention to her surroundings. After the third ring, a man grabbed Erica from behind. She tried to fight and get away, but he was too strong for her.

"Get off me!" she screamed out, followed by, "Somebody help me, please!"

The guy couldn't take anyone hearing her, so he hit her in the head. Right after, everything went blank, and Erica was knocked out.

"Man, hurry up and get that bitch in the van!" the driver yelled.

The guy roughly threw Erica in the back of the van. After shutting the door and opening up the passenger-side door, he looked down and saw her phone lying on the ground. He picked it up and got into the van.

"Drive off, nigga, and hurry up!" he yelled.

Chapter 11

Pierre stepped out of the shower. As he walked into his room, he grabbed his phone off the dresser and saw that Erica had called him over five times. At first, he hesitated to call her back. He just knew that she was calling to break up with him. It just seemed that her dad had that type of power over her.

After he put on his boxers and climbed in the bed, he decided to finally listen to the voicemail that she had left.

Pierre listened to the voicemail and instantly jumped out of the bed. "Man, what the fuck!"

He called Erica's phone. He wasn't sure what the hell was going on, but he knew it didn't sound right at all. Hearing her scream out for help did something to him. He kicked himself for not being able to answer her calls before.

After the fourth ring, he heard a stranger's voice answer Erica's phone. "What's up, nigga? You got my bread, and I got your bitch."

"What the fuck you say, my nigga?" P wasn't sure
if he heard the voice on the phone right, so he had
to make the nigga repeat himself.

Tim chuckled, then got serious. "Nigga, you
heard me. You got my fucking bread, and I got
your bitch."

Pierre stood up from his bed. What he was hearing over the phone had him completely fucked up.
"Ay, nigga, you must not know who you fucking
with right now."

"Now, now, Mr. Miller, I don't believe you're on
the right side of the game to be playing Billy Bad
Azz. I think it's time that you shut your fucking
mouth and just listen before I smoke this li'l pretty
bitch right after I make her suck my dick."

Pierre wasn't used to following orders, especially from some bum-ass nigga. As bad as he
wanted to go off, he sat back down on the bed and
listened to the muthafucka who he promised to kill
once he got his baby back.

"All right, go ahead and talk," Pierre ordered.

Tim smiled at the fact that he had P right where
he wanted him. P was known to be so hard in the
streets, and here he was bitching up for a bitch. It
was crazy to find out that a lot of these so-called
street niggas became an average nigga when a
bitch was involved. Especially when they fucked
around and caught feelings for a ho.

"I know it was y'all ho-ass Brick Boyz who hit up one of my spots on the east side and killed some of my workers before running off with my shit. Now return my shit and you can have this bitch back," Tim hollered into the phone.

"This that ho-ass nigga Tim? I swear if you hurt my girl, I'm gonna kill your whole fucking family from youngest to oldest," P said, catching on to the voice.

"Don't say my fucking name, bitch. Just take notes. I'm gonna need all my shit back plus an extra fifty Gs for my pain and suffering. And fuck you and that threat, nigga."

P shook his head. The money wasn't a thing. He was just pissed that he had even gotten Erica involved in this bullshit. He kicked himself in the ass for not answering when she first called him. He would have been wherever she needed him to be.

"All right, I got the dough, man. Just tell me where and when I need to drop it off at."

Tim sat back in his chair in the dark basement where he held Erica. He looked over to her weak body laid out in the corner. She had slowly begun to wake up in the van, so he had hit her again. He really didn't wanna hurt her at first, but knowing that her nigga had just beaten his ass and he had his money, Tim made sure to leave a mark so she would never forget him.

"I'm gonna give you a call back with a time and place. Just wait on it, nigga," Tim ordered.

"Wait a minute, nigga. How do I know she okay and still alive and you ain't just trying to get some bread?" P hated to have to ask, but he needed to know that she was okay before he made his next move.

Tim got up from his chair as he put the phone on speaker. Standing over Erica made her become frightened. She could barely open her left eye from his punch, but seeing him made her flinch. "Ay, bitch, your man on the phone trying to get your ass back. But the way that dress fits around that ass got me thinking if I even wanna return you."

"Don't fucking play with me, Tim, and she better not be hurt, or that's gonna be your ass," P yelled as he texted Mekco and Cross.

"Say something to this nigga before his bitch ass starts crying," Tim said to Erica, who was now crying. Tim held the phone in front of Erica, waiting for her to say something.

When she didn't say anything, P started to worry. "Baby, I swear I'm about to come get you. Just hold on tight. I love you, ma." P had to get himself together after talking to Erica. He hated that he had shown Tim his weakness. He knew Tim was really gonna try to play with his emotions now.

"Ay, Tim, where the fuck you wanna meet up at? I really don't even wanna drag this shit out with you."

Erica finally opened her mouth to say something, but Tim snatched the phone away. He had P exactly where he wanted him: weak and in need. "At two a.m. I'm gonna call you back with a location. Just be there with my dough if you want this li'l bitch back." Without letting P get another word in, Tim ended the call.

As he went over the conversation he just had with Tim in his head, P slipped some clothes on. Never had he thought that someone would be so stupid to come for Erica. He knew it was possible, but he never knew somebody wanted to die so fuckin' bad.

P was gonna make sure he made Tim pay for the bullshit that he was on. He thought about how he was gonna kill each family member one by one if anything was wrong with Erica. Then he decided to go on a killing spree just because Tim was dumb enough to act like he really was about that life. Anyone who knew Tim for real knew that he was all bark and no bite. That also made P think about who was the real mastermind behind this whole thing.

Pierre picked his phone up from the bed and dialed Mekco's number. He knew if he wanted to find Erica, he was gonna need some of his boys in the streets. He had a feeling that Tim was still somewhere in the hood, and it should be easy to find his ass.

"What's up, nigga? How was dinner with your father-in-law?" Mekco jokingly asked.

"Man, that shit not even important right now. I have a bigger problem going on right now. Did you get my text, bro?"

Mekco quietly climbed out of the bed, trying not to wake Nicole up. "Just got back up. What's good?"

P hated to have these painful words leave his mouth, but he needed to get his team out in those streets and look for his girl. "Ay, you remember that nigga Tim who we had to stomp out at the club?"

"Yeah, I remember that shit. We eating good off that nigga and his weak-ass crew," Mekco said.

Pacing the floor, P told Mekco the bad news. "Man, that nigga and his crew just snatched Erica up. He on some other shit holding her for ransom and shit."

Hearing that made Mekco's face turn into stone. What he heard wasn't shit to laugh about. "What the fuck you say? You need to repeat that shit. I don't think I heard you right."

"You know I play a lot, but I would never play about no shit like this. That nigga grew some balls and snatched my baby like that wasn't him signing his death certificate," P said as he put his shoes on.

"Ay, bro, you know I have your back on this shit. What do you need? What's the ticket?" Mekco questioned.

"This nigga talking about he want the shit we took from that house plus an extra fifty Gs. He said he was gonna call me later with the time and place where we could meet up. Mekco, I swear once I get Erica, I'm killing that nigga and whoever with his ass."

"I feel you, but who the fuck that li'l dirty nigga think he fucking with? Somebody must have gassed this nigga up or something."

"That's what the fuck I said."

P held the phone thinking about Erica. He knew she was still alive, but at the same time, he was scared for her. She was a good girl and never went through shit like this before. He just hoped Tim wasn't crazy enough to hurt her.

Mekco was also upset and pacing the floor. The news had his blood boiling, and he was ready to kill a muthafucka. "Ay, bro, I'm about to make some calls and get the team out in these streets. Don't worry. We gonna find your girl and kill them niggas."

"All right. I'm about to hit the streets my fucking self."

Mekco never went through this type of shit before, but he could only imagine how he would feel if a nigga snatched Nicole up. He was surprised that P sounded as calm as he did.

Not being sure about how P wanted things to play out, he had to ask, "If we find this nigga Tim, how do you want him?"

Without a second passing, P hurried and said, "Keep his ass alive. I wanna be the one who makes his mama buy that black dress."

Once Mekco made that call to the team, everyone was hitting the streets in search of Erica or Tim's bitch ass. They all were locked and loaded ready to kill whoever.

Knowing how P was feeling, Mekco knew that Tim and whoever were gonna have to die even if Erica wasn't hurt. There were certain lines that a nigga should never be able to cross and still be able to walk on this earth.

Having one more call to make, he went ahead and called Cross. He usually wouldn't get him involved in their bullshit, but this situation was serious.

Mekco had called Cross's number three times before he finally answered. "It's late as hell, Mekco. This call had better be about some money, especially since I had to climb out of some wet pussy to answer my phone," Cross said, lighting his cigar up.

"My bad, Cross. Some shit popped off, and I needed to let you know what the fuck was going on."

"What you stalling for? Come on and let that shit out," Cross demanded.

"So check this shit out. That nigga Tim kidnapped Erica and demanded some dough to return her," he said, putting his clothes back on.

"Come pick the money up," Cross said without hesitation.

"We have the money. I was just letting you know that P is about to paint the city red."

Cross shook his head right before pushing Brittany's head from his lap. For the last couple of months, Mekco and his team had been taking losses left and right. He wanted P to keep his hands clean, but tonight he understood if he murked somebody.

"It's simple. Pay that nigga, get Erica home safe, go kill all his loved ones, then double back and kill his ass."

With a smirk on his face, Mekco nodded his head in agreement. "Yeah, boss, you right. We can't let that retarded bastard have one up on us. We about to go hard in these streets and bring Erica home before that nigga P kills everybody in Detroit."

Cross held the phone, thinking about the situation at hand. "You know what? That nigga might be retarded, but we don't know who is behind this shit. I can't believe he would have come up with this on his own."

"You right. Me and P was just saying that shit when he first called me with this shit. That nigga might have snatched Erica up, but I'm willing to bet money that it wasn't his idea."

"What the fuck did you just say?" Nicole asked as she sat up in the bed.

Mekco knew that she had heard him. She was trying not to cry. He kicked himself, wishing that he had gone into the living room to talk.

"What did you say?" she asked again.

Placing the phone back to his ear, he stared Nicole in the eyes as he ended the phone conversation with Cross. "Ay, Cross, I'm about to handle that business, and I'll hit you up later if we hear anything." He slid his phone into his pants pocket.

"Nicole, baby, why don't you go back to bed?"

Nicole watched as Mekco started pacing the floor again. "Don't do me like that, Mekco. Tell me what the fuck is going on with Erica now!" she yelled.

He slowly walked over toward Nicole and wrapped his arms around her. He allowed her body to fall onto his. The more she cried out, the harder he held her. He felt bad that she had to hear about Erica like that. He wasn't planning on telling her until they got Erica back. He just didn't want Nicole to be worried. Knowing that she was fucked up and all in her feelings, he didn't even wanna leave her at the crib by herself.

After letting Nicole cry her eyes out, he finally broke free from the tight grip that she had on him. "Baby, stop crying. I know that's your girl, but you're gonna have to let me go. I have to get out in these streets so we can find her."

"Mekco, who did this?" she questioned.

"Baby, just chill for me. I got the whole team out looking for her. She'll be home soon."

"Before you leave, can you promise me that y'all will bring her home and kill whoever is behind this shit?"

"I promise, baby."

After placing her back in the bed and tucking her in, Mekco placed a kiss on her lips. "Baby, get some rest, and I'll be back in no time."

Nicole didn't respond. She knew the Brick Boyz were gonna handle their business and make sure whoever was crazy enough to pull off some stuff like this would pay, and with their life at that.

Mekco walked out the door, leaving Nicole in her feelings. He hated to see her crying like that, but he couldn't get shit done sitting in the house holding her.

Erica sat in the corner of the dark basement floor that her kidnappers had held her in. Even though she was scared to death, she still looked around to see if there was anything that could tell her where she was or who had her. The moonlight shining through the small basement window helped her see that she wasn't in an abandoned house but in a house that was clean and nicely put together.

Hearing Pierre's voice over the speakerphone gave her hope that he would come and rescue her. Sitting down there gave her a chance to think about everything that he had told her. He warned her about people who would try to hurt her just to hurt him. She knew this but chose to stay with him because of her love for him.

Hearing the basement door open, followed by footsteps, Erica lay back down on the carpet. She believed that if she acted like she was still knocked out, then her kidnapper would just go away and leave her alone.

Before he reached Erica, he made sure to put his mask back on. Tim kneeled down with a sneaky smirk on his face. Slapping Erica across her face, Tim made her sit back up.

"Ay, get your ass up. Now let me break some shit down to you. If your nigga be on some bullshit, I'm gonna kill him and your ass. That nigga and that bitch-ass muthafucka Mekco think they the shit, like can't nobody touch them. I bet they rethinking that shit right now. Me taking you is just the beginning of our plan."

"Please just let me go. I never saw your face. I can't tell on you," she pleaded with her kidnapper.

"Nah, it ain't that easy," Tim said, rubbing up and down Erica's leg. He had been feeling her since he first saw her. It was about two years ago when he dropped his girlfriend off at church. Ever since then he had fantasized about being with her. Once he found out about her dating P, he knew that he had to make her part of his plan. Tim slowly started working his way toward her panties.

Feeling his hands touch a place that she had only allowed Pierre to touch made her feel very uncomfortable, and she then began to cry, trying to move away from him.

"Please, sir, I'm begging you. Please don't do this. My father has money, and he could give you anything that you want. Just let me go."

All of Erica's cries went unheard. Tim didn't give two flying fucks about the shit she was talking about. He knew what he wanted, and it was her. Besides, the dress that she was wearing showed off every curve on her body, and he couldn't get it out of his mind.

Tim stood up to unbuckle his jeans. His dick was already hard and standing at attention. "You see this shit? You did this. You must have some good pussy if I can get hard just thinking about sliding in you."

Erica cried harder as she prayed that Pierre would hurry up and save her from the pervert who wanted to have sex with her. "I'm begging you not to do this to me. I told you before that my daddy can pay you," she cried out.

"Fuck your daddy, bitch. He ain't got shit to do with this pussy I'm about to get," Tim said as he pushed Erica back down on the carpet.

Erica tried to fight him off, but with her hands tied together, things were difficult. Since she couldn't push him off her, she tried moving around and keeping her legs closed. Tim was tired of her fighting him, so he did what he knew would make her do as he wanted. He hurried and pulled his pocketknife out from the pair of jeans he had balled up on the floor.

He pressed the knife under her neck. "Be still, bitch, before I slice your fucking neck open. You acting like you don't want this dick when I know you do. The way you twerked that ass on me at the club wasn't for nothing."

That was when it hit her that it was the guy named Tim who had her. Erica was scared out of her mind. She had never been raped before and never pictured something like this would have happened to her.

Erica lay there crying and begging Tim to stop, but he was so into it that he wasn't paying her any attention. Tim had a lot of nerve moaning like they were making love. It pissed Erica off even more when he kept trying to kiss her on her mouth. He was enjoying her so much that he didn't hear the basement door open and his girl walking down the steps.

"Tim!" she yelled. "Are you out of your fucking mind? Why would you bring that bitch here? And why her? I thought you were trying to get Nicole."

Erica was relieved when he finally climbed off her. "Bitch, shut the fuck up. You talk too fucking much. Now take your stupid ass upstairs before I leave your ass again," he yelled to Chanel as he hurried to grab his pants and put them back on.

Chanel knew she couldn't live without him, so she turned around and hiked back up the stairs. Tim was only a few steps behind her.

Once Erica heard the basement door shut, she lay there crying. Her night couldn't get any worse than it already was. She could hear Tim arguing with the female who had come in the basement. She couldn't make out what they were saying, but she knew the female was pissed. The lady's voice sounded familiar, but she just couldn't place it with a face.

"Please, God, help me get out of this basement alive. I lived by your rules up until a couple of months ago, but I swear I'm still a good person. Please help me."

Before Erica could finish praying, she heard the basement door open and footsteps rushing down the stairs again.

"I just got rid of that bitch so we could be alone. Are you ready for round two or what? I'm ready."

"I just want to go home," she cried. Erica was scared and could tell that this guy wasn't playing with a full deck, and she was starting to lose all faith in going home alive.

Chapter 12

After picking Li'l Trey up, then driving for a minute, P picked up his ringing phone. Seeing Erica's number, he already knew it was that bitch-ass nigga Tim.

"Where the fuck we meeting at? I got your bread, so don't be on no bullshit," P said as he secretly made his way toward the house Devon had told him about.

"All right, big fella. Meet me downtown at the Rosa Parks Terminal. I want you to drop the money off at Bay 11," Tim spoke into the phone.

"All right, nigga. I hear you, but where you gonna leave Erica?" P asked, making sure this was a good plan.

"I'm gonna leave her inside the building. I told you she is unharmed and ready to go home."

Before hanging up, P said, "Okay, nigga. I'm on my way now."

"Man, I'm about to go down here and see what the fuck is up, but I swear I'm gonna kill his punk ass. There really ain't no way out of this shit."

While making his way downtown, P didn't say a word. He was happy that he was about to get Erica back, but at the same time he was worried that she wasn't gonna fuck with him after this shit. He had warned her about shit like this, but he just had to have her to himself.

Finally arriving at the meeting spot, P called Erica's phone. "Ay, bitch-ass nigga, I'm down here. Where the fuck my girl at?"

"Nigga, get out the car and drop my money off at Bay 11, then go inside of the building, and you'll see her sitting there."

P hung the phone up, but before getting out of the car, he looked over to Li'l Trey. "Look, I'm about to handle this. You just keep an eye out."

"All right, I got your back," Li'l Trey said, stepping out of the car as well.

P set down the bag full of fake money and newspaper clippings that Brandon and Brian had left for Mekco. He then walked off as if nothing were going on. As he got closer to the building, he saw that there were only a few people inside waiting for a bus. He frantically looked around for Erica. He checked the bathrooms, but she wasn't in there. Seeing that he had been played, he ran out of the building and went toward the bay where he'd set the bag down. He was hoping to catch Tim slipping and kill his ho ass, but once he got there, he could see that the bag was already gone.

"Fuck!" P yelled as he jogged back toward the car.

Reaching the car, he saw Li'l Trey slumped over. He rushed to his side of the car to check him out. Apparently, someone had snuck up and knocked him out. His head was bleeding, but not from a gunshot. He was hit with a blunt object.

P jumped in the car and hopped on the phone so he could give Mekco a rundown of what just happened.

"All right. Drop bro off at the ER." Mekco was trying to find the right things to say to P. He didn't need him to spazz out right now. He needed him to remain cool during this situation even though it was hard.

"Yeah, I'm about to handle this shit now," P replied.

"You know you my nigga, right?"

"Yeah, nigga."

"Look, don't even trip. We're gonna get her back. This little stunt was just a minor setback, but we on it."

"Yeah, I know, but I'm gonna hit you back when I'm done with him."

Dropping Li'l Trey off at the hospital wasn't as simple as he thought. As soon as he parked the car and ran in asking for help, six different people started asking him a million questions at once. P wasn't trying to do all that. He was just trying to get him help and then bounce.

"Look, I don't know this man. I was just being a good citizen and getting him help," he yelled as he rushed out the door. The nurses had him fucked up if they thought he was gonna sit around and fill out a thousand forms just for Li'l Trey to be seen by a doctor.

After the third knock, P decided to knock a little harder. There was no way he was gonna give up.

"Boy, have you lost your entire mind? Do you know what time it is?" Pastor Collins asked Pierre.

"Yeah, I know what time it is, but believe me, if it weren't an emergency, I wouldn't even be here right now, would I?" Pierre said calmly.

The pastor stared him up and down. For a moment he started to get a little nervous. All he saw was a thug dressed in all black, and he knew that only meant one thing. "So what, you came to kill me? Is that the only way you think you could have my daughter?"

"Nah, honestly, I'm not on no shit like that. I actually came to talk to you about something, so can I come in?"

Erica's dad stood there for a minute. He wasn't sure if he could trust the thug standing in his doorway.

"Look, sir, I love your daughter with everything in me. I would never hurt you because I know she loves you, and me hurting you would only hurt her."

"I'm not trying to hear all that love crap. And I'm not letting you in my damn house, you murderer. Now go away." Pastor Collins tried to shut his screen door, but Pierre grabbed it, stopping him dead in his tracks.

"I'm not trying to hurt you. Somebody kidnapped Erica, and we have to find her before the mutha-fucka kills her," Pierre yelled, his voice cracking.

Hearing what sounded like pain in his voice, the pastor stepped to the side and allowed Pierre to step inside.

Pierre took a seat on one couch, and the pastor took a seat in his favorite recliner. "Now what did you say, boy? If I heard you correctly, you said someone snatched my daughter?"

"Yeah, that's what I said. I have been out looking for her all night. The guy who got her just pulled a fast one on me. I think I fucked up, so I came to you for help."

Pastor Collins started to laugh. "Why did you come to me? My daughter wanted to be grown so bad and mess around with you, a common criminal. Now you go find her your damn self," he hollered.

Pierre didn't let what he was saying get to him. He could tell that the man was just putting up a front, trying to play tough guy with him. "Pastor, I wouldn't have come here if I thought you couldn't help. So are you gonna help me or not?"

Shaking his head, he quickly responded, "Pierre, I don't know how I could help you. Right now all I can do is pray and ask the Lord to bring my baby home."

"Okay. If you believe that will work, pray for her then," Pierre suggested.

Pastor Collins caught Pierre off guard when he walked over and grabbed his hand. Pierre snatched his hand back with the quickness. "Man, what are you doing?"

"You want my daughter back just as much as I do, right? Go ahead and pray with me, Pierre."

Pierre hadn't prayed since his grandma died, and he wasn't sure if God really was in the mood to hear from him. Truthfully, he was scared.

Eric grabbed his hand again. "We have to drop to our knees and do this the right way."

Pierre allowed him to take over the situation, and the next thing he knew, he was on his knees still holding his hand as he led them into deep prayers. He prayed for what seemed like forever but was only a good ten minutes.

Once they got up, they both took their seats. Pierre felt like a thousand pounds were lifted off him. He felt good, but he knew that he wasn't done killing. He already had plans for a few muthafuckas.

"Pierre, I'm staring at you now, and I can see in your eyes that you are not as hard as you think. I can see that you really do care for my daughter, and maybe I was wrong for judging you. Now I'm not into all this street crap, but I know who to call."

Pierre didn't say a word as he watched the pastor pick up his house phone then dial a number. He couldn't make out everything that he was saying, but he did hear him tell the person on the phone that he would see him in a minute.

It surprised the hell out of Pierre when he witnessed Cross walking through the door. "What the hell you doing here, Cross?" P asked, standing from the couch.

"Shit, I could be asking you the same thing," Cross said, stepping in and taking a seat on the love seat.

Eric came back into the room. "Clifford, this is your niece's little boyfriend, Pierre."

Pierre had a smirk on his face. He was surprised at how he was still learning something new every day. "Wait a minute, Cross. You're Erica's uncle?"

"So Erica is my niece's name?" Cross asked Eric.

Pierre sat there with a confused look on his face. From what he was picking up, Cross and Erica's dad really hadn't fucked with each other in years. It had to be that way, because he didn't even really know her name.

"Eric, it shouldn't have taken you no fucking twenty-five years to reach out to me. I thought dropping them huge donations to our father's church should have told you that I was always gonna have your back. You are a coldhearted muthafucka. You've been spending my dirty money, but you couldn't tell me I had a niece walking around," Cross said with an attitude.

"You know we're living two different lives, and after that trip to jail for two years, I wasn't about to give them any more of my life. That's why I decided to move away and get right with the Lord. Cross, I wasn't about that life. I couldn't have my daughter around that type of stuff, and that's why I kept her in the church. That was, up until she ran into him. I still don't understand what attracted her to someone living like that," Pastor Collins explained.

P interrupted their conversation. "Okay, it's good that y'all reunited, but my girl is still out here with a retarded muthafucka. Y'all do remember that, right?"

The brothers turned their attention toward the young man who was clearly in love. Eric was about to say something until Cross cut him off. "I got Mekco on his way over here now. I just had him dig up some info that probably could help us out."

Just like clockwork, Mekco popped up. Cross opened the door and allowed him to walk in. Eric sat there not saying a word, but frustration was written all over his face. He couldn't believe that his baby girl was mixed up in this street foolishness.

"Ay, Cross, I got that address you asked for. Me and P about to go check this shit out," Mekco said, trying to ignore the deadly look that Erica's dad was giving him.

P stood up from the couch. "Come on, let's go knock these niggas' heads loose."

"I don't care what you have to do to get my daughter back, but please try not to discuss your plan in front of me," the pastor said.

They both looked at him strangely, but at the same time they understood where he was coming from.

"Pierre, when this is all over, please come back to visit me. I could help you ask the Lord for forgiveness and clear your soul from all the sins you committed."

Pierre didn't say anything as he walked out the door with Mekco. He got in the car and thought about the pastor and what he had said. To him, that man had a confused soul of his own.

"So what the fuck did I miss, and how the hell did we all end up at Erica's daddy's house?" Mekco asked, more confused than ever.

P took his time explaining how everything went down. Mekco was just as surprised to learn that Erica was related to Cross.

P was quiet for the rest of the ride. He prayed that he didn't fuck up his chances finding Erica. He also prayed that Tim was as retarded as he thought and hadn't checked that money yet. P had a feeling that if Tim checked that money before they found her, then he was gonna kill her for sure.

His feelings had him caught up. He had never loved someone other than his grandma as much as he loved Erica, and he was at the point where he was willing to kill whoever was in his way of proving his love.

If you called yourself trapping on the east side of Detroit that night, you and your whole team were feeling the Brick Boyz's pain. P and the team were kicking in doors, killing whoever was down with Tim and his team. Knowing that Tim wasn't on no bullshit, he was determined to find her. Any nigga who really wanted their bread back would have had a time and place ready for a drop-off. That was why he had to find her ASAP. He knew Tim was a retarded nigga and would probably hurt Erica just because.

P pulled up to the dark street and killed his lights and engine. Tim was known for hanging on this street, so he was about to make the whole block rock. The house was the third house from the corner, and to his surprise, the front room's lights were on.

P jumped out of the car, ready to murk another nigga for the night. Mekco was right behind him with his gun in his hand. He was ready to pop off if needed.

The two stood on the porch listening for any movement coming from inside of the house. "You ready?" Mekco asked.

"Nigga, you already know what tip I'm on."

Mekco nodded his head, letting P know that he was ready for whatever.

Boom!

Pierre kicked the door so hard that it flew off the hinges. The guys were surprised that they didn't hear anyone move. They made their way toward the back of the house where they could see light coming from the TV in the room.

Mekco looked at P as he held his hand up. He quickly did a countdown, dropping finger after finger. Opening the door with their guns drawn, they saw a nigga in the bed knocked out asleep.

Busting him in the head with the gun, P yelled, "Where the fuck that nigga Tim at?"

The guy was still asleep, plus the blow to the head had him confused. "Man, that nigga not here, and he ain't been here since he ran off with my shit."

"Where the fuck that nigga be at then?" P asked.

"Ay, what tip you on?" the sleepy guy asked.

P pushed the gun into the right side of his head. "Bitch-ass nigga, I'm on that tip that if you don't start talking, your brains gonna be all over this muthafucking dirty wall."

Von was scared shitless. But seeing that P and his little sidekick weren't playing with his ass, he was ready to sing like a bird. Besides, Tim had just done him grimy, and he had no problem snitching, especially if it was gonna save his life.

"Ay, I swear I don't fuck with that nigga no more, but he be at his girl's house all the time. He be fucking with a bitch from the west side."

"Where at, nigga? Don't get shy now," P yelled.

"Man, he fucking with a bitch over there off Chicago and Wyoming. It's a white and red house. She got a bunch of flowers all over her yard. It's hard to miss."

With a smirk on his face, P dropped his arm down to his side. "Thanks, nigga. You all right with me."

Von finally was able to breathe, thinking he was gonna live another day. P walked out of the room while giving Mekco a strange look. He wasn't a dummy and knew exactly what that meant. He lifted his gun up and pointed it toward Devon.

"Wait a minute now. I told y'all everything that y'all needed to know. Please let me live," Von pleaded.

Without saying a word, Mekco put a bullet between his eyes. The two ran out of the house and made their way back to the car.

"That nigga must not love you like you thought he did, Erica," Tim said as he walked over toward Erica.

"What are you talking about?" Erica asked. She really hadn't said anything to him, but to hear him question P's love for her, she needed to know what he was talking about.

He grabbed the bag off the pool table. As he got closer toward her, he unzipped the bag and began to pour the contents out over her head. "Bitch, do I look stupid to you? That muthafucka thought I was stupid enough to fall for the same bullshit Mekco fell for."

Being so angry, he kicked Erica on the side of her head. The blow caused her to fall back down on the carpet.

Erica screamed out in pain. She wasn't sure how much more abuse from him she could take.

P hurried and drove in the direction that Von gave them. As they pulled up to the house, they noticed that he knew exactly what he was talking about. He'd described it to a T.

"Bro, she better be in here or I'm gonna go crazy. I don't know what the fuck I'll do if that retarded nigga hurt her," P admitted.

Mekco knew his boy must really love Erica, because for once he acted like he actually cared about someone else's well-being instead of just acting out.

"Come on, let's run up in this bitch and get shit popping."

Just as they were getting out of the car, they witnessed a young lady trying to open up the side door of the house. P rushed out of the car with his gun in his hand.

"Bitch, you bet' not scream, or I'll blow your fucking head clean the fuck off. Now open the fucking door," he mumbled with the gun to her head.

Chanel fumbled through the keys, trying to find the right one without getting shot. Once she opened the side door, she received another warning.

"You bet' not make a sound. Now tell me where the fuck Tim at."

Chanel was scared, but to save her life, she pointed down the basement stairs. Mekco grabbed Chanel by the hair, holding her back as P tiptoed down the stairs. He could hear Erica scream and Tim yelling at her. His blood boiled as he reached the bottom of the steps and saw Tim standing over her, buck-naked, trying to get her to open her mouth.

Without hesitation, P pulled the trigger. It was just his luck that, at the same time, Tim moved, so the bullet went through his shoulder.

P rushed over to Erica and hurried to pick her up from the floor. "It's okay, baby. I got you now."

Erica cried in his arms. She was happy that he found her before Tim killed her. She had heard him repeat over and over again that he was gonna kill her.

"Kill him, baby. Please kill him!" Erica begged.

P wasted not a second, blasting half of his head off. Erica screamed out loudly, even though she got exactly what she wanted. Even after seeing him dead, she had no regrets behind it all.

"What the fuck did you do?" Chanel yelled as Mekco walked her down the steps.

She cried out seeing that Tim was laid out on the floor dead.

Erica turned her attention toward the female. Earlier she thought that her voice sounded familiar, but now that she wasn't blindfolded, she could see the lady who was sick enough to allow her boyfriend to rape someone in her home.

"Chanel!" she screamed as she slowly turned in her direction. Before P and Mekco could even respond, Erica charged at her full speed. Now Erica was the one to use foul language, but this was one time that the Lord was gonna have to forgive her.

"You stupid bitch!" she yelled, and busted Chanel in the mouth. After that, Erica gave her the business. Pierre could see that Chanel wasn't a match for Erica, so after letting her beat the bitch down to the ground, he grabbed her.

"Come on, baby. Let's get you the fuck out this house."

Mekco stood there in his thoughts. He had run into Chanel a few times when the girls went out, but he never would have thought she was up to no good.

"What are we gonna do with this bitch?" he finally asked.

"Please don't kill me. I didn't do anything to Erica. I promise I won't tell anybody about what happened down here," she begged.

Pierre stared at Erica and could see that the bullshit that Tim had put her through had changed her. He saw something in her eyes that told him that the little naive church girl was long gone. P was all for killing Chanel, but he left that up to Erica. "Baby, it's your call," P told her.

Without blinking or even a tear falling, Erica coldly said, "Kill that bitch, baby."

Pierre lifted his gun back up and gave her a hot one to the forehead. "Let's get the fuck out of here."

"You go ahead and get her home. I'm gonna wait for that nigga Kirk to pull up. We gonna go ahead and just torch this bitch the fuck up."

"Good looking, my nigga. Hit me up later," P said as he grabbed Erica's hand.

Erica was a little shaken up, but she knew that she had made the right choice that night. People like Tim and Chanel didn't deserve to live.

"Ay, Erica, when you up to it, call your girl. She probably at home going crazy," Mekco yelled up the stairs.

He then heard Erica whisper, "Okay."

Mekco sat on the basement stairs waiting for Kirk. It might have seemed like everything was over, but something still didn't sit right with him. He still wasn't sure who was behind the whole thing. For all he knew, the real nigga was somewhere watching and waiting for them to slip up again.

After waiting for ten long minutes, Kirk showed up, and they started tossing gasoline all over the house. Kirk started upstairs and Mekco started in the basement. Once they were done, something popped in Mekco's mind. He hurried to check Tim's pockets. He grabbed Erica's phone, and then he found Tim's phone. Mekco knew he was about to get some answers now.

The ride home for P and Erica was somewhat quiet. Erica wasn't sure what to say. That night her life had changed forever. She was no longer sure exactly whom to trust outside of her small circle.

Pierre held her hand as he drove. "E, you know that I love your ass, and I promise that I will never let some shit like this happen again. I promise I'll do whatever it takes to make things right with you. I just don't want you hating me because I fucked around and slipped up. I let a muthafucka put his hands on you, but I made him pay for that shit, baby."

Erica was mad at what happened to her, but she never blamed Pierre. He warned her about this type of stuff, and she still decided to stay with him. If she had a chance to start over, she probably would still have chosen to be with him.

After reaching his place, Pierre helped her get into a hot bubble bath. She lay back, deep in her thoughts as she tried to soak her aching body. She silently cried as she thought about the way Tim had hit her and forced his nasty penis inside of her. In the tub, she decided to never speak on that night again, especially to Pierre. Telling him that another man had entered her body was gonna be a secret that she was gonna take to the grave.

That night in the bed, Pierre held Erica in his arms like he was scared to lose her again. He apologized what felt like a thousand times, and each and every time, she forgave him.

Chapter 13

Two Months Later

Pierre sat on the phone with Cross, discussing the BBQ they were planning on having at the park. Whenever Cross put an event together, he went all the way out for everybody. One thing for sure, when his name and the Brick Boyz's name was attached to anything, the whole hood came out to have a good time.

Erica walked in the living room just as Pierre was getting off the phone. "Who was that?"

"Damn, girl, you all in my business," he said, laughing. She gave him a funny look, and then he said, "I'm just playing. That was your uncle. You know we are trying to get everything together for this park shit next weekend."

"I still can't believe he turned out to be my uncle. I swear, my dad kept a lot of stuff from me growing up."

Pierre pulled Erica down on his lap. "Damn, you starting to get a li'l thick," he announced as he allowed his hands to roam all over her body.

Feeling embarrassed, she pushed his hands off her. "Shut up, boy."

"Damn, don't be mad. Ain't nothing wrong with that. You are still the most beautiful girl in the world to me."

While blushing, she managed to say, "Thank you, baby."

"I'm for real. You're so beautiful. Plus, I love the way you be so low-key with the shit. You never go overboard with your makeup, and I never saw you half dressed."

Still blushing, she turned his way and planted a kiss on his lips. "Okay, baby." She giggled.

"Yeah, let me stop before you be walking around with the big H," Pierre jokingly said.

"So, baby, Nicole wanted to come pick me up so we could go find something to wear to this BBQ."

At first Pierre wasn't gonna say anything about her still not driving her own car. He thought that maybe it was too soon to bring it up. He still wasn't sure how she was really feeling since she never brought that night back up. Plus, whenever he tried to talk to her, she always changed the subject.

"E, I know that night fucked you up and scared the fuck out of you, but when do you think you'll be able to drive yourself around?" Pierre questioned.

Erica got up and started to walk off toward the bedroom that she shared with Pierre. Of course he was right behind her.

"Baby, I'm sorry. I wasn't trying to hurt you. I just thought that sooner or later we are gonna have to talk about it. We can't continue acting like that night never happened."

Erica sat at the end of the bed and cried. "He hit me and kicked me before telling me that you didn't love me enough to pay him his money back."

Pierre took a seat next to her and held her. One thing for sure, he hated when she cried. Seeing her tears fall always made him feel like he failed her. Before he could respond, Erica continued to talk.

"He told me that you didn't give him his money for my return. That you called yourself playing him by giving him some fake money that some guys named Brandon and Brian had given Mekco. The girl, Chanel, was from our church, and that was his girlfriend all this time. He was using her to get close to me and Nicole. Tim was supposed to get Nicole and not me. He said he took me because he thought I wanted him because of that dance. Baby, I swear I didn't want him."

"E, don't cry. I'm sorry that you had to go through all that, but you know that I love your ass, and I was only trying to find you. If I didn't care about you, I wouldn't have popped them muthafuckas for you. I hate that you even doubted my true feelings for you."

Erica buried her head in his tattooed chest. The truth was sitting on the tip of her tongue, but she couldn't find the courage to tell him that Tim had raped her three times that night. It was killing her not to tell him, and that was the real reason why she never liked talking about that night.

Pierre held on to her tightly, trying to calm her down. Her crying slowly stopped as he rubbed her back. "Look, I'm sorry for even bringing the shit up. Let's just chill until Nicole comes to get you."

Erica lifted her head and gave Pierre a peck on his lips. "I'm sorry for being so difficult lately. I'm not mad at you, and if I didn't know anything else in this world, I know for sure that you love me. I never questioned Mr. Miller."

He then lightly lifted her head back up by her chin and kissed her. The two were all into it, and Pierre was getting happy thinking that she was finally about to give him some. Taking his time climbing on top of her, he slowly placed soft kisses on her. Erica got caught up in the moment, and for the first time in two months, she thought that maybe she was ready to have sex again.

As she felt him rubbing at her T-shirt then snatching at her panties, she panicked. Her chest felt heavy, and her breathing was out of control. She could have sworn Tim was there about to rape her again. Before Pierre could ask what was wrong, she pushed him away from her, running into the bathroom. She sat on the toilet and cried her eyes out.

Pierre knocked on the door and waited for her response. "I'm sorry. What did I do wrong?"

Her not answering only pissed him off more. It had been very frustrating not being able to make love to the person he loved for two whole months, and he had promised himself that he wasn't about to go out and fuck another bitch. Cheating was out of the question. He could never do her like that, but he still wanted to know what the problem was.

"E, open up the door and talk to me."

Erica tried to calm down, but she couldn't control her body from shaking. "Pierre, I'll be out in a minute. Please just give me a minute," she yelled.

Pierre stood there for a minute waiting for her to walk out, but she never came out. He knocked again once he heard the shower running. "Man, what the fuck?" he mumbled.

Stepping back and kicking the bathroom door open, Pierre finally walked into the bathroom. Erica stood in the shower, zoned out in her own little world.

"Baby, what the fuck is wrong with you?"

Feeling him grab her arm to get her attention, she finally turned his way. "What do you want?"

"Shit, I wanna know what the hell is wrong with you."

She quickly got her act together. "Nothing, baby. I just felt dirty. I'll be out in a minute."

Pierre always heard folks talk about how women were bipolar, and he now understood what they were talking about. There was clearly something wrong with her, and he planned on getting to the bottom of it.

He walked out, looking at the door that he had just fucked up, and made his way to the bedroom.

After her shower, Erica felt much better. She returned to the room with her robe on. She smiled seeing his tatted body lying there, watching a game on TV with nothing but his boxers on. After repeatedly telling herself that she had to get her act right, she felt like she was ready to give herself to the man she loved.

She climbed in the bed and straddled Pierre. He instantly got hard. As they began to share a passionate kiss, Pierre flipped her over on her back.

"I love you, Pierre," she whispered into his ear as he slowly entered her.

Just above a whisper, he replied, "I love you too, baby."

For the first time in two months, the two made love. Erica couldn't help but silently cry. Not because of what happened that night, but because she had forgotten how much power Pierre was packing between his legs.

Soon after they cuddled up, she fell fast asleep. He held her sleeping body and repeatedly placed kisses on her forehead. For some strange reason, he couldn't let their conversation from earlier go. Her words kept playing over and over in his head. Something wasn't sitting right with him.

After another ten minutes of thinking, he slid from under her and grabbed his phone. Not wanting to wake her up, he went into the living room to talk on the phone. He hurried and dialed Mekco's number.

"What's up, bro?" Mekco asked.

"So listen to this shit. I was talking to Erica about that shit with Tim, and I think she might have just given us some information that we could use. Tell me why she said that nigga was talking shit about the bag of money being the same shit Brandon and Brian gave you."

Putting his blunt out, he responded, "Damn, really? The only way he would have known that is if him and them niggas talked, which means them ho-ass niggas were behind the whole thing."

"Exactly, and she said that bitch mentioned that Nicole was the one who was supposed to have been there, not Erica," P added.

"Either way, that nigga was gonna leave the earth that fucking night. Anyway, I'm gonna hit you back up a little later," Mekco said, smirking at Nicole, who had just walked in with nothing on.

***

After a long-overdue makeup session and a power nap, Nicole took a shower and got dressed. She was so ready to go shopping and hang with her best friend.

"Damn, Nicole, why did you get out of bed? Come lie back down with me."

"Mekco, I told your ass I wasn't about to cake up with you all day. Me and Erica are about to go to the mall and find an outfit for this barbecue y'all having."

"You got enough time to do that shit. You can chill with me today. Plus, she probably booed up with bro right now as we speak. She ain't thinking about your yellow ass."

After laughing at him, Nicole started looking in the closet for the right sandals to match her outfit.

"So you really about to leave me like this? Okay, I got your funky ass. That's why I'm only giving your ass twenty dollars. You better go hit up the Goodwill and find an outfit."

They both had a good laugh at his joke before Nicole could respond. "Yeah, that was funny, but my best friend's uncle is your fucking boss, and do you know what that means? That means one phone call to Uncle Cross and I'll have whatever I want."

Mekco stared at Nicole like she was crazy. "Don't fucking play with me like that. I'll fuck your ass up if you ever call another nigga for shit, and I mean that."

"Oh, so you mad now, daddy?" she asked, still joking around.

"Hurry up and get your funky ass out my house before I throw your ass out one of these windows."

Still thinking things were funny, Nicole laughed even more. "This is not even your house. We in my shit."

"But who the fuck pay all the fucking bills in this bitch? You don't do shit but spend my fucking money and run your fucking big-ass mouth."

By this time, Mekco had jumped out of the bed and was putting his clothes back on. He had been tired of her, and today she really had gotten on his fucking nerves with that mouth of hers.

Nicole stopped smiling seeing him get dressed. "Baby, what are you doing? Where are you going?" she asked as she started grabbing at his shirt to stop him from walking away from her.

He pushed her out of the way and started to head out the bedroom door. That was when she placed her arms up in the doorway. "Mekco, why are you tripping? You know I was just playing with you."

"Man, get the fuck out of my face!" he yelled.

Being the stubborn person she was, she stood there like she didn't hear him.

Mekco stood there thinking about if he really felt like dealing with her ass any longer. "Move now before I move your ass myself," he coldly said.

"I'm sorry, baby. Please don't go. I'll make it up to you," Nicole cried out.

Mekco wasn't trying to hear that shit. He had been getting tired of her for a minute now, and for some reason her little joke about calling Cross had pushed him to the point of no return. His mom had told him before that she was a gold digger using him for his status and money, but he was in love with her and didn't see it until recently.

He tried to walk closer to the front door, but she wouldn't let him get out of the house. So he did what he had to do. Without using much force, he snatched her up by her neck. "Stop fucking playing with me. I will fuck your ass up for real," he yelled.

He noticed how the grip around her neck got tighter and how her face turned red as her tears began to flow down her cheeks. He never had been the type to lay hands on a female, but she had it coming. He then tossed her ass on the couch, not wanting to choke her ass out.

"Look, I'm done with this shit," he said before walking out the door.

At that very moment Nicole felt her whole heart jump out of her chest. Him saying he was done hurt her more than him choking the shit out of her. She lay on the couch and cried her eyes out. She was stuck and couldn't see herself without her true love.

"Well, baby, it looks like it's just gonna be you and me tonight. Nicole just texted me saying that she wasn't up to shopping and she's gonna stay in for the rest of the day."

Pierre sat up in the bed. "Good, now we can chill for the rest of the day. It's too hot for you to be out anyway. I'm not trying to see my chocolate melting."

Erica fell out in laughter. "Boy, you so damn silly. I can't believe you just said that."

Pierre couldn't help but watch Erica. For the first time in a minute, she actually laughed and just seemed to be back to herself. He wondered if finally getting some dick had anything to do with that.

It had been a whole week, and Erica still hadn't talked to Nicole. Her friend had been dodging calls and texts, making Erica worry.

"Nicole, you've been flaking on me for a whole week now, girl. Are we gonna go shopping or what?" Erica said over the phone.

Nicole had been in the house, stuck in her feelings. She had called and texted Mekco over forty times, just for him to still ignore her before just blocking her altogether.

"Boo, I just don't feel like it. I'm sorry, but we will go before the party. I promise," Nicole dully mumbled.

Erica could tell that something was wrong with her best friend. There was never a time where she wasn't full of life. "Nicole, are you okay?"

Nicole fixed her mouth to say she was okay, but instead of it coming out, she started to cry. "No, Erica. No, I'm not okay. Everything is fucked up, and I just can't deal with this shit right now. I'm scared and hurt, and I just don't know what to do right now." She managed to let all that out before she started to cry harder.

"I'm on my way, boo," Erica quickly said before hanging up and climbing out of the bed.

As she slipped some clothes on, Pierre walked back in the room. "Where you going, baby?"

"Something is wrong with Nicole, and I'm gonna go check on her. You know it's not like her to be crying," Erica explained.

Pierre walked over to the closet and pulled out a shoebox. "So that means you are fine with driving?"

Without giving it a second thought, she answered, "I was gonna catch an Uber."

"Drive your car."

"But—"

"But nothing. Ain't shit gonna happen to you," he tried to install in her head.

"Okay then, baby," she said, finally giving in.

"Here, catch this," he said, pretending to toss a small handgun her way.

"Boy, are you freaking crazy?" she yelled out in fear as she raised her hands to cover her face.

"Girl, you the one crazy as bat shit. You really believed I was gonna throw a fucking gun at you?" he asked while laughing at her.

Thinking about it, Erica laughed to herself. "You play too much, Mr. Miller."

Usually he would say something about her calling him that, but lately it really wasn't bothering him. In fact, he had to catch himself a few times from calling her Mrs. Miller.

That's right. Pierre was ready to make Erica a part of his life permanently. Since the night he rescued her from Tim, he realized that it wasn't just a simple love thing between them. The connection between them had him going from not wanting to go back to jail to not giving a fuck, everyone had to die. Pierre knew in his heart that it was time to have that talk with the pastor. When she cried out for him to kill Tim, he did that shit with no hesitation. He knew she held his heart then.

"All jokes aside, I'm happy you're feeling better now," he said, watching her get ready. It wasn't until she pulled out her makeup case that he began to frown.

"Baby, you don't need that shit. You're perfect without all that shit on. Plus, it's too fucking hot, and that shit gonna melt anyway," he said with a laugh.

"Pierre, what's wrong with you today?"

"Shit, I'm good. What you talking about?"

"I know you like to joke a lot, but I've noticed that when you start joking too much, it means you're really nervous about something. So what's on your mind, Mr. Miller?"

Pierre wore a smirk on his face. He thought it was cute how she thought she knew him like that. But the truth was she was right. He was nervous about the next Sunday dinner they were having with her dad.

He had planned to pull the pastor to the side and ask for permission to marry his daughter. Pierre and Erica's dad had become cool with each other. Pastor Collins had a new respect for him now, and Pierre couldn't deny that the man had grown on him and had helped him pray and ask for forgiveness after killing a few people in one night.

"Baby, ain't shit wrong with me. Matter of fact, I was just about to make some runs and link up with Mekco."

Erica walked over toward Pierre and planted a kiss on his lips. "Okay, I'll see you later."

"Love you," he hollered as she walked toward the front door.

His sweet words still made her blush like a schoolgirl. "Love you too, Mr. Miller."

After Erica left, Pierre grabbed his phone to call Mekco up.

"What's up, bro? We're still linking up today?"

"Hell yeah, I'm about to be your way in a minute. You at your girl's crib or at the house you paid all that money for and never at?"

"I see your ass got jokes, muthafucka, but I'm at my crib, nigga. I didn't say shit before, but I had to cut Nicole's ass off the team," Mekco admitted.

"Man, you playing, right? I know y'all muthafuckas ain't called it quits."

Mekco really didn't feel like talking about the shit for real. Not even to his bro at that moment. "Look, I'll see you when you get here."

They ended the conversation, and P hopped in his new all-black Suburban truck to meet up with Mekco. After that night of driving around like a madman killing and shit, he had to get a new ride. As he rode to Mekco's house, he thought about what his bro had said, and he now knew why Nicole had been so upset when Erica had spoken to her earlier.

Erica sat on the couch as she waited for Nicole to come back from the kitchen. In a matter of seconds, Nicole came back with two glasses and a bottle of Hennessy. Erica watched as her puffy-eyed friend filled her glass halfway up.

"Boo, you ready to talk? Clearly something is bothering you. It's all on your face."

Nicole sat there speechless and killed her drink.

"Nicole!" Erica yelled as she snatched the glass from her hand. "What are you doing? What's your problem? So, are you trying to mess things up?" Erica continued to yell.

With a nonchalant attitude, Nicole looked at Erica like she was crazy, then responded, "What's your problem? I'm just trying to have a good time. And what am I messing up?"

Erica paused for a minute. "Nicole, what happened to you not drinking 'cause you and Mekco were trying to work on having a baby?"

"Girl, fuck Mekco's bitch ass," Nicole yelled before she burst into tears.

Erica stood up from the couch and took a seat closer to Nicole. As she held Nicole in her arms, she repeatedly told her everything was gonna be okay, even before she knew what was going on.

"What happened? Tell me what happened, Nicole."

Nicole managed to stop crying long enough to yell out, "He broke up with me. He don't love me anymore."

For the next fifteen minutes, Erica listened to Nicole spill her heart out about what all went down the day Mekco walked out on her.

"Boo, it'll all be okay. You know that boy loves your crazy self. Maybe he just needed a break. Don't trip. You know he'll be back," Erica explained, trying her hardest to calm her bestie down.

"Bro, you really telling me that you cut Nicole loose? Why the fuck would you do that? I thought y'all had a good thing going."

P and Mekco sat in Mekco's basement, taking shots and discussing business. P could sense a change in Mekco's attitude. Since he had mentioned breaking up with Nicole, he blamed that for the way Mekco was acting

"I love the fuck out of that girl, but she's just not who I need to be with right now. I got her too spoiled, and she just got comfortable not doing shit. All she cares about is my fucking money. Then on top of that, I'm starting to believe that was the only reason she was with me," Mekco explained.

P stared at him like he was crazy. "You really have lost your mind. That girl is crazy in love with your ass. Bro, call your girl and get her back. You and I both know you can't live without her."

Mekco killed his shot as he thought about what P was saying. "Nah, I'm a free agent. Bro, I'm about to be out of here."

P laughed at Mekco, then continued to drink as he watched his boy pretend to be happy with his decision. He knew somewhere deep inside, Mekco still loved Nicole and he was faking because he didn't have a real reason to break up with her.

"Erica, I'm so happy that you talked me into getting out of the house. I've been fucking crying over that nigga," Nicole said. She then stepped out of the dressing room, showing off the tight-fitted dress that she was thinking about wearing to Cross's party. Nicole turned around, showing off her figure. "I look good. Those niggas not gonna be able to get enough of my fine ass."

"Girl, you are a mess. You know Mekco's not for that. He'll kill every guy at the park for paying you too much attention, then choke your ass up when he's done."

Nicole gave Erica a funny look before saying, "Girl, please, he let me go, and now I'm about to show him what he'll be missing out on."

"Whatever. Anyway, how do I look in this dress?" Erica asked, spinning around, looking like America's Next Top Model.

"Oh, my Gawd, bitch, you look pregnant," Nicole yelled.

Feeling embarrassed, Erica rushed back to the dressing room.

Nicole followed right behind her. "I'm sorry, boo, but it does look like you have put on a few pounds. You're starting to spread like butter."

"Nicole, I cannot be pregnant. My dad would kill me, and ain't no telling how Pierre is gonna act. We never even discussed having kids."

"Girl, bye, Pierre loves the fuck out of you. He's gonna be so happy."

Erica stood there looking lost. Having a baby was not in her plans at the moment.

Nicole stared at her bestie. She wanted to be as supportive as she could. "Come on, we need to go buy a test to make sure I'm about to be an auntie."

"I don't need a test. I'm not pregnant. Stop speaking that negative into my life," Erica said as she started to put on her regular clothes.

After Nicole paid for her dress, she turned her attention back to Erica. "Are you sure you not buying that dress?"

"Nah, I'm not about to wear anything that's gonna fit me tight like that," Erica said, feeling a little down.

After leaving the pharmacy, the two made their way back to Nicole's house.

"You go handle your business, and I'll be out here waiting for you."

Erica couldn't believe that she had let Nicole talk her into buying one of those stupid home pregnancy tests on their way to her apartment. Nicole could never take no as an answer.

Erica made her way into the bathroom. As she sat on the tub waiting for her results, everything started to invade her mind from how everyone in her life would feel to if she was ready for this. She still had school and a whole life ahead of her. Those were the longest five minutes in her life.

Nicole waited patiently as she heard the bathroom door open. Erica walked out with her eyes filled with tears. She slowly passed Nicole the test.

"Damn, you're having a baby," Nicole said with a smile. Even though Erica was in her feelings, Nicole was happy for her.

"Nicole, this really can't be happening. I can't be pregnant right now," she cried.

"Well, it looks like it's too late now. The way you are looking, you're probably a couple of months already. When was your last normal period?"

"I don't know. To be honest, it hasn't been normal in a while. I really thought it was from being stressed out all the time."

"Whatever. That test is right," Nicole said, giving Erica attitude. "Spend the night, and we can go to that free clinic. They take walk-ins, too."

Erica called Pierre to tell him her plans about spending the night. She didn't bother to tell him about taking the pregnancy test. She didn't want to believe that she was knocked up, so she wasn't gonna talk to anyone about it outside of Nicole.

***

The next morning, the girls made their way to the clinic. They arrived around 9:00 a.m. Erica started to get irritated and inpatient. They had already been sitting in the lobby for an hour, and she was ready to leave. "Come on, Nicole, let's go. I'm sleepy and hungry."

As soon as Nicole started to stand up, a nurse's assistant from the back came up front and called Erica's name. "See, girl, God's trying to tell you something." They both laughed before Erica made her way to the back with the assistant.

As she went into room 4 like she was told, she started to cry. She undressed from the bottom down and waited for the doctor to come into the room. She was cold and scared at the same time. Feeling lonely, she wished she had allowed Nicole to come in with her.

That night, Erica took a hot shower while she cried her eyes out. She hated bad news. To some a baby was a blessing, but right now a baby would only bring up a lot of pain.

As soon as her head hit the pillow she was knocked out. It wasn't long before Pierre came into the house. He walked into the bedroom and saw that she was knocked out. He placed a kiss on her lips before hitting the shower.

Chapter 14

"Pierre, I'm headed out for church now. I'll see you around five at my dad's house for dinner," Erica reminded him before leaving.

"Wait a minute, baby. Let me look at you first."

Erica walked over to his side of the bed. "Baby, you gonna make me late. What do you want?"

Sitting up in the bed, Pierre responded, "Come give me a kiss before you walk out."

Erica held her arms out as he got up. As they hugged, he planted small kisses on her neck and on her lips. Erica smiled as he hugged her and squeezed her behind. "Damn, girl," he mumbled.

"What now?" she asked as he released her.

"You're getting thicker, but I like that shit. It looks nice on you," he said but quickly wished he hadn't said anything. The look on her face told him that she didn't wanna hear that shit.

"All right, I'm out. I'll see you later."

He lay back down, not giving it a second thought. His mind was on tonight. He was building up the nerve to talk to the pastor about asking Erica to marry him. It was crazy how he never imagined falling for someone like her and actually being deep in love the way that he was. Tonight he was gonna prove his love to her.

Erica took her seat next to Nicole in the front row. Nicole asked, "So did you talk to Pierre yet?"

A little irritated, Erica responded with a slight attitude. "No, and I'm really not in the mood to talk about it to anyone right now."

"Well, excuse me then," Nicole replied. She turned her attention to the choir. She knew this was all new to Erica, so she wasn't gonna pressure her to talk to her. When she was ready to accept the fact that she was indeed pregnant, and when she was ready to talk, Nicole was gonna be right there waiting.

"Dad, the food is just about ready, and Pierre should be on his way," Erica yelled into the living room.

Pastor Collins was so into the game that he barely heard her or the doorbell.

Erica walked into the living room. "Dad, did you hear me? The food is ready."

"Oh, okay. I'm sorry, but this game got all my attention," Eric admitted.

"I see, 'cause you got Pierre standing outside like he's not welcome," she said, walking to the front door and opening it for her love.

Pierre walked in with some flowers for Erica like he always did. "Hey, baby," he said, placing a kiss on her lips.

"Hey, baby."

"Hey, Mr. Collins. How have you been?" Pierre asked, trying to stay on his good side.

"Oh, I'm doing fine. Just watching this game. I'm not too sure who is gonna win tonight, because if you ask me, both teams are drunk and the ref is drunk too. He is going back and forth cheating for both teams."

"Well, let's go to the table. The food is ready," Erica suggested.

The three went into the dining area and took their seats. After blessing their food, they all dug in.

"Dang, girl, this food is wonderful. You really did a great job," Pierre admitted as he stuffed his mouth with the gravy-covered meatloaf.

"Thank you, Pierre. My dad and Nicole's mom taught me how to cook growing up."

Erica noticed how her dad's body language changed once she mentioned Nicole's mother, Teresa. He never said anything about them dating, but she had noticed little things between them. Plus, Teresa had been dropping little hints around Nicole, and she had no problem reporting it to Erica.

The three engaged in small conversations that led into Erica asking Pierre when he was gonna join them in church for service. Any other Sunday, Pierre would be quick to tell them that he wasn't sure, or he'd just say church really wasn't his thing. It surprised Erica and Eric when Pierre proudly told them that he would join them the following Sunday.

Both father and daughter smiled and were very excited.

"I'm so happy that you're ready now. Let me go wash these dishes and allow you two to get back to that game," Erica said before taking the empty plates into the kitchen.

Pierre and the pastor went into the living room and turned the game back on. Pierre was sweating bullets and was actually scared. For the first time in a long time, he doubted himself. He wasn't sure if he could pull this off.

Finally after twenty minutes of just sitting there, he turned his attention to the pastor. "Can we step outside for a minute? I need to talk to you about something, and I really don't want Erica to hear us."

Eric stood up from the couch. "Sure, come on. This game sucks anyway."

The two went outside on the porch. Pastor Collins had a feeling what Pierre wanted, but he wasn't about to let this go down. He had gained a lot of respect for him, but he still didn't believe he was good enough for his daughter. No matter how many people he killed to prove his love for her, it didn't impress him one bit. He had been playing nice just so he wouldn't lose his daughter completely.

"What is it?" Eric asked.

"Look, I know we didn't start off on the right foot, but I've been doing all that I can in order to prove to you that I care about your daughter. So I came to you tonight to ask if I could get your blessing to marry your daughter."

The pastor burst into laughter. "Boy, have you lost your freaking mind? I'm only tolerating your black ass because my daughter is stuck on stupid and acts like she can't stay away from you. There's no way in hell that you'll ever have my permission to marry my daughter."

Pierre was pissed, but still he tried not to go off. "Look, I wasn't trying to get your permission for shit. I was doing the right thing asking for your blessing. Truth be told, it's up to Erica and what she wants to do. That bullshit and all that fake shit you've been on is irrelevant. She got the final word," Pierre said, standing up for himself.

"You know what, you piece of tatted-up shit? Get the fuck away from my property before I call the police on you. I'm sure you're wanted for something," Pastor Collins threatened.

"Man, fuck you!" Pierre yelled.

Just then, Erica came outside with a beautiful smile on her face like always. "Dad, I put the leftovers away, and all the dishes are clean."

"Thanks, baby girl. You know your daddy loves you so much, don't you?"

"Yeah, I know. I love you too." Erica looked over toward Pierre. She noticed how he looked upset. "Baby, what's wrong with you?" she asked, giving him a hug.

"Nothing, baby. You ready to go home?"

"Yeah, I'm ready. Dad, we are about to get ready to go. I'll see you Wednesday at Bible study."

He didn't even bother to respond. He just turned around and went into the house. He didn't care if Pierre told Erica what happened. He was tired of being fake about the whole thing.

After a hot shower, Pierre climbed in the bed. He really couldn't understand why she didn't want to get in the shower with him but jumped in when he got out. She had been acting strange, and he didn't know what the problem was.

Erica stood under the hot water and rubbed the soap over her skin. Just touching her stomach made her feel sick. She hated the secret that she carried but was too scared to tell anyone.

"God, why me?" she mumbled while still crying.

Pierre got out of bed to get the remote from the dresser. He had remembered that he had placed it there when he was changing the batteries earlier that day. Just then he heard Erica's phone ringing. He went into the living room and saw her purse on the couch. Thinking he was doing her a favor, he opened her purse to take her phone out. He then thought about placing her phone on the charger for her, but instead some papers fell out at the same time. He started to place them back in her purse, but seeing the word "clinic" on them made his senses tingle, and he just had to know what was going on with her.

"What the fuck?" he mumbled as he read the papers from the clinic saying that she was pregnant. He was happy about the baby but pissed that she didn't tell him right away. He now knew why her hips were spreading out and her moods were all fucked up.

He set her purse and phone back down on the couch and stormed to the bathroom.

When he walked in, she was slipping on a T-shirt. "Hey, baby, what you want?"

"E, what's the deal with keeping secrets now? I thought we were better than that," Pierre said, holding the papers up in the air.

Her heart jumped out of her chest once she saw those papers, and she hated herself for not tossing them. Crying, she asked him, "Why were you in my purse?"

"Nah, fuck all that crying shit. Why the fuck you didn't tell me you were pregnant? You didn't think I would want to know that I was gonna be a father?"

Pierre watched as she stormed past him out of the bathroom and into the bedroom. She sat on the bed and cried.

"What the hell are you crying for? This baby thing could be a good thing, right?"

Erica sat there not saying anything, and that had Pierre worried.

"What's the problem, E, and why couldn't you tell me you were pregnant? You don't wanna have my baby or something? You gonna have to talk to me. All that crying ain't helping shit."

"I'm scared, Pierre. I was so confused about everything. And plus, I didn't want you to be mad and leave me," she cried out.

"Why the fuck would I be mad and leave you if you were pregnant? Do you know I just asked your dad if I could marry your ass? That's how much I love you. Why would I leave you?" Pierre yelled in her face.

His words caused her to grab her chest as if she were slowly having a heart attack. She was at a loss for words and could only cry harder. He wanted to marry her, but she was full of secrets that could jeopardize everything that they had worked so hard for.

"E, you pissing me the fuck off. Just calm down and be real with me, okay? Do you love me for real, or is this just something fake like your dad admitted to me earlier? Come to find out he has been faking about the way he really feels about me and been all friendly with me just to keep you around."

"I never faked any feelings for you. I do love you, and that's why I couldn't tell you. I was so scared to lose you," she yelled back to him.

"Why would you lose me? I'm happy about the baby. E, just talk to me please. I promise I won't get mad."

Erica stood up and walked closer toward the dresser. She tried to get herself together before she began to talk. "I just found out I was pregnant, and then I went to the clinic. The doctor did an ultrasound. He said I was around a few months pregnant, and I panicked."

Erica broke down crying again. The truth was so close to the tip of her tongue that she could taste it, and it made her sick. She stood there holding her stomach as she began to feel ill.

"Erica, is that all you wanna tell me?" Pierre asked, but by the look on her face he could tell that there was more.

She cried harder as she shook her head no.

"Talk to me, ma, please," he begged.

Erica grabbed Pierre's hands and held them in hers. "Baby, I was scared to tell you because the baby might not be yours, and—"

Before she could finish what she was saying, Pierre turned into P. He snatched his hands from her. He was so pissed that he wanted to beat her ass, but instead he punched the wall that she was standing in front of.

"What the fuck, man? What type of shit you on?" he yelled.

Erica cried even more as she tried to grab him. Before he realized what he was doing, Pierre blacked out and had his hands wrapped around her neck, pinning her to the wall.

"Do you know I will fucking kill you, girl, huh?" he asked as his grip got tighter.

"Please," Erica barely said over a whisper.

Pierre stared into her teary eyes for the first time and instantly let her go. It was her eyes that he noticed when they first met, and since that day, he knew he was in love and he needed her in his life. It was her eyes that saved her that night.

"Damn," was all that he could say as her body slid down the wall and her tears continued to flow.

"I'm about to get the fuck out of here before I end up hurting you for real. How the fuck you playing that good-girl shit when you been doing what the fuck you wanted to do all along? What the fuck? E, I really thought you loved me."

"Pierre, I really do love you, and that's why I was so scared to tell you everything."

"You been fucking somebody else? I'm confused as hell. How does that mean that you love me?" he asked as he pulled some clothes out of the closet.

Erica's feelings were hurt, and she hated how quick he was to judge her. She knew she had no choice but to tell him the complete story about the night she was kidnapped.

"Pierre, I swear it's not what you think, and I swear I would never do anything to hurt you. Please don't walk out that door before you hear the whole story," she begged.

Pierre already had his pants on but decided to take a seat on the bed. "Look, Erica, I wish you would stop playing games with me and just say what the fuck you gotta say. You really ain't on my good side right now, and the way I feel about you ain't good. So go ahead and talk."

"Pierre, I love you, and I was scared to death to tell you the truth about that night. I was scared that you wouldn't want me anymore if you found out what happened to me, and that's why I didn't say anything. When the doctor told me how far along I was, I knew that I was gonna have to either tell you everything or just get an abortion. I just couldn't live with carrying this baby not knowing the truth. I had thought it over and had scheduled an appointment for Thursday to end this pregnancy." She spoke so fast, trying not to cry but to get everything out.

Pierre listened, and the story fucked him up because even though she didn't say it, he thought he knew what she was saying. He stood up and walked over to her. She was scared and started walking backward until her body hit the wall.

"Pierre, I'm so sorry," she whispered.

Pierre wrapped her up in his arms. "E, what are you really telling me?"

She had said so much already, but he just needed to hear her tell him everything.

"I don't wanna say it, Pierre. Please don't make me," she cried.

"Baby, just let me know what happened, and I promise you won't ever have to tell another soul."

While he was still holding her, she continued to cry on his chest. She never wanted to repeat these words, but right now she didn't have a choice. Her future with her soul mate was on the line.

"When he kidnapped me, he kept hitting me, and he raped me over and over. When you showed up, he was gonna do it again, but you saved me. I was so scared that night. That's why I begged you to kill him. I hated him so much for what he did to me. You are the only person I ever wanted to share my body with, and he took it. Pierre, he took something from me that I will never be able to get back."

Pierre held on to her tight. He found himself in his feelings about this situation. He felt bad for going off on her and mainly for putting his hands on her. "E, I'm so sorry for tripping on you like that. You know if I had heard the whole story, I wouldn't have acted like that. I'm so sorry, baby."

Erica knew that if she had told him, things would have been different, and she quickly forgave him. "I'm not mad at you, and I hope you are not mad at me. Can we just forget tonight even happened?"

"Not everything, but most," Pierre jokingly said.

Pierre continued to hold her. He felt so bad for tripping on her. He should have been smart enough to know that she wasn't fucking anyone else.

"On a serious note, we need to discuss this whole baby thing. I can't let you get an abortion. I know you against abortions and all that, and you only want one because of what happened, but I strongly believe that this is my baby. You can't kill my baby. I love y'all, man."

Erica hugged him tighter. "I love you so much, baby."

The two ended up in the bed cuddled up as if nothing happened. Pierre slowly rubbed her lower back as she drifted away on his chest. He couldn't fall asleep with the news that he had just received. He thought about that bitch-ass nigga Tim taking advantage of Erica and how she killed herself trying to spare his feelings. Erica had lived with that secret for months, and now that he knew the truth, everything was making sense.

After he rescued her, she was acting strange and shit, like she use to tense up and cry whenever he tried to have sex with her. That was her way of telling him that something was wrong without saying anything. He then thought about her saying that she was gonna get an abortion just because she was scared that the baby wasn't his. That type of shit made him realize how much she loved him for real. From what they talked about before, she had always been against abortions because of religious reasons.

That night Pierre couldn't sleep at all, but Erica was knocked out as long as he was holding her. Every time he moved, she was moving too. He loved that girl, and that she could look past him choking her and calling her out as if she were a ho let him know that she was down for him. He was mad at himself because he should have known better than to put his hands on her, regardless of what was going on.

The sun was shining bright and the birds were chirping when he was finally able to get some rest. It didn't last long when he heard Erica across the hall puking out her guts.

"Damn," he mumbled before climbing out of the bed and walking into the bathroom. Once he got into the bathroom, Erica was getting up and flushing the toilet.

"You okay, baby?" he asked.

Erica grabbed her toothbrush from the medicine cabinet. "Yeah, I'm fine. Let me clean myself up, and then I'll cook some breakfast."

Pierre left her alone in the bathroom. He knew she probably was still gonna be sick, so he wasn't thinking about no breakfast. He didn't even want to put that on her.

When Erica walked in the living room, Pierre was putting on his shoes. "Baby, you look so tired. Where are you going?"

"I see you sick as shit this morning. I was about to go get you some crackers and shit," he answered.

"Pierre, I was about to make you breakfast."

"Nah, you need to go lie down. I wouldn't feel right having you cook while you fucked up like that. Don't worry about me. Let me take care of you and our baby."

Hearing him say "our baby" brought a smile to her face. His sweetness was why she loved him so much.

"Baby, don't overthink it. Go get back in the bed and let daddy take care of everything."

With that being said, Erica went back to the bedroom and climbed back under the sheet. Pierre made his way to the market to get them something to eat. Since he wasn't a fan of actually cooking, he grabbed a couple of boxes of DiGiorno pizzas. He made sure to grab her some crackers and a big Vernors pop. He was gonna make sure she felt better.

He was determined not to be like his dad. His dad had been in and out of his life but had let the streets take over him. Pierre loved his daddy for what he was, but he never really had a real daddy in his life to teach him right from wrong. Pierre Sr. had gone from the nigga selling the work to the nigga smoking the work. Then after some years had passed by, he ended up making the prison system his new home before he died after serving six years. Pierre was gonna make sure he stayed in his child's life no matter what.

After returning home, Pierre wasn't even hungry anymore. He put the food away and went to the back. Standing in the doorway, he just stared at Erica asleep. She was the most beautiful girl in the world, and he was grateful for her being in his life. He smiled when he noticed how her hand rested on her belly. There wasn't much there, but it was a beautiful sight to see.

When he returned to the living room, he pulled out his cell phone and dialed Mekco's number. He wanted his bro to be the first one to know about his baby.

"What's up?"

"I got some good news," he said, cheesing as if Mekco could see him.

"What's up, bro?"

"Man, I'm about to be a daddy. Can you believe that shit?"

Mekco pushed Toya off his chest and sat up in bed. "Bro, you fucking kidding. Cross gonna kill your ass about his niece," Mekco jokingly teased.

"Man, whatever, dog," P said, laughing.

"Don't say I didn't warn your ass."

"Anyway I asked her dad if I could marry her ass, and he flipped the fuck out on me last night. I told that muthafucka 'fuck you' before we left."

Mekco laughed before getting serious. "You a fucking fool, my nigga. That nigga gonna be at church praying extra hard that his baby girl leave your ass for real now."

"Mekco, I'm not worried about that shit. My girl ain't going nowhere. Fuck that nigga if he on that bullshit."

Toya rolled out of the bed. Mekco watched her fat ass jiggle as she walked out of the room and into the bathroom. "Ay, let me hit you up in a minute. I need to handle something right quick."

P hung the phone up and climbed back in the bed with Erica. As soon as his body hit the bed, she slid her body right on his. Before he knew it, he was knocked out with her.

Chapter 15

It was the day of the picnic, and the Brick Boyz and Cross had really showed out. Between the food, DJ, and the bounce houses for the kids, everyone was out having a good time.

Erica had spent the night with Nicole so they could get ready together. Instead of wearing the dress that she had picked out, Nicole put on some short shorts and a fitted T-shirt to match Erica.

"Come on, Erica. This shit started over an hour ago and you still not ready," Nicole yelled out.

Erica walked out of the back and into the living room. "I'm ready now. This damn baby be having me messed up when I try to eat."

Nicole laughed a little before saying, "Come on, girl. You all right now?"

"Yeah, let's go."

The two took Nicole's car to the park. She was lucky that they could even find a parking spot close enough to the gathering.

"Oh, hell nah, I see this nigga got some stupid bitch all on his lap."

Erica shook her head. All she wanted was to have a good time, but then she saw that Nicole was gonna be on some bullshit. "Let's just go find us some seats and chill."

Nicole rolled her eyes at Erica. "Yeah, that's easy to say when your man don't have a ho on his lap."

"Come on, Nicole, y'all did break up. Let him have his fun and you have yours," Erica suggested.

Nicole kept walking straight to the table where Mekco and most of the Brick Boyz were sitting. Nicole took a seat and quickly spoke to everyone. Mostly everyone spoke back, but at the same time they all looked at Mekco and the girl who was sitting on his lap. Everyone felt awkward and was confused. Some of them instantly started plotting to get her in their bed.

Seeing that Erica was about to take a seat by Nicole, P called her so she could sit next to him.

"I'll be back, boo. Let me go see what Pierre wants," Erica whispered to Nicole.

"Okay, I'm about to drink and chill right here. Don't be down there talking to that bitch. Y'all not about to be cool," she said loud enough for everyone to hear.

"Bye, girl," Erica said, laughing at her best friend.

"Hey, Erica. How have you been?" Mekco asked as she took a seat on Pierre's lap.

"Hey, Mekco. I've been good," she responded.

"Congratulations on the baby."

"Thank you."

Erica felt funny holding a conversation with him because the female on his lap was looking at her funny. It was crazy how females were all in their feelings when the guy they were sleeping with talked to someone else. It was like she didn't even see her sitting on Pierre's lap.

"What's up, baby? What took y'all so long to get here?" Pierre asked.

"Man, I tried eating this morning, and this baby had me so sick."

Rubbing on her little belly, Pierre smiled to himself. Just the thought of a little him running around warmed his heart. "E, I told you to keep some of those crackers in your purse to help with all that."

"I know, but Nicole had made breakfast, and it smelled so good. I had to try a piece of bacon and a little bit of eggs," she said giggling.

"Well, that's what you get for being greedy. My baby ain't want that shit," Pierre said, laughing.

Nicole watched from a distance with jealousy all in her eyes. It hurt her feelings that Erica was living her life. She had the man with money, a baby, and happiness. Nicole knew that if it weren't for her, Erica would have never even paid P any attention. She made that shit happen, and she wanted what they had.

Mekco peeped how Toya was giving Erica a funky look, so he did what he thought was right and introduced the two. "Toya, this is P's girl, Erica. And, Erica, this is my friend Toya."

Toya stretched her hand out for a handshake, but Erica just gave her a funky wave. Those who were close laughed. Toya was pissed but turned her attention back toward her phone.

"Baby, don't act like that," Pierre whispered in Erica's ear.

"Forget her. She is not my friend."

Toya heard her and turned in Erica's direction. "What did you say?"

Before Erica could respond, Mekco stepped in. "Toya, chill your ass out before you be walking home."

"Mekco, I was only trying to be nice. I don't know why she acts all funky like that. Shit, I wasn't trying to be her friend. I was only speaking out of respect."

Erica looked back to where Nicole was sitting, but she was gone. She tried looking around for her, but she was out of eyesight. Erica just figured she was somewhere talking or just having a good time away from the table.

"What's up, Nicole? Why you not sitting over there with the rest of the team?" Jamel asked. He really didn't care what her reasons were. He was just looking for a way to start a conversation with her. For the last few years, he had watched her walk around being comfortable being Mekco's girl, but he wanted her for himself. Even though he wasn't a member of the Brick Boyz and really didn't fuck with them niggas like that, he came out for the free food. When he noticed Mekco didn't have Nicole glued to his hip but some other bitch, he decided to put his plans in motion.

"'Cause I'm my own woman. I don't need to sit with them to have a good time," she said, sounding bitter.

Jamel took a seat next to her. "I feel you on that shit. You wanna hit this blunt?"

Nicole wasn't a smoker for real, but seeing Mekco all over that girl had pissed her off, so she was ready to feel good. "Hell yeah, pass that shit over here."

Twenty minutes later, Nicole was up dancing on Jamel just having a good time like she planned on doing.

"Ay, Mekco, you see your girl over there with that nigga Jamel?" Li'l Trey asked.

"I see her over there fooling. She acting like I won't go over there and snatch her ass up. And that nigga Jamel know I don't fucking play. He probably only came so he could eat for the day."

"Mekco, what the fuck you worried about that bitch for? Ain't you here with me?" Toya asked with an attitude.

"You not my fucking girl, so you can chill with all that shit. I brought your ass to the park, and you are already trying to claim me."

Toya was embarrassed. She jumped up and started to walk away. Mekco didn't give a fuck about her leaving. His main concern was Nicole and her being a THOT with that bum-ass nigga Jamel. Seeing her grind all on him made his blood boil.

"Man, let me go get this bitch," he mumbled.

Mekco made his way over to where they were dancing. Things happened so fast that neither saw him coming. Mekco roughly grabbed Nicole by her arm.

"What the fuck you out here thinking you doing?" Mekco yelled.

"Let me go. I'm out here having fun just like you. What the fuck you thought, only you could have fun?"

"Man, stop fucking playing with me. Don't make me fuck your simpleminded ass up."

By this time Erica and Pierre were coming back from their walk.

"Ay, let her go and let's go chill. Don't be out here in front of everybody tripping on her," Pierre told Mekco, trying to calm him down.

"You okay, Nicole?" a concerned Erica asked.

With an attitude, Nicole got loud. "Yes, I'm okay. I wish y'all would get out my fucking face and let me enjoy myself. Go back to y'all little table and leave me alone."

"Nicole, why you tripping, girl?" Erica asked.

"Look, Erica, I'm not tripping, so go back over there and be with your man. Shit, get the fuck out my face. Go feed that baby and chill with that big-head bitch Mekco's fucking now," Nicole yelled.

Erica was now starting to feel like her best friend was jealous of her. It was embarrassing how she cut up in front of everyone, so to keep the drama down, she turned and walked away. She was not about to argue with Nicole. She knew she was acting out because Mekco didn't wanna be bothered with her lately, but the fact that she mentioned her man and baby told the real story.

Erica walked back to the table to sit on Pierre's lap. Pierre placed a kiss on her lips before asking if she was okay.

"Yeah, baby, I'm ready to go home."

"Baby, don't let her attitude get you down. Just chill a li'l longer." Pierre had something planned and didn't want it ruined by that extra-girly bull-shit.

"Ay, young boy, what is my niece doing on your lap?" Cross jokingly asked Pierre as he gave him a handshake.

"What's up, Cross?" P responded, not taking him seriously.

Jumping up from Pierre's lap, Erica greeted him
with a hug. "Hey, Uncle Cross."

"What's up, baby girl, and why are you out here
with these gangbangers?"

Laughing, Erica responded, "Whatever, Uncle
Cross. Why are you in my face sounding like my
daddy? Besides, Pierre is one of your workers."

They all laughed.

"Anyway, let me get up on this stage and do my
little speech."

"Ay, Cross, are we still good on that?" P yelled
behind him.

"Hell yeah. I'm all here for that," Cross responded.

Cross walked over to the DJ booth and whispered in the DJ's ear. Soon after, the music stopped,
and DJ Ricky was talking on the mic.

"Hey, everyone, and good afternoon. I hope you
all are having a good time. Let's all give thanks to
the Cross and his crew for getting us all together
this great afternoon."

Everyone cheered and clapped their hands in
excitement.

Cross then took the mic and began to talk to the
crowd of people. "Thank you all for coming out for
the fifth year in a row. There's plenty of food, so
make sure you all eat good. Kids make sure you
get your face painted, get some balloons from the
clowns, and enjoy jumping in the bounce house
without losing your shoes. Parents, we all know

school is coming up in a few weeks, so before you leave, make sure your kids get a backpack. We already filled them up with supplies. Enjoy the rest of your day."

The crowd cheered and clapped louder. They loved the love that Cross and his team showed the hood. Cross might have earned his money doing bad, but he took care of the hood.

Everyone was having a good time, and Toya eventually came back to the table. Mekco had gone looking for her and dicked her down somewhere, so now she was acting right with a huge smile on her face.

Erica was sitting with Toya and Li'l Trey's girlfriend, Ashley. She was used to always being around Nicole, but for the first time she really gave the other girls a chance, and it wasn't really all that bad.

"Erica, they brought all this food and you over there picking over your plate," Ashley spoke up after noticing she wasn't eating.

"I swear I'm trying, but this baby doesn't like anything. Every time I eat, it all just comes right back up. I'm so over this pregnancy stuff."

"Aww!" Ashley and Toya said at the same time.

Erica smiled. It felt good to tell people about the baby and to see them happy for her blessing. She loved that feeling and wished that things could go this smoothly when it was time to have this talk with her father.

Erica watched as Pierre, Mekco, and Cross circled around each other and talked in private. She wondered what that was all about but knew better than to be in their street business.

Pierre walked over to the table where Erica was sitting. "Hey, you okay over here?"

"Yeah, I'm okay. I just can't eat this food. I'm so mad because it smells so good."

"It'll be okay soon. That shit don't last the whole pregnancy. Why don't you go ahead and get up right quick? Come over here with me."

He held his hand out to help her up. She wasn't sure what was going on, but she got up. While doing so, she noticed Mekco and her uncle smiling. As P got on the stage, the DJ handed over the mic.

Pierre was nervous as hell, but he had to do what he had to do. "What's up, everyone? Are you all having a good time?"

The crowd cheered to show how much of a good time they were having.

"I need y'all help right quick. I want everyone to show some love to my baby, Erica."

She stood on the steps with Cross and Mekco, smiling hard.

"Come up here and let these folks meet your beautiful ass," he ordered.

Erica shook her head no repeatedly.

Mekco playfully pushed her. "Go ahead and get your scary ass up there."

Pierre laughed at her before asking her to come up there again. This time, Cross took her by the hand and walked her up onto the stage. He then stepped up with her and grabbed the mic from P. "This is my beautiful niece, Erica."

The ones who were watching clapped for her but didn't have an idea why at first. That was, until they saw Pierre drop down to his knee. The crowd went crazy, and Erica took her attention off the crowd and started to look around. Once she saw Pierre on one knee, she instantly began to cry.

"Baby, will you marry me?"

As she cried, she shook her head yes. This was the moment that she dreamed about, but there was only one thing missing. Her best friend wasn't there next to her to celebrate her engagement.

Pierre stood up and wrapped his tatted arms around Erica. He then kissed her before placing a rock on her finger. She smiled hard before turning to the crowd and showing them her finger. As everyone cheered, she continued to search the crowd for Nicole, but when she laid eyes on her, Nicole's face was frowned up, and she was getting up to leave the party.

That made Erica cry harder. Not having her best friend in her corner broke her heart.

Pierre hugged her tighter and whispered in her ear, "I love you, baby, and don't ever doubt that shit."

***

It had been two weeks since Nicole had talked to Erica, and she didn't give a fuck. She stayed in the house feeling betrayed by everyone, starting with Mekco. He had hurt her the most, and then he had the nerve to be flaunting his new bitch off like she was as beautiful as her.

It was 10:00 p.m., and she was up, drunk, talking to Jamel. She was so gone that she had to put the phone on speaker just because she couldn't hold the phone up straight. She laughed at how he was so sprung over her already. She was feeding him the attention that he loved, but she hadn't fucked him yet. She thought about it a few times just because she knew it was gonna get back to Mekco and destroy his ego. But at the end of the day, she knew it would only kill her chances of getting her true love back.

"You playing games, Nicole. You know a nigga been feeling you for the longest and you bullshitting. Just your voice got a nigga's rock hard. Let a nigga slide through."

"Damn, boy, calm the hell down. I told you I wasn't ready for all that yet. I just got out of a relationship that I was in for a couple of years," she said, trying to sound innocent and convincing him that she wasn't the freak she really was.

"Bro, fuck that nigga Mekco!" he yelled with much pride knowing he couldn't fuck with a Brick Boy even on their worst day.

Before Nicole could say anything, Mekco snatched her phone off the bed. "Ay, dirty nigga, when I see you, that's that ass."

Nicole was stunned to see Mekco standing in her bedroom. She had completely forgotten that he still had the keys to her place. It was a good thing that she didn't invite another nigga over there. She would have been dead for sure.

"Man, fuck you and that freak bitch. I was just trying to get the pussy," Jamel yelled before hanging up the phone.

Mekco slapped Nicole hard across her face, then snatched her up from the bed right before tossing her on the wall. "What the fuck you think you're doing? You think I won't smoke your stupid ass and that dirty-ass nigga?"

Nicole couldn't respond because of the grip he had on her neck. After a minute he let her go, then watched her grab at her chest as she hit the floor. Mekco didn't pay her any mind as he started to undress, then went into the bathroom to take a shower. Once he was out of sight, she calmed herself down, then climbed in the bed. Even though she was somewhat scared, something in her was happy that he was there.

Mekco jumped out of the shower, then dried off. Walking in the room, he saw that Nicole was in the bed pretending to be asleep. He knew better than to fall for that shit. He knew she was pretending to sleep so he wouldn't touch her again.

When Mekco walked over to the bed, he roughly grabbed her by her legs and dragged her closer toward the edge of the bed. He then snatched her panties off. "So you was just gonna give my pussy up to the first nigga who said hi to you?"

Being scared, she didn't say anything.

"Nicole, I know you woke, so you better answer me now," he ordered.

"Mekco, you the one who said you were done with me. What was I supposed to do? Was I supposed to just sit around and wait for you to come back to me?"

Mekco was still upset about her talking to another nigga. Just the thought of her fucking somebody else made his blood boil. Mekco didn't respond with words. Instead, he picked up her phone and dialed Jamel's number back.

"What are you doing, Mekco?" Nicole asked.

He didn't say a word as he placed the phone on speaker. Nicole then heard Jamel say hello. Mekco was gonna make sure Jamel knew exactly who Nicole's pussy belonged to. He wasted no time burying his face between her legs. He began to feast on her just the way that she loved, causing her to moan loudly.

"Oh, my Gawd!" she yelled out at the top of her lungs.

Mekco didn't ease up, not one bit. He needed to show her that she was his pussy and she'd be out of her mind to fuck with another nigga. He knew no other nigga could make her cum the way he did or fuck her the right way.

Nicole's legs started to shake, and he knew exactly what time it was. He stood up and grabbed his T-shirt to wipe his face off. "Damn, bae, you wet as fuck," he mumbled.

Mekco roughly flipped her around on her stomach and entered Nicole from the back. His stroke made her arch her back and moan out in pleasure. She screamed out Mekco's name repeatedly until she came again. It wasn't long before he was shooting his seeds deep inside of her. Once he was done, he placed a kiss on her forehead.

They both heard Jamel moaning on the phone. They had forgotten that they even had an audience. Mekco hung the phone up laughing. "That bum-ass nigga nasty over there beating his meat to us fucking."

"You the one who called him, and I still don't see the purpose of that shit."

"The purpose was for that nigga to know who that pussy belongs to. After all that name screaming, I think he knows it's mine, and he won't ever step to you again," Mekco said, glowing with his own pride.

"Boy, I tell you, you're so fucking cocky."

Mekco replied by saying, "And I have every right to be, muthafucka. You can turn your ass around. I'm not done yet."

"Mekco!" she cried out, but there wasn't any use. He was punishing her in the worst way, but she truly loved it.

After the third round, both were laid out in the bed, out of breath, sweaty, and tired. Nicole smiled to herself as she laid her head down on his sweaty chest. She was happy to have her man back.

"Baby, I don't want us to ever break up again. I love you, and it's not about the money, I swear."

"Look, I'm not saying we're back together just yet. I love your crazy ass, but we need to have some space between us while I figure out what I wanna do," he said, being as honest as possible.

Nicole sat up, pissed off. "So what, you just wanna hang on to me to make sure I'm not fucking nobody while you out fucking whoever you wanna fuck? I'm not for that."

"Do you love me?" he asked.

"Yes, I do love you, and you know that. Why can't we just be back together like we were before? Why are you trying to make things hard?"

"I'm tired. Let me sleep on it. I need to get my thoughts together," he said, thinking she was just gonna say okay and leave it like that.

"So basically you just came over to prove to yourself that you could fuck me whenever you wanted to. I'm nothing to you but free pussy?" she yelled.

Without saying a word, Mekco climbed out of the bed and turned the light on. He then opened the closet and started looking for something to put on.

"You got what you wanted. Now you're just gonna leave like that?"

"Look, this is why we can't be together. You talk too fucking much. I give you everything that you want and need, and all I want is for you to shut the hell up sometimes."

Pulling herself together, Nicole coldly said, "I'm not about to let you run in and out of my life. If you're not gonna be with me a hundred percent, then just leave right now. Walk out those doors and don't come back."

"Why can't you just chill and see what happens between us?"

Nicole shook her head at what he was saying. "Look, stop trying to play me like a weak bitch. That's not me anymore. I have grown up since we first got together. What you fail to realize is that I want you, not need you."

"But at the same time, I'm paying your rent and all your bills," he reminded her.

"I had a job when we first started kicking it, remember that? You said you didn't want me to work, remember that?"

Mekco didn't respond. He knew she was right. He had made her become who he wanted her to be.

He stared at her with love in his eyes. He couldn't deny the love that he had for her, but all that love shit had him scared, and he wasn't sure what to do.

Nicole was tired of his wishy-washy ass. She got up and started putting on her clothes.

"Where the fuck you going?"

"Boy, I'm not about to play these games with you. I'll go back to my mom's house so that you won't ever have to worry about me again."

Mekco really didn't want to lose her for real. He started snatching at the clothes that she was trying to put on. For a moment she fought against him, but soon she realized that he wasn't gonna let her leave without a fight.

As Mekco pulled her in, he gave her a passionate kiss, which calmed her down. "Nicole, I swear I love you. I really do. But you're gonna have to let me get me together. Don't question my love for you, 'cause you got my heart. Just let me fall back for a minute."

"If it's really like that, then why can't we just be together?" she cried.

All Mekco could tell her was that it wasn't her. It was him.

Going against how she really felt, she shook her head yeah, which told him that she was gonna allow him to continue to play with her feelings. Mekco held her as she cried in his arms. His plan wasn't to hurt her but to better himself.

As they calmed down and climbed in the bed, Nicole ended up crying herself to sleep as Mekco held her. Soon after, Nicole was knocked out. Sleep didn't come easy for Mekco, so without waking Nicole up, he snuck out of the bedroom and went into the living room. He turned the TV on and lay on the couch. His thoughts were getting the best of him.

The next morning, Nicole woke up to an empty bed. Mekco had crushed her, then left her for the last time. She silently cried her eyes out. It hurt her so bad to lose someone she truly loved. Then on top of that, she didn't have anyone to talk to because she had run her best friend away.

Being jealous of Erica and her happiness caused her to act out and become the green-eyed monster. Nicole was depressed and thought that she wasn't gonna be able to continue living like this. She felt like she had hit rock bottom, and for once, sexing Mekco really good didn't even work.

She walked into the bathroom and opened up the medicine cabinet. She found two bottles of pain pills that Mekco had left at her house. She thought her days of being a weak bitch were over until now. She thought this would be the only way out of all her problems.

Mekco walked through the door with some breakfast from Coney Island. He had gotten up early to get breakfast for himself and Nicole. He

had allowed her to fall asleep the night before so
he could think things over. By the time he got up in
the morning, he had a clear mind and was ready to
be the man she needed him to be. He was going
to make things right between them if that was the
last thing that he did.

Mekco set the breakfast along with the roses
that he had bought for her on the dining room
table. He was ready to get his baby back. "Nicole!'
he yelled, trying to get her attention.

After a few minutes and still no answer, he
called out again. "Nicole, baby, we need to talk."

He yelled again, but he still didn't get an answer
from her.

Mekco made his way to the back of the house to
her bedroom, but he didn't see her. His next stop
was to the bathroom. He thought he might have
heard the shower going, so he opened the door
without knocking.

Mekco pushed the door open and couldn't believe his eyes. After seeing the empty pill bottles in
the sink, he hurried and pulled the shower curtain
back. Mekco's heart dropped when he saw Nicole
sitting in the tub with the shower water running
on her. He quickly snatched her out of the tub and
took her into the bedroom. He repeatedly shook
her, trying to wake her up.

"Nicole, baby, get up!" he yelled as he lightly
slapped her face, trying to wake her up.

Seeing that she wasn't responding, he pulled out his phone and dialed 911.

"911, what's your emergency?" the phone operator asked.

"I just got home, and I found my girl in the tub. It looks like she took some pills, and she won't get up. Please send someone out. Please save my baby."

Mekco was full of emotions and was scared for Nicole. He really wasn't sure what he would do if something were to happen to her.

He was surprised that it only took the ambulance ten long minutes to get to her place. Mekco was also happy that they rushed her to the hospital.

As he followed the ambulance to the hospital, he said a silent prayer, begging God not to take the woman who had his heart. He even vowed that if she made it, he'd do right by her for now on.

Erica, Pierre, and Mekco sat in the waiting room waiting to hear an update on Nicole's condition. They all were worried, especially Erica. The last time she and Nicole had talked she could sense that something was really bothering her, but never in a million years would she have thought that her best friend would have tried to take her own life.

Teresa and Pastor Collins rushed into the waiting room. It was clear to see that Nicole's mom had been crying.

"What the hell happened to my baby, Mekco?"

Mekco stood up and greeted Teresa with a tight hug. "Hey, Ma, I found her in the tub passed out. It looked like she tried to kill herself. They got her here as quickly as they could."

Teresa started crying even more. The news broke her heart that her daughter didn't want to live anymore.

Erica got out of her seat, then gave her a hug. "I'm so sorry, but I know she will be all right," she whispered in her ear.

The pastor spoke to everyone but Pierre. He still couldn't get over the fact that he had cursed at him the last time they had dinner together. Pierre didn't give a fuck. As long as he had Erica by his side, he was all right. He would tell him fuck him again if he had to.

Teresa took a seat, and Erica's dad followed right behind her. He placed his arms around her and just allowed her to cry. By the way he touched her, Erica could tell that the two were very close and probably had been intimate with one another.

Erica knew it wasn't the time or place for extra drama, but she still wondered why her dad was looking at her all crazy. After a while it had started to really bother her. She stood up and went to the restroom. She really didn't have to use it. She just needed to clear her mind. It hurt her that her best friend was laid up in the hospital bed. How could someone with a full life ahead of them try to take their own life? Erica knew that Nicole had always been full of life, and she just couldn't wrap her brain around what she had done. That question ran through her mind repeatedly.

Erica walked out of the restroom only to be frightened by her dad standing there. "Dad, you scared me," she said, clutching at her chest.

With a firm look on his face, Pastor Collins stared his daughter up and down. He knew when he first came in the waiting room that his eyes weren't playing tricks on him, but he didn't say anything. He had seen that huge engagement ring on her finger. "I don't know why you have to be so hardheaded. Do you get joy out of life for going against me, young lady?"

"What are you talking about, Daddy?" she asked, confused.

Eric roughly grabbed his daughter's hand. "You think I didn't notice this on your hand? As big as this ring is, did you think you could hide it from me?"

"Daddy, I was gonna talk to you about it when I came over for Sunday dinner. I wasn't trying to hide it from anyone. You have to understand and respect the fact that we are in love."

"That's some bullshit and you know it. You barely know this criminal. Just because he is probably buying you nice things and keeping your ass wet, that doesn't mean you're in love. You have really let me down, and I know your mother is not proud of your behavior. How can you think loving a drug dealer was the right path to follow for a bright future? You know what, all I see for your future is you laid up somewhere with a bunch of kids while he's locked up for being a big dummy."

At first Erica couldn't respond, but she felt her tears starting to build up. Her dad had an evil smirk on his face like he had just won a war between him and his biggest enemy. Erica knew her father all too well and knew the only way to beat him was to fight back. She wiped her face dry with the piece of paper towel that she had taken out of the restroom.

"Look, I know you don't like Pierre and he told me about you fake liking him. That was really messed up on your part, because that man has done everything to get on your good side. Oh, and just to let you know, Pierre and I are expecting our first child in a few months."

Pastor Collins's heart dropped to the floor as he took in the words that she had just said.

"That's right. I'm pregnant, and if you keep acting the way that you've been acting, my child will not know you."

With that being said, Erica coldly turned around and walked away. But the pastor wasn't having that. Just as she was entering the waiting room, he hurried behind her, snatching her left shoulder and pushing her against the wall.

"You will not have that boy's baby!" he yelled.

Pierre jumped up and pushed him off Erica. "Ay, bro, watch yourself," Pierre yelled as he grabbed Erica and sat her down in one of the empty chairs.

"Teresa, I see that I'm not wanted here. I hope you can find a way home," Eric said while fixing himself up.

"Ma, I'll take you home," Mekco said, finally speaking up.

Before walking out of the room, Pastor Collins looked toward Erica and Pierre. "Y'all all going to hell, and I'm gonna be the one who delivers you there."

"Man, get the fuck out of here with that shit," Mekco yelled. He was pissed that Erica's dad was even trying to start some shit while he was sitting there praying that Nicole was gonna be okay. It wasn't the time or place for all of that extra bullshit.

Eric walked out of the room, feeling defeated.

"I'm sorry, Erica, but that man is too much. Are you okay?" Mekco asked.

"I'm okay. I just hate how he acts. Then everyone in church praises him like he is God Himself. I love my dad, but he is so quick to judge everyone like he is better than them."

"It'll be okay, baby. I promise," Pierre assured her.

"Yeah, I know. I just told my dad that if he continued to act up, then he wasn't gonna be able to be around my baby."

Pierre had a lot to say behind that. "I see where you're coming from, but to be honest, I don't have any family, and you have your dad and uncle. If our baby doesn't have its granddad in his life, he won't have much family. We gotta get shit together."

Erica looked at him with a smile on her face. That right there was one of the reasons that she loved Pierre. No matter what her dad did to make her wanna walk away from him, Pierre always tried to make stuff right between them. Her dad did act out and pissed both of them off, but Pierre was the one to remind her that he was still her dad at the end of the day.

"You right, baby."

"Family for Nicole—" Before the doctor could get her whole name out, everyone was on their feet waiting for the update of her condition.

"Hi, I'm Dr. Jones, and I am one of the doctors working on Nicole. She is doing fine right now. We did have to pump her stomach out for the contents that she swallowed."

"So can I see my baby?" Teresa asked.

"Yes, you can. She might be a little out of it, but she is awake for now," Dr. Jones told them.

Teresa went in first to see her daughter. "Hey, baby, Mommy is here now. Please talk to me and tell me what was bothering you so much that you would want to leave me."

"Ma, I really don't want to talk about it. Just know that I will never try this again. I love you, and I never wanna leave you."

Teresa sat in the chair, holding her daughter's hand. She wasn't gonna force her to talk about nothing that she didn't want to talk about. As she held her hand, she said a silent prayer asking the Lord to watch over Nicole.

"Baby, you got a few more visitors out there, so I'm not gonna be selfish and keep them waiting. The doctors said you could come home in a few days, and I'll be here to get you. I love you, and don't ever do anything like this to scare me again."

"I love you too, Mommy, and I swear I won't."

Nicole watched as her mom walked out the door and Erica walked in. She could tell Erica had been crying, and she felt bad for putting everyone through this. As Erica walked in, she noticed the ring and her small baby bump. She wasn't sure why she hated Erica, but she turned the opposite way and stared out the window.

"Nicole, I know you're not talking to me, but I still love you. You're not just my best friend. You're my sister. If you wanna talk about what's bothering you, I'm here for you."

"Erica, please save all that shit. I don't want to talk to you, Ms. Goody Two-shoes. You walking around with my life, and truth be told, if it weren't for me, you wouldn't even know Pierre," Nicole coldly said, not holding back her true feelings.

"What? You gotta be kidding me. You did all this because you're jealous? Girl, if you only knew the bull crap that I went through or, better yet, am still going through, trust me, you wouldn't wanna walk in my shoes. Nicole, you need to grow up for real."

"Get the fuck out my room. I no longer wanna see your face."

"I'm not going anywhere. We need to talk this out," Erica demanded.

Nicole pressed the button on her remote that called the nurse into her room.

"Yes, ma'am, is there a problem?" Nurse Henderson asked.

"Yes, there is. I asked her to leave, and she refuses to go away. Can I have security escort her out?"

The nurse turned toward Erica. "Ma'am, I'm sorry, but I'm gonna have to ask you to leave right now."

Erica stood up with tears in her eyes. "Nicole, we should be better than this. Why are you such a"—it took her a minute before she let the words leave her mouth—"Nicole, you're such a bitch."

Nicole didn't respond as she watched her so-called best friend walk out of the room.

Erica went straight to Pierre and cried on him before telling him that she was ready to leave. After they said their goodbyes, they left hand in hand.

It was Mekco's time to see Nicole, and he was actually scared. He knew how broken she was about their breakup. Then to find her passed out really did something to him.

As he entered the room, he saw the sweet girl he had run into a few years ago. She was so beautiful to him, and that was something that he couldn't deny.

"Hey, baby. I'm so glad that you are okay. You scared the shit out of me this morning," Mekco admitted.

"I'm sorry."

"Why would you do something so stupid like that?" he asked.

"Mekco, where were you this morning?" she asked, ignoring his question.

"I stepped out to grab up some breakfast. I knew you had been drinking and wasn't gonna get up to cook."

Nicole started to cry. She was actually trying to kill herself because she thought that he had walked out on her for good. Now she was laid up in the hospital looking crazy because he went to buy them some breakfast.

Mekco sat on the side of the bed and held her. "Baby, it's gonna be all right. You my baby, and ain't nothing changing about that."

Nicole held on to his every word. The only thing that was bothering her was the fact that she just tossed away her friendship thinking nobody gave a fuck about her.

Chapter 16

"Your girl finally home from the hospital, and Mekco said she is doing much better," Pierre said, taking a seat next to Erica on the couch.

"That's good, but you know we're not friends anymore. Her words, not mine."

"Whatever. I'm not trying to hear that shit. But anyway, what you doing on the computer?" he asked, seeing that the computer had all of her attention.

"I'm getting my schedule ready for class. You know I'll be back in school later this month?"

"How are you gonna work around school and the baby?"

"I have everything worked out. I'm only gonna go to school part-time. And for the second semester I was thinking about doing online classes. That way, even if I'm in labor, I can have my laptop with me."

They laughed at the whole labor and laptop joke.

"E, you know I have your back on everything, but don't try to overdo anything. Anyway, I really can't wait for you to get bigger so we can see what the sex of our baby is."

"I think it's a girl, to be honest," Erica admitted.

"Nah, a li'l girl won't do. I need a soldier coming out of you. We're gonna make a football team with no cheerleaders allowed."

"Whatever. After two I'm done having babies," Erica said, laughing.

"Shit. I keep trying to tell you I'm in control, not your spoiled ass."

Instead of Nicole's mom coming to pick her up, Mekco was there to make sure she was good. He felt guilty and blamed himself for Nicole trying to kill herself. What Nicole didn't know was that Mekco was battling his own demons. He was somewhat like his father but trying to go a different route. His father was a good guy until shit got too serious or he smelled a responsibility.

The first two years of Mekco and Nicole's relationship, he wore a condom because he was scared of commitment and knocking her up. He tried his hardest to break that cycle, and in doing so, he talked to Nicole about having a baby. He really wanted a baby, but then the whole relationship thing had him scared. He then decided to take the easy way out and just break up with her. He thought that just fucking hoes was the answer to his problem. That only worked for a minute because Toya started being too attached and thought they were in a relationship. Mekco wasn't feeling that and thought that if he was gonna be with anyone, it would be Nicole. Shit was crazy how one minute he was fine and the next he was tripping.

Nicole lay in Mekco's bed, thinking over everything that she had been through and what she put everyone else through. She wanted to apologize to Erica, but her pride was in her way. Since Mekco had promised to be by her side, she had been feeling much better.

"Hey, baby, I ordered us some food. It should be here in twenty minutes," Mekco said, walking into the room and sitting next to her.

"Mekco, I have a question for you, and no matter what, I want you to tell me the truth."

"Nicole, didn't the doctors tell you that you needed to get some rest?"

"Yeah, I am, but I still can talk, can't I?" she asked with an attitude.

"What's the question?"

"Do you think I was wrong for cutting Erica off?"

Mekco had his opinion about the situation, but up until now he remained quiet about it. "Honestly, you were dead-ass wrong. You cut that girl off like that because bro was in love with her. You mean to tell me all those years of being her friend didn't mean shit to you?"

"Damn, tell me how you really feel. I know I was being a bitch, but what if I call her and she doesn't forgive me? That's what scares me the most."

"Nicole, you've been on that bullshit, and for you to admit it might mean a lot to her. Call your girl up and get things right between y'all. Not only have you been through a lot, but she has too," Mekco said, thinking about the story Pierre had shared with him about Erica.

He remembered his boy feeling fucked up about her being raped by Tim and how she was scared to tell him. Pierre had also told him that the only reason he even found out about Tim was because she popped up pregnant and was scared. That was a moment that Erica really needed her friend to talk to.

"Baby, call her and tell her you're sorry for being a bitch."

Nicole sat there and thought about what he was saying, and she knew he was right. The two had been friends all their lives, and she let her jealousy turn her against her best friend.

Mekco tossed her cell phone to her. "Go ahead and own up to your bullshit." After that, he walked out the door.

Erica had just gotten her schedule completed for the following semester and was looking at how much her classes were gonna cost her father. She knew he was probably still mad at her, but that shouldn't have anything to do with her continuing her education. She was planning on calling him later that day to go over everything with him.

Her phone ringing knocked her out of her thoughts. She looked at her cell phone and saw that it was Nicole calling. She smiled for a minute, then thought about their last conversation, and that smile quickly became a frown.

"Hello," Erica said, answering the phone.

"Hey, boo. Just listen to me right quick. I know you're mad at me, but I do understand now that I was being a jealous bitch. I should have been there to celebrate with you instead of being a hater. I'm sorry can you forgive me?"

Erica held the phone for a minute, thinking stuff over. She wanted Nicole to apologize and for things to go back to normal. She was happy that Nicole was now acting like she had some sense.

"Nicole, I do forgive you. Please don't ever in life think we are gonna be beefed out over some crap. Even if I had to come and beat you up, we were gonna be back friends."

Nicole laughed, then asked, "So how are you and my godchild doing?"

"We are doing good. I'm slowly being able to eat, so that's a plus," Erica replied.

The girls sat on the phone for almost two hours before they agreed to go out to breakfast in the morning and to spend the day together.

The next day, Erica picked Nicole up from Mekco's house. As she pulled up, she dialed Nicole's phone to tell her she was outside.

"Hey, I see my baby growing. You gonna be big as fuck in a minute," Nicole said, rubbing Erica's stomach.

"Girl, don't start that. I'm still at the beginning of my pregnancy. Anyway, where are we going to eat?"

"You the pregnant one. What you got the taste for, baby mama?" Nicole asked.

"Forget breakfast, let's go get some tacos. That's all I really eat anyway."

Nicole laughed before jokingly saying, "Your baby gonna come out a fucking Mexican. Watch what I tell you."

The girls arrived at one of their favorite Mexican restaurants. Once they took their seats and ordered their food, they dug straight in.

It was crazy how their friendship picked right back up where it left off. They sat and talked about mostly everything. It felt like old times again.

"So, what do you think you're carrying?" Nicole asked.

"I want a girl, but you know Pierre wants a boy. Boys are bad, so I don't know about all of that," Erica truthfully answered.

Nicole started to laugh but was quickly distracted by a familiar face across the restaurant.

"What's wrong, Nicole?"

***

"Girl, we got to get the fuck out of here. Like right now."

Erica could tell by the look on her friend's face that she wasn't playing when she said that. They both jumped up and started to leave the restaurant.

"Hey, Nicole, where your ho-ass nigga?" Brandon asked with much attitude.

Nicole saw the gun on his hip and got frightened. She grabbed Erica's hand and rushed out of the restaurant. "Come on, Erica. Run!" she yelled.

Erica and Nicole ran to the car without looking back. They were so scared that Erica almost hit a car leaving the parking lot. "Oh, my God. Nicole, who the heck was that?" Erica yelled as she drove off.

"That's a nigga who use to work for Mekco, but he ended up fucking him over, and now Mekco wanna kill him and his brother."

Erica looked in the rearview mirror. "I think he is following us. I'm scared."

Nicole pulled her phone out and dialed Mekco's number. "Mekco, baby, Brandon got a gun and is following me and Erica. We scared as fuck right now."

"Ay, where the fuck you at?" he asked, placing his gun on his hip, then leaving the house.

"We just left the Mexican restaurant in Dearborn, baby," Nicole cried into the phone.

"Damn, it's gonna take a minute for me to get to y'all, so tell Erica to hit 94, then jump on 96. She should ride that bitch until she is able to come up to the Livernois exit and make a left. There's a police station right there."

"Police station?" Nicole questioned.

"Yeah, baby. Don't question shit. Just tell Erica what I said," he ordered.

"I got you on speaker, so she can hear you."

"Look, don't worry about shit. I'm headed that way now."

"Okay, baby."

"Let me set this shit up. Then I'm gonna call you right back. Y'all be safe, and do everything that I told you to do."

Erica followed the directions that were given to her. She was scared out of her mind, but Pierre talked to her plenty of nights about remaining calm in situations like this. He promised that he would make sure no one ever hurt her again.

"Erica, I'm getting scared. This nigga is riding our ass."

"I'm going as fast as I can. Just chill for me. If you start tripping, that's gonna make me nervous, and I'm trying to stay cool."

As Erica got closer to the police station, both girls' nerves somewhat calmed down. Mekco had called right back as promised, and everything was in motion. His people were on the job, and all they had to do was pull up in the driveway.

It was just lucky that Brandon got caught at the red light. Like she was told, she hurried and pulled up in the parking lot. Brandon saw this and slowly drove past the police station. He wanted to kill them bitches, but he wasn't about to do that shit in front of the fucking police.

Brandon drove past with hate in his eyes. What he didn't notice was an unmarked police car following him and that Mekco wasn't too far behind them.

Officer Peterson and Officer Shepherd went over to Erica's car. "Mekco wants you guys to go straight home from here. We're gonna follow you and make sure you make it safe."

Nicole spoke up for the both of them. "Okay, thanks."

Erica was a little nervous, so they just sat there for a minute. "I'm about to call Pierre and have him meet me at your house. I don't even feel right driving anymore."

She pulled out her phone and dialed his number. After a minute, she placed her phone back in her purse. "That's strange. He is not answering for me."

"Maybe he is with Mekco about to handle things and can't talk right now," Nicole explained.

"Yeah, you right, but let's get away from here."

Erica drove off and made her way back to Nicole's house. Once they were inside the apartment safely, the officers turned around and went back to the precinct.

"Erica, I was so scared. That guy was crazy as hell. I don't know why he was following us when he was the one who fucked over Mekco and ran off with his money. I don't know why his bitch ass is so mad, but I know my baby is gonna take care of him."

Erica didn't even bother to respond to Nicole's rant about this crazy street-life crap. She couldn't understand how Nicole had gotten so comfortable living like this was a normal way of life.

"I'm tired. I'm about to go lie down and get some rest. This baby is having me so sleepy," Erica said, standing up from the couch.

"Go ahead. You know you still have your room back there."

Nicole watched as Erica disappeared to the back. She could tell that something was really bothering her, but instead of digging for answers, she lay back on the couch and prayed that Mekco was okay.

Erica closed the door behind her and got situated in her bed. She tried to get her rest, but her mind was running a thousand miles per hour. She tried calling Pierre again, and once again she got no answer.

As she lay there in the bed, she started to cry. The last few months had been great with Pierre, and she really loved him, but this street life was starting to be a little too much for her. Before she got with Pierre, all she did was go to school and church, and from time to time she stayed over at Nicole's house. Since she had been with Pierre she had been kidnapped, raped, and chased by a man with a gun. She was starting to have second thoughts of being the wife of a Brick Boy.

Erica ended up dialing Pierre's number one last time before she fell asleep with heavy thoughts.

Officer Knolton and Officer Moore drove behind the burgundy Chevy Impala waiting for the right time to put some work in. They had been on the force for many years, but they got the most excitement when Cross or his team needed them to do some dirty work.

"I think this nigga done drove far enough and he probably thinks everything is all good now," Office Knolton said.

"Hell yeah, let's go ahead and pull this bitch-ass nigga over. The quicker we get this over with, the quicker we get this bread," Officer Moore added.

Officer Knolton turned the sirens on, alerting Brandon to pull the fuck over.

Brandon slapped the steering wheel. He had only been in town for three days and was already in trouble with the law.

"Yes, Officer, what's the problem?" Brandon asked.

"License and registration please."

"What was I pulled over for? If you don't mind me asking."

With a firm tone in his voice, Officer Knolton repeated himself. "License and registration now."

Brandon stupidly reached over to the glove compartment. As he searched around, the officers looked around, making sure no one was watching them. Moore went back to the officers' car. Officer Knolton quickly pulled out his Taser, then stunned Brandon.

Brandon tried to let out a scream before the officer stunned him again. "Bitch-ass nigga."

Office Knolton then pushed his body over toward the passenger side of the car. Just then, Officer Moore pulled up on the side of Brandon's car and yelled, "Hurry the fuck up. Somebody coming this way."

Knolton got into Brandon's car. They both hurried and drove off. Officer Knolton followed his partner, playing everything off. As he looked through his rearview mirror, he laughed to himself, seeing that the car that was coming up behind them was only Mekco's. The games were just about to start.

Mekco had followed the unmarked police car. He was pissed that the nigga Brandon had the nerve to even show his face in Detroit again after he and his brother ran off with that money. Now he was about to pay them back with his life.

The three cars ended up at one of Cross's vacant buildings. He had bought the building but never took the time to get it fixed up. Since it was just sitting there, they used it to do their dirty work.

Mekco finally walked in with an evil grin on his face. He looked at Brandon, whose face was now pale. It looked as if he had just seen a ghost.

"So your bitch ass really gonna step to my girl like her nigga wouldn't kill your bitch ass," Mekco said as he slid his black leather gloves on.

"Man, fuck you and that THOT bitch," Brandon yelled without any fear in his heart.

Without a second thought, Mekco slapped Brandon. "You got a lot of mouth for a dead mutha-fucka."

"I know your faggot ass gonna kill me anyway, so I might as well say what I wanna say. So like I said, fuck you and that bitch."

It was Mekco's plan to torture Brandon, but he couldn't handle his smart-ass mouth, so instead he let a hot one in the middle of his forehead end the whole thing.

"Bitch-ass nigga," he mumbled.

***

"Damn, if you were gonna just do that, what the fuck we here for?" Officer Moore said.

"My bad. I got tired of his mouth, but y'all still gonna get your bread," Mekco assured them.

Officer Knolton jogged out of the building, then returned with a gas container in his hand. "Fuck this shit. I gotta do something."

Officer Moore and Mekco laughed as they watched the dirty officer walk around Brandon's lifeless body, pouring gasoline all over him.

"This muthafucka crazy," Mekco said, still laughing.

Officer Moore turned his attention toward Mekco. "Shit, did you forget that's my partner?"

With that being said, he pulled out his matchbook and threw a lit match on Brandon's body. "How the fuck you like your meat: medium or well done?"

"Y'all some sick muthafuckas, but make this nigga well done."

Mekco walked out of the building with a smile on his face. He had always been a huge fan of a happy ending.

About the Author

T. Friday was born and raised in Detroit, Michigan. At the age of 36, she is the mother of five children: three handsome boys, ages 19, 15, and 13, and two beautiful girls, ages 10 and 8.

At a very early age, T. Friday became in love with reading books such as *The Baby-Sitters Club*, *Sweet Valley High*, and *Goosebumps* by R. L. Stine. It wasn't until she was in her early teens when she was introduced to urban fiction. That was when she knew that she wanted a career in the book industry. In January of 2016, T. Friday had her left leg amputated, and that was when she realized that she had been taking her life for granted and it was time to make her dreams come true. She picked up a pen and some paper, then started writing. In May of 2017, T. Friday signed her first contract with Racquel Williams, who is the owner of RWP. As of 2021, she was the author of twenty-six books. She has plans to continue writing until one day all of her books are turned into movies.

T. Friday's Book Catalog

Intrigued by a Savage's Love (Standalone)
Finding Love in a Real Boss 1
Finding Love in a Real Boss 2
Nasir & Kennedy: Luv in the Gutta (Standalone)
In Love with a Street Princess (Standalone)
To Be Loved by a Brick Boy 1
To Be Loved by a Brick Boy 2
To Be Loved by a Brick Boy 3
Yearnin' for the Love of a Thug (Standalone)
All Cried Out: Lovin' a Detroit Nigga 1
All Cried Out: Lovin' a Detroit Nigga 2
When Love Calls the Shots (Standalone)
Saving all my Love for a Young Boss 1
Saving all my Love for a Young Boss 2
Jewel and Javarri: His Love Wasn't Enough
(Standalone)
Tears Shed from Loving a Trap Nigga 1
Tears Shed from Loving a Trap Nigga 2
A Detroit Nigga Finessed my Love (Standalone)
Pretty Bitches get Even (Standalone)
Aaliyah & Marcel: Side Chicks Wanna Be Loved
Too (Standalone)
Prettier in Pink (Standalone)
Boo'd Up With a Young Outlaw for Christmas
When a Street King Wants You
Upgraded to a Real Boss
Upgraded to a Real Boss 2
Thot Girl Summer Detroit

Author's Contact Information

Facebook: Author T Friday
Instagram: Authortfriday
Twitter: @TFriday9

If you haven't already signed up for my email blast for new updates on all my books, please do; Messiah.nf@gmail.com

ALL MY BOOKS CAN BE FOUND ON AMAZON.COM

Read a book, leave a review on Amazon or Goodreads, and tell a friend.